RICK LAI'S
MAJOR SABBATH

AIRSHIP 27 PRODUCTIONS

Rick Lai's Major Sabbath

"Thy Name is Sabbath" and "Origins of Major Sabbath" © 2016 Rick Lai
"City of Enemies" © 2016 Erik Franklin
"The Mission of Shanghai Joe" © 2016 Frank Schildiner

Published by Airship 27 Productions
www.airship27.com
www.airship27hangar.com

Interior illustrations © 2016 M.D. Jackson
Cover illustration © 2016 Patricio Carbajal

Editor: Ron Fortier
Associate Editor: Gordon Dymowski
Marketing and Promotions Manager: Michael Vance
Production and design by Rob Davis

ISBN-10: 0-9977868-4-1
ISBN-13: 978-0-9977868-4-2

Printed in the United States of America

10 9 8 7 6 5 4 3 2 1

RICK LAI'S
MAJOR SABBATH

VOLUME ONE

TABLE OF CONTENTS

THY NAME IS SABBATH
BY RICK LAI

*J*immy Ballantrae, a professional gambler, was serenading the patrons of the Jean Lafitte Saloon in Bougival Junction as he played on the piano. Suddenly a harsh voice with a Germanic accent interrupted Jimmy's rendition of "For the Love of Barbara Allen."

"Judas! You betrayed us in Mexico!"

Abruptly ending his singing, Ballantrae turned around to behold a thin man with a mustache cut in the style of European army officers.

"Do I know you?"

"Don't pretend not to recognize me! I am Otto Stejar!"

"Stejar…Forgive me. I have a bad memory for names. That's why I write everything in a book."

Ballantrae reached for a thick journal on top of the piano. He flipped through the pages.

"Here you are. We met last year. You were under the command of that Austrian mercenary who hired me to paint his portrait. It's a pity what happened to Heinrich. The notorious Black Indian threw a knife into him."

"You were the Black Indian's accomplice. The two of you conspired to steal the gold that Heinrich was guarding for Emperor Maximilian."

"Even if what you said is true, Maximilian is dead. A firing squad plugged him full of holes. Don't you realize where you are? You're in Texas."

"And Texas has a tradition of settling differences by the gun." Stejar pulled back his jacket to expose a holstered gun resting on his right hip.

"Wait a minute, Stejar. I'm unarmed, and we're in a crowded saloon. The owner is letting me lodge here. My revolver is in my room upstairs. Wait outside while I get my gun. We'll settle this in the street."

"It shall be as you wish, but you are only delaying your doom. Even if you manage to kill me, Heinrich's cousin is looking for you."

Stejar turned around. Before the Austrian had reached the saloon's doors, Ballantrae had pulled out the revolver secreted in the hollowed out back of his journal. The gambler shot Stejar twice in the back.

Stejar was murdered in 1868. Four years later, a deadly duel transpired in Mexico.

A bullet exploded into the head of the Major's horse. As the animal fell to the ground, the rider was hurled from the saddle. His right hand lost its grip on the Winchester. Sprawled on the ground, the Major groped for his rifle. Before he could touch the weapon, another bullet slammed into the Winchester pushing it farther away. A third and fourth bullet followed. The rifle now rested a far distance from the Major. His right hand reached for a holstered gun slanted sideways near the left side of his belt buckle. Before the revolver could be pulled out, a bullet tore into the holster severing it from the belt. Another bullet hit the holstered gun propelling it away from the Major.

"You may think I'm out of ammo," stated a commanding voice. "Don't delude yourself. My rifle's magazine carries my lucky number . . . Seven. I still have one bullet left."

The speaker looked like an undertaker in rawhide as he stood over the Major. Massive rope-like fringes of black leather hung from his black leather shirt and pants. A black hat with a wide rim covered a shaven skull. Hanging over his chest was a gold ring tied to a leather thong around his neck. A smoking cigar was clenched in his teeth.

The rifle in his hands was quite unique. It had a short cut-off barrel with a horizontal magazine. It was aimed directly at the Major's head.

"Nice rifle, Sabbath," coldly remarked the Major.

"It was made by Gordon Munitions, but we aren't here to discuss firearms. I've never seen you before in my life. I have one question. If I don't like the answer, I'm going to blow your head off. Why are you trying to kill me?"

A derringer slid from the Major's sleeve into his right hand. Two bullets ripped into Sabbath's chest. Dropping his rifle, Sabbath fell on his back. Rising from the ground, the Major picked up Sabbath's rifle.

"Why?" murmured the dying Sabbath.

"To settle an old debt, Christian Sabbath." Reaching into his vest pocket, the Major pulled out a watch. The sweet melody of a lullaby filled the air once the watch was opened.

"What the hell is that?" asked Sabbath.

The Major placed the portrait inside the locket directly in front of his vanquished adversary's eyes.

"Remember my sister?"

"Mister, I never saw that woman before," were the last words uttered by Sabbath.

The Major retrieved his rifle and pistol from the ground. One of Sabbath's bullets had shattered the rifle's trigger. The Major threw the useless rifle away. Removing the revolver from the severed holster, the Major tucked it under his belt. He then picked up the Sabbath's rifle.

"Major!" yelled the red-headed rider rapidly approaching on a horse. He had a banjo tied around his back. When the horse halted in besides Sabbath's corpse, a look of shock overran the rider's face.

"Major, what have you done?"

"Avenged your brother and my sister, Galloway. Their killer roasts in Hell."

"He didn't kill them!"

"WHAT?"

"You were right five years ago. The Black Indian and the Crazy Indian are two different men. The *Federales* just captured the Crazy Indian."

"You assured me that Sabbath was the killer!" The Major's hand reached up to grab Galloway's left arm.

"It wasn't my fault!" protested Galloway. "L'Ollonaise lied to me!"

Yanking Galloway out of the saddle, the Major threw him on the ground. By the time Galloway rose to his feet, the Major was seated on the horse. Starting to reach for the banjo hanging on his back, Galloway stopped when the Major pointed Sabbath's rifle at him.

"Don't even think about it," warned the Major. "I know all about the rifle hidden inside that banjo. Sabbath must have a horse tethered around here. You're going to look for it after you perform a certain task. Start gathering rocks. We're not leaving the Black Indian for the vultures."

Nearly ninety minutes later, Sabbath's body was covered by rocks in an improvised grave. A cross made from two wooden sticks stood at the head of the gunfighter's final resting place.

During the construction of the grave, the Major had remained on the horse.

"I'm headed back to Texas, Galloway. You should stay in Mexico. With me in the north, and you in the south, we'll both live to a ripe old age."

The Major rode away.

No sooner had the Major gotten off his horse in El Paso, then he was accosted by a scrawny old man with a white beard.

"My name is Isaiah, stranger."

"Like the prophet?"

"Yes, like the prophet. People say I know everyone, but I don't know you. I'll make a bargain with you. You tell me your name, and I'll tell you anything that you want to know about El Paso."

The Major gave his name. "Where is Gordon Munitions?"

"That's easy. It's on the side of the street opposite my house. I live next to the railway station. Those damn Brockston-Morton trains keep me up all night!"

"Maybe you should move."

"I was born in that house, and I intend to die there!"

Within less than a half hour, the Major was in the office of the owner of the armaments firm. In 1872, the fifty-five year old Arthur Gordon was quite a legend. He had been a leader of a band of guerillas during the Texan War for Independence, but his critics claimed that he had been little more than a bandit. In the Civil War, he had commanded a ship that regularly ran the Union blockade. His enemies whispered that Gordon had earlier gained his nautical skills by engaging in the overseas slave trade outlawed by Congress in 1807. Since the war, he had helmed an armaments firm based in El Paso.

Gordon's income came primarily from two sources. To the Spanish colonial authorities in Cuba, he sold weapons to suppress the rebels seeking independence. Inside the United States, he arranged for specially made firearms for a select coterie of purchasers. Nearly all of those orders were filled by Leroy Bailey, an ex-Confederate gunsmith. Originally he was based in New Orleans, but Bailey fled to Mexico when the city fell to Farragut. Living in a remote house on the seashore, Bailey made guns for the clients of Gordon Munitions. A few valued patrons were even permitted by Gordon to visit Bailey in Mexico.

"I've heard of you, Major," acknowledged Gordon, a tall man with gray hair. "You served with the Hellbender Regiment in Tennessee, but I always thought you were a Colonel."

"I was a Colonel in the Union Army during the Mexican War. My rank in the Confederate Army was Major."

"Regardless of your rank, you're still considered to be the best shot in South Carolina. I would be honored to have you as a client."

"Do you recognize this?"

"That's the rifle that my partner made for Christian Sabbath. There's a similar one that Bailey made for a fellow named Randall. The difference is that Randall's has a standard magazine. Something happened to Sabbath?"

"He's dead. It was my misfortune to supervise his burial."

"You were friends?"

"No, I'm the man who killed him."

Valentin L'Ollonaise owned the Sunlight Saloon in Signo Amarillo, New Mexico. There was a Sheriff in Signo Amarillo, but he had no reason to harass L'Ollonaise. All indications were that the gambling establishment ran an honest game. L'Ollonaise employed a trio of armed bodyguards called the Three Aces, but that was not unusual considering the large amount of money that was kept in the proprietor's safe.

A man wearing a dark Inverness cape entered the saloon. A black hat covered a receding hairline. His hawk-like countenance had penetrating eyes and a gray mustache. A drooping pipe hung from his mouth.

"Want to order a drink?"asked the blond bartender.

"Whiskey," replied the stranger.

The bartender poured the drink. "There's an old legend that the Angel of Death sometimes walks the Earth as a living man. Your style of dress reminds me of that legend."

"You're very poetic for a bartender."

"People call me Coeur."

"Isn't that French?"

"It means 'breast.' As any woman will tell you, it's my favorite part of their anatomy. Would it be presumptuous of me to ask to ask where you bought your clothes?"

"They were made by a tailor shop in California. Why are you curious about my attire?"

"I'm thinking of buying a suit just like it."

"You won't be able to afford it on a bartender's salary."

"Maybe I'll find some way to augment my income, but Sheriff Ramsey doesn't make it easy to earn a dishonest dollar,"

"Ramsey? I've heard of a Texas Ranger named Priam Ramsey."

"'He's the same man. Ramsey came here with his family in '69. You don't want to get on his wrong side. He's a very stern man."

"How stern?"

"There's a town ordinance that no one can carry a gun unless they are 21 or older. Ramsey had his own 20 year-old son arrested for violating that ordinance."

"I'm looking for the proprietor of this establishment."

"Mr. L'Ollonaise is in his office in the back." Coeur pointed to a door guarded by a huge cowboy. "You have to pass inspection by Spade first."

Leaving the bar, the stranger approached the bodyguard. "I have business with your boss."

Spade drew a Colt revolver from his holster. "You have to leave any weapons with me."

The stranger opened his Inverness coat slowly. "There's a derringer in my right vest pocket."

Seeing a gun handle rising from the vest pocket, Spade pulled out the weapon.

"Four barrels? I've never seen one of those before. What's in the bag?"

"Something that will interest your boss," The stranger opened the satchel.

Viewing the contents, Spade's eyes sparkled. "What's your name?"

"Morgan Douglass. I'm a professional gambler."

"Mr. L'Ollonaise, there's a Mr. Douglass here to see you." Opening the door, Spade ushered the gambler inside.

Seated behind a large desk, Valentin L'Ollonaise was a handsome man with golden hair.

"I understand that you run a very special poker game, Mr. L'Ollonaise."

"It's scheduled for two o'clock tomorrow night after we close the saloon. You must have at least one thousand dollars to be allowed into the game."

Douglass deposited his bag on the desk. "There's five thousand dollars inside."

Opening the bag, L'Ollonaise counted the bound stacks of cash. When he had finished, he opened a brown book and began to make an entry.

"Do you spell your surname with one 's' or two?"

"Two."

"And your first name."

"Morgan. Do you always write down everything?"

"Yes. I have a bad memory. I'm never without this book." L'Ollonaise extended his hand. "Welcome to the game."

The two men shook hands.

"I couldn't fail to notice your unique physical feature, Mr. Douglass. You're missing the last joint of the middle finger on your right hand."

"It was shot off in the Battle of Stones River in 1862."

"How did you hear of my card game?"

"Last year, a friend of mine named Hatfield played a game here."

"You must share the same tailor as Hatfield. Your clothes are nearly identical to the ones he usually wears."

"We buy our clothes from the same establishment."

"If I remember correctly, Hatfield's tailor is Paolo Di Marco of San Francisco."

"Hatfield's clothes are made by Paolo's nephew, Gino."

"I remember now." L'Ollonaise consulted his book. "I even wrote down Gino's name after Hatfield mentioned him. As I mentioned before, I have a bad memory."

"Apparently your bartender's memory is equally bad. He commented on my clothes, and neglected to mention that Hatfield wears similar attire."

"Coeur? I hired him a month ago. He never met Hatfield."

When the private game was held the following night, there were two other card players present besides Douglass and L'Ollonaise. Their names were Philip Holden and Marty Heywood. Proving himself to be a thoroughly incompetent gambler, Holden was cleaned out early. Heywood managed to survive for an hour more before his cash was depleted. Under the rules of the game, a player vacated the saloon once he lost all his chips. Besides Douglass and L'Ollonaise, the only people apparently remaining in the drinking establishment were the Three Aces. Armed with holstered revolvers, the gunslingers called Spade, Diamond and Club were supposedly there to prevent anybody from stealing the pot in the poker game. Neither L'Ollonaise or Douglass were wearing a gun belt, but the latter had his four-barreled derringer in the right pocket of his vest. Resting on the poker table near L'Ollonaise's right hand was his journal.

More than 13,000 dollars rested on the table. Included in the pot was nearly all of Douglass's money.

"I raise you 1,000 dollars," announced L'Ollonaise.

"I only have only 519 dollars left to bet. Will you let me cover the remainder of the stakes with collateral? I have on my person an item that is worth at least the amount in question."

"I'll need to see this item."

"Of course." Douglass opened the canvas bag and revealed a secret compartment in the bottom. Pulling out of the compartment an object, the gambler deposited it on the table. It was Sabbath's rifle. The horizontal magazine wasn't loaded with any bullets.

"A most unusual weapon, Douglass," noted L'Ollonaise. "How did you acquire it?"

"An American gunsmith designed the rifle for an adventurer named Christian Sabbath. After the Civil War, Sabbath was hired by the Juaristas to steal a gold shipment guarded by Austrian mercenaries loyal to Emperor Maximilian. Jimmy Ballantrae, a swindler with multiple aliases, also desired the gold. A skilled artist, Ballantrae arranged to be hired to paint the portrait of Heinrich the Butcher, the mercenary leader entrusted with the gold. Offering his services to assist Sabbath and the Juaristas, Ballantrae intended all long to steal the gold for himself. The Butcher died in a brutal battle with Sabbath. The greedy Ballantrae ran off with the gold, but Sabbath made sure his treacherous ally crossed the American border empty-handed.

"One of Heinrich's former subordinates was a soldier named Stejar. When Maximilian was overthrown, Stejar came to the United States and got a job with Brockston-Morton Railways. In a Texas saloon, Stejar stumbled upon Ballantrae. Seeking to punish Ballantrae for betraying the Butcher, Stejar challenged the swindler to a duel. After shooting Stejar with a concealed weapon, Ballantrae fled the state. The railroad company didn't take kindly to the murder of one of their employees. They posted a 10,000 reward for Ballantrae?"

"Dead or alive?'

"Alive. Ballantrae's not even worth a plug nickel if he's a corpse." Douglass looked squarely into his opponent's eyes. "Ever hear of Red Galloway?"

"Hatfield brought him here about a year ago."

"Red's younger brother, Bob, married a wealthy heiress from South Carolina. When the war broke out, Red served with the Confederate Army in Arkansas while Bob remained behind to manage the family plantation in Texas. When Red returned home after the war ended, he discovered that both Bob and his wife were dead. They were murdered by a Mexican bandit called the Crazy Indian."

"Indian? Didn't you say he was Mexican?"

"He's Mexican, but he likes to take peyote, the drug cultivated by the Tonkawa Indians. The brigand's usage of peyote has led to the false rumor that he's an Indian. Remember that Sabbath fellow? He was the son of a Texas farmer and a Tonkawa squaw. Sabbath liked to dress in black. People dubbed him the Black Indian."

"How can you be sure that the two Indians aren't the same man?'

"Originally Red Galloway suspected that they were. In 1867, he went searching for the Black Indian *in* Mexico. Joining Red was a former Major in the Confederate Army. The destruction of the Major's plantation in the war reduced him to being a bounty hunter. His sister had been the ill-fated wife of Red's brother. Although they never found the Black Indian, the Major quickly concluded that Sabbath wasn't his sister's slayer. By all accounts, the Crazy Indian has white hair and a beard. Not only did Sabbath always shave his face, but he also shaved his head. He was as bald as a billiard ball. Supposedly Sabbath saw a photograph of King Mongkut of Siam. That monarch had shaved his skull as part of a religious ceremony. Sabbath thought Mongkut looked incredibly handsome without hair, and decided to emulate him.

"Convinced that Sabbath was innocent, Red and the Major returned to the United States. About four years later, Red met Ballantrae. The wanted murderer had established a new identity outside of Texas. After telling the incognito Ballantrae about his futile search for the Crazy Indian, Red became the victim of an elaborate ruse. Ballantrae desired revenge against Sabbath for foiling him during the gold robbery. The accomplished swindler told a false account of his own adventures with the Juaristas in Mexico. Ballantrae claimed that Sabbath frequently disguised himself with a fake wig and beard. Furthermore, Ballantrae supposedly saw Sabbath listening to the melody of a watch with the cameo photo of a woman.

"Before the war, the Major had a trio of musical watches made. Each of them had a cameo portrait of his sister inside. The Major kept one of the timepieces for himself, and gave the other two watches to his sister and Bob Galloway on their wedding day. When the bodies of the Galloways were found, their two watches were missing. The Crazy Indian must have stolen them.

"Red thought he had proof that Sabbath was the Crazy Indian. Contacting the Major, Galloway convinced him to travel to Mexico to track down Sabbath. The Major killed Sabbath just before hearing that his sister's true killer had been apprehended by the Mexican authorities, Following Sabbath's death; his rifle came into my possession. Now that you know the rifle's history, Mr. L'Ollonaise, will you accept it as collateral?"

"I will indeed, Mr. Douglass, but I don't want to cheat you. That rifle is worth more than four hundred and eighty-one dollars. I shall add a piece of collateral of my own to balance the stakes."

L'Ollonaise reached into his vest pocket and pulled out a round item. He deposited it next to Sabbath's rifle.

"A watch," observed Douglass.

"I won it in a poker game in Mexico. The previous owner didn't mind losing it. He had another timepiece that was identical to it. We should put all our cards on the table."

"Three Kings," said Douglass exposing his cards.

"Three Aces, Major." L'Ollonaise didn't brother to reveal his cards. Spade, Diamond and Club had all drawn their revolvers. Each weapon was pointed at the seated man in the black Inverness cape.

"Morgan Douglass? A rather obvious alias. Red Galloway told me your true name. In fact, I wrote it in my book. You have the distinctive trait of wearing your gun on your left side. You moved it to the right since you were using a false name. Why go to all the trouble of switching the position of your gun, and then undercut that ploy with an easily discernible pseudonym?"

"You think that Valentin L'Ollonaise is a more believable name, Ballantrae?"

"Actually it's my real name. Jimmy Ballantrae is just a *nom de guerre*. I come from a prominent family. I am a direct descendant of Francois L'Ollonaise, the pirate who sacked the Venezuelan port of Macaibo in 1667. That missing joint on your finger makes you an easy man to identify, even when you lied about how it happened."

"What are you talking about? I told you the truth."

"Red Galloway isn't your only acquaintance who played poker with me at the Sunlight Saloon. Remember Lieutenant Tervis?"

"He served with me in the Confederate Army, Even won a medal for saving my life."

"Let me see." L'Ollonaise opened his book. "According to Tervis, you chewed off your finger in wartime just to spend your 20 days of convalescence with Colonel Leland's wife."

"That's a damn lie! Jonas Leland was a brute. He often beat his wife. I warned Jonas that I'll kill him if he ever laid a hand on her again. She later committed suicide. I was never her lover, but Jonas spread that lie to damage my reputation. Tervis never knew the truth. He joined my unit after I was wounded."

"I'm curious, Major. Red Galloway must have told you all about his dealings with me and Hatfield. How did you discover my earlier activities as Ballantrae?"

"I talked to the man who sold Sabbath that rifle. My informant knew about your actions as Ballantrae, but was totally ignorant about your

L'Ollonaise identity. Nevertheless, my source mentioned that Ballantrae had a habit of writing everything down in a journal. Galloway mentioned you had a similar eccentricity. As a condemned man, may I have a last request?"

"You can make the request, but whether I grant it is another matter."

"Could you show me your last poker hand?"

L'Ollonaise flipped over his cards. "A pair of Aces and a pair of Eights. You may not believe me, Major, but I would have allowed you to win that pot if you were merely a gambler. You are unfortunately a bounty killer. I imagine that you have a wanted poster bearing my likeness in that fancy coat of yours."

"Yes. I was going to show it to Sheriff Ramsey in order to take custody of you."

"You should have done before engaging in these foolish histrionics. With Ramsey on your side, you might have stood a chance against me and my Aces. Diamond, remove the derringer from the Major's waistcoat." Once his order had been carried out, L'Ollonaise issued more commands. "Aces, escort the Major to the side of the saloon that's opposite the bar. Our guest's back must be against the wall. Major, extend your right arm so it points in front of you. Now bend your elbow. Diamond place the derringer in the Major's hand. Make sure the barrel is pointing towards the ceiling."

"You plan to have Ramsey find my bullet-riddled body holding a gun. You're going to tell him that I drew my derringer in anger after losing the last hand."

"Don't fret, Major. I'm going to give you a fighting chance." Before rising from the table, L'Ollonaise picked up the watch. "My Three Aces are standing in front of you. I shall open the watch to play the melody. When the music ceases, you can lower your arm and try to shoot my Three Aces before they shoot you."

"Considering your Aces have their guns already pointed in the direction of my chest, I'm a dead man already. You're a real bastard, L'Ollonaise!"

"Only in a figurative sense. You're the genuine article. How old are you, Major? Forty-five?"

"I'm forty-seven."

"You would have been in your late thirties when you had that cameo made, but your sister looks over fifteen years younger!"

"Rosemary and I had different mothers."

"You're neglecting to mention that only Rosemary's mother was married to your father. Tervis told me the whole sordid story. Your mother was a whore. Your father married late in life. He only legitimized you when his wife failed to produce a male heir."

"Rosemary ignored the circumstances surrounding my birth. She always accepted me as her brother."

"Considering that you robbed Rosemary of her exclusive claims to the family fortune, her acceptance of you indicates that she was a moron or a lunatic."

"L'Ollonaise, I'll remember that remark at your execution."

"The only execution you'll be attending is your own." L'Ollonaise released the lid of the watch. An entrancing tune filled the air.

The Major knew that musical strain by heart. He could calculate exactly the second that the melody would cease. The Three Aces weren't closely listening to the music. Their eyes were riveted on the Major's right arm. If the bounty hunter's limb so much as twitched, the Three Aces would fire with deadly accuracy.

The music stopped. The barrel of the Major's raised derringer still pointed upward when the bottom of its handle opened on a hinge. Three exposed barrels shot bullets directly into the foreheads of the Three Aces. The Major ran towards the owner of the Sunlight Saloon.

Dropping the watch, L'Ollonaise leaped towards the journal lying on the poker table. Opening the book in the middle, he seized a revolver from its hidden compartment. Before L'Ollonaise could fire, the Major's left hand seized Sabbath's rifle by its barrel and slammed the butt into the swindler's face. L'Ollonaise fell unconscious to the ground.

"You're damn lucky that I need you alive."

The Major suddenly heard a sound behind. Without turning around, the Major dropped the rifle and seized the edge of the poker table with the tips of his fingers. Flinging the table on its side, he dropped behind it. The money scattered on the floor in all directions. The table top functioned as a shield as three bullets slammed into it.

"Let me guess. The Ace of Hearts."

"Right, Major," admitted Coeur. "My French nickname does mean 'breast,' but it more properly means 'heart.' L'Ollonaise considered me his Ace in the Hole. l was hiding behind the bar during the entire game."

"Someone in town would have heard all those shots. Sheriff Ramsey should be arriving soon."

"If I kill you and destroy the wanted poster before he arrives, my boss is in the clear."

"Not if I kill you first."

...three bullets slammed into it.

"You have to move from behind that table to take your shot. The odds favor me shooting you first."

"You might miss. We might even kill each other. Neither of us had to die. Let's make a deal."

A few minutes later, Sheriff Ramsey and his two deputies, Burnett and McDade, entered the Sunlight Saloon. They found the Major and Coeur standing amidst the carnage. A slumbering L'Ollonaise was still sprawled on the ground. The three lawmen quickly took possession of all the weapons in the room. The Major identified himself using his real name. He removed a wanted poster from inside his coat.

"I'm a bounty hunter. L'Ollonaise is Jimmy Ballantrae, a man wanted for murder in Texas. When I came to Signo Amarillo, I wasn't completely sure that Ballantrae and L'Ollonaise were the same man. I joined the poker game to observe L'Ollonaise up close. My plans ran awry when L'Ollonaise deduced my identity. He ordered the Three Aces to kill me. I was fortunate indeed that Coeur intervened."

"I had been working late the last few weeks, and not getting enough rest," asserted Coeur. "Unbeknownst to everyone, I accidentally fell asleep behind the bar. The angry altercation between L'Ollonaise and the Major woke me up. I had no idea that my employer was crooked. There's a revolver hidden behind the bar just in case any customers get unruly. I couldn't let the Three Aces murder the Major. I had no choice but to shoot them."

"L'Olloniase will lodge in the town jail until we sort out the proper legal procedures," decided Ramsey. "Major, you and Coeur will need to come to my office."

"What about all the money lying on the floor?" challenged Coeur. "There's about 13,000 dollars there. The Major won it all fair and square."

"McDade, stay here and pick up the poker stakes. Bring them to the office when you're finished."

Picking up L'Ollonaise, the Major and Ramsey carried him over to the Sheriff's office. There they deposited the swindler on a cot in a jail cell. After locking the cell, Ramsey went over by his desk and pulled a drawer open. He took out two sets of pen and paper. He left one set on his desk, the other he brought over to a small table with a chair.

"Major, I want you seated at my desk. Coeur, you sit at this table. Write a statement summarizing what happened tonight. Don't forget to date and sign it. Don't say anything until you're finished."

When the two statements were finished, Ramsey compared them. He found no discrepancies, but he was a little perplexed by Coeur's signature.

"Your father was Mexican?"

"And my mother was from Louisiana. My real name is Jake Sartana."

Carrying the poker money, the other deputy came in. "All together, I picked up 12,515 dollars."

"Samson McDade, you always were good with figures." stated Ramsey. "It's better that I keep this money locked here in my office. Major, I'll need to verify your stories with the other gamblers, Holden and Heywood. If everything checks out, you can claim your money along with your prisoner and weapons. By the way, do you have the time?"

The Major pulled out a pocket watch in his right pocket. "It's three minutes to six."

"You probably need some shuteye at your hotel. Come back around noon. That's a lovely pocket watch. Who's the pretty lady?"

"My late sister, Sheriff. She died very young,"

"My condolences. I noticed you have another watch in your left pocket. That's mighty unusual. The only other fellow that I heard about with dual timepieces was that crazy Englishman who made a bet this year about traveling around the world in 80 days."

The Major showed Ramsey the other watch. "It's part of a matching set. See it has the same photograph of my sister. There is one favor, Sheriff, that you could do for me. Could you and your deputies witness a deal of gift? I'm consigning 5,000 dollars of my winnings to Jake."

Ramsey raised an eyebrow. "What prompts this act of generosity?"

"The reward for Ballantrae is 10,000 dollars. Jake deserves half of it for all his help. Of course, I won't be able to collect the money until I conduct the prisoner to Texas. There's no reason for Jake to travel with me to Texas. I'm going to pay him in advance."

The document was prepared, signed and witnessed. "Jake, you can collect your money at noon as well."

"Seems like an open and shut case," commented Burnett.

"Heck!" exclaimed Ramsey. "Burnett, you've got to learn a lot if you ever want to someday be a Sheriff. You may only be 21 years old, but youth is no excuse for stupidity. McDade, do you concur with your fellow deputy?"

"I found three bullets in the poker table. Three different bullets killed the dead Aces. Sartana's gun was missing three shots. The Aces' guns were never fired. Neither the revolver owned by L'Ollonaise nor the four-barreled derringer were fired. The statements by the Major and Sartana don't explain the facts."

"Then what really happened?" wondered Burnett.

"Anybody know what Coeur means in French?" said Ramsey.

"When Coeur drifted into town, I looked up his name in a French-English dictionary," disclosed McDade. "He always joked that 'couer' meant 'breast.' It could be translated that way, but 'heart' is the more common translation."

"After Spade, Diamond and Club, Sartana was a hidden fourth ace for L'Ollonaise," reasoned Ramsey. "Sartana didn't fall asleep behind the bar. He was crouched there to kill the Major if his fellow Aces failed. Before the poker game started, L'Ollonaise must have realized that his Texas past was known to the Major. That bounty killer must have another gun somewhere. He shot the other Aces, and then Sartana tried to kill him. Using the poker table as a shield, the Major negotiated a truce where they split the bounty.

"I don't like being lied to. I'm not turning over L'Ollonaise to the Major. I'll arrange for a Federal Marshal to take L'Ollonaise to Texas. The Major will eventually get paid the bounty, but it will take longer since he won't be turning over L'Ollonaise himself."

Laughter interrupted Ramsey's theorizing.

The Sheriff turned his gaze towards the jail cell. "Well, Mr. L'Ollonaise, you're awake. How long have you been listening."

"Since the Major and Sartana left. You're totally wrong, Sheriff. Before the game began, the Three Aces did a little target practice using the poker table. That's why there are three extra bullets."

Ramsey handed the two statements to L'Ollonaise through the bars. "Do you dispute anything in those accounts?"

"Every word is absolutely true, Sheriff."

Ramsey saw no reason to deny the Major custody of L'Ollonaise at noon.

The Major had brought two sets of old slave shackles with him. Riding on horseback to Texas across New Mexico, L'Ollonaise wore the shackles on his wrists with his arms extended before him. At night when the bounty hunter slept, the prisoner's arms were chained behind him while his legs were chained. The Major largely avoided the towns, and bought supplies at isolated trading posts and stagecoach stations.

The Major was sleeping peacefully on the ground. He was dreaming of Rosemary's luxurious wedding where he substituted for their late father and gave the bride away. These blissful thoughts were interrupted by the muzzle of a rifle butt pressing against his face.

"Get up!" growled a guttural voice.

The Major reached instinctively behind the rolled up blanket that functioned as a improvised pillow.

"If you looking for that fancy derringer behind your headrest, we already removed it," said the man with the rifle. Dressed in a black frock coat and bowler hat. He was a massive man with a beard. There were four other men with rifles. They were dressed in similar hats and coats.

Rising to his feet, the Major confronted his captor.

"Who are you?"

"We are the Gentlemen of the Night," replied the bearded man.

"I thought that secret society of cutthroats only existed in London."

"In the 1830's, His Honor, Fergus O'Breane, dispatched agents to North America to establish branches of the organization throughout the continent."

"Enough of the history lesson, McIntock!" decreed L'Ollonaise lying on the ground. "Get these chains off me. He keeps the key in his waistcoat."

The bearded Smith did as he was instructed. He quickly removed the shackles from L'Ollonaise. Once the swindler was back on his feet, McIntock bowed on his knees before him.

"*Gentlemen of the Night,*" uttered McIntock.

"*Family's Son,*" responded L'Ollonaise.

"*Will there be daylight.*"

"*It will be daylight from midnight to noon if it's the will of the Lord of the Night.*" L'Ollonaise extended his hand. Lifting himself up, McIntock surrendered the Major's derringer.

"Before our little poker game," related L'Ollonaise, "I sent a coded telegram to my cousin in Redstone. The L'Ollonaise clan is a prominent family in the Gentlemen of the Night. We run all American operations for O'Breane's successor in London. My cousin was informed that if she didn't receive a following telegram within 48 hours to assume that I was your prisoner. She took the proper steps. Jason McIntock is one of her most trusted subordinates."

"Your cousin stationed patrols on the Texas borders to intercept the Major," added McIntock.

Ollonaise chuckled. "Sheriff Ramsey figured out the deception that you and Sartana concocted. He was so peeved that he intended to turn me over to a Federal Marshal. Being confined in a prison wagon with armed guards would have made my cousin's rescue operation very difficult. A few convenient lies convinced Ramsey that he had erred. I gladly accepted being turned over to your custody in the certainty that the Gentlemen of the Night would liberate me."

"What should we do with the Major?" said Smith.

"This bounty killer hoped to see me hang. Lynch him!"

A noose was quickly tied to the branch a tree. After placing the Major on his horse, The Gentlemen of the Night fastened the noose around his neck.

L'Ollonaise positioned himself behind the horse. "Give my regards to your sister!" shouted L'Ollonaise as he slapped the horse's rump.

A bullet sliced through the rope. Instead of being suspended in the air, the Major rode the horse away from the Gentlemen of the Night. Five further bullets collided into the bodies of McIntock and his four underlings. Another bullet smashed into the muzzle of the four-barreled derringer held by L'Ollonaise. The gun went flying out of his hand.

Jake Sartana emerged from the darkness. He was holding Sabbath's recently fired rifle. Removing his right hand from the trigger as he continued to grasp the rifle in his left, Sartana drew a revolver from a holster.

"You're lucky, L'Ollonaise, that the bounty requires you to be alive. Otherwise, you would be crow's meat like your friends. You weren't the only one who took precautions regarding the long ride to Texas. The Major hired me to watch his back. He even gave me an extra suit and coat he packed." Sartana was dressed very similarly to the Major, but his coat had a red interior lining. "I've been discretely following the pair of you."

"What's your game, Sartana? You hope to earn a harp in Heaven?"

"I don't expect to go to Heaven. Besides, I don't play a harp. I play an organ."

The Major rode his horse back into the camp. "You took your damn time before shooting!"

"Sorry, Major," apologized Sartana. "It took me awhile to get in the proper position to dry-gulch your attackers."

"Luckily for me, you can shoot like Rocambole."

"Who's Rocambole?"

"A famous French crook. He once rescued a condemned man from a London gallows by shooting the rope."

The Major picked up a pair of shackles and placed them on L'Ollonaise's wrists.

"Was Rocambole ever in these parts, Major?" asked Sartana

"Not to my knowledge. Why?"

"During the war in New Mexico, I saw an unknown sharpshooter save a bandit from a hanging just like I saved you."

The Major lifted the four-barreled derringer from the ground. After examining it. He tossed it away. "Your shot busted the muzzle, Jake. I'll have to buy another one."

"Who did you buy it from?"

"Arthur Gordon in El Paso. His gunsmith makes really fancy weapons."

"After all this is over, I'll appreciate it if you introduce me to this Gordon fellow. I wish to peruse his merchandise."

"Sure, Jake. I want you to travel with me and the prisoner. What do you know about the Gentlemen of the Night?"

"First time I ever heard about them. L'Ollonaise never mentioned them in Signo Amarillo."

"If McIntock spoke the truth, there are other patrols looking for us. We better cross into Texas before dawn."

Once they were in Texas, L'Ollonaise remained defiant.

"You may think that you've won, Major, but our contest is far from over. A jury could easily acquit me. I shot an armed man in a saloon. I can easily claim self-defense."

"You also have the fact that your victim, Stejar, was a foreigner associated with the corrupt Maximilian regime. Furthermore, Stejar was employed by Brockston-Morton Railways. That firm is very unpopular in the state of Texas. The majority of citizens here view that company as a pack of land-grabbing carpetbaggers."

L'Ollonaise smiled. "You understand the situation exactly."

"Indeed. I do. For your information, we're on the outskirts of Bougival Junction, but we won't be riding into town. We're going to that ranch over there. Jake and I have a little surprise in store for you."

A huge fence encircled the ranch. A large sign on it bore the caption "Trespassers Will Be Shot." Two guards with shotguns were stationed behind the gate that acted as an entrance to the ranch.

Riding up to the gate, the Major addressed the guards. "I'm here to see Bill Gordon."

"There's no Bill Gordon here," answered one of the guards, "but there's a Frank Gordon."

"Is he from El Paso?"

"Yep."

"He's the man I need to see."

"I'll go fetch him," said the other guard before leaving for a bunkhouse. After a few minutes, the guard returned with a lean man. His right hand bore a large ring with a crest in the form of a black "G." The ring was identical to one worn by Arthur Gordon. The newcomer's blue eyes skeptically looked at the Major and his two companions.

"State your business."

"Is your father Arthur Gordon?"

"That's right."

"He told me your name was Bill."

"My full name is William LeFrank Gordon. Only Pa and my brothers call me Bill. Everyone else calls me Frank. You must be that bounty hunter that Pa wired me about. Your proper title is Major. Isn't it?"

"Yes. Does the Baron's offer still stand?"

"It sure does. Your prisoner must be Ballantrae. Once the Baroness identifies him, you'll be paid. Who's the other man?"

"That's Jake Sartana. We're temporary partners for the duration of this affair."

"Open the gates, boys," ordered Bill Gordon. "I'm taking these men to the boss's residence."

Upon entering the enclosure, the Major and Sartana dismounted and tied up their horses' reins to the fence. They helped the chained L'Ollonaise to dismount. Bill Gordon escorted the visitors to a large mansion. On the porch was a red-haired man with a monocle. His gloved hands were holding a small satchel. A belt with a holstered gun was around his waist.

"Baron, your expected visitors have arrived," announced Bill.

"It can't be!" shouted L'Ollonaise. "You're dead! Sabbath killed you!"

"You mistake me for my cousin, Heinrich Von Skimmel. We always bore a strong resemblance to one another. In fact, in order to avoid being confused with him, I cut my hair short in the traditional military style. You will also notice that that my mustache lacks the accompanying side whiskers cultivated by my cousin. I am Gustav Von Schulenberg. I believe that you know my wife and stepdaughter."

The Baron was joined by a gorgeous brunette who was obviously pregnant. With her was a six-year old girl with similar raven hair. She carried a wooden pole with a doll attached to it by a string.

"Traitor!" screeched the Baroness. "My first husband treated you as a friend of the family. You helped murder him. His death left me and Heidi at the mercy of the Juaristas." Her brown eyes shifted towards her second husband. "They were going to rape me when my gallant Gustav intervened."

"Calm yourself, Gretchen," cautioned the Baron. "You must think of your condition." He mercilessly gazed at L'Ollonaise. "I served as a captain in the Austrian Navy under Archduke Maximilian. Years later when he accepted the throne of Mexico, I organized a group of Austrian and Hungarian mercenaries to fight along the French and Mexican forces supporting him. Among those men was my cousin. After the French withdrew their support in 1866, my mercenaries continued to fight for another year. When Maximilian was defeated, I managed to rally a large portion of the surviving mercenaries and their families and cross the Rio Grande into Texas.

"I am independently wealthy. However, I am a soldier by nature. I could not return to Europe. Emperor Franz-Joseph disapproved of his brother's Mexican enterprise. I am *persona non grata* at the Viennese court. My services were offered to the American cavalry, but they were refused. Seeking to curry favor with the Mexican government, the American authorities did not wish to employ a prominent adherent of Maximilian. Brockston-Morton was beginning its operations in Texas. While many other firms employ the Pinkertons to protect them against robbery, Brockston-Morton was enlightened enough to hire me to organize their own security force. Many of my former mercenaries returned to Europe, but some like Otto Stejar agreed to be server under me at Brockston-Morton. Otto recognized you in a Texas saloon, Ballantrae, or whatever your name is. "

"His real name is Valentin L'Ollonaise." said the Major.

"Thank you, sir," replied the Baron. "Herr L'Ollonaise, Stejar did the honorable thing by challenging you to a duel. You cowardly shot him in the back with a gun concealed in a book. Brockston-Morton was generous enough to post a 10,000 dollar reward for your capture. "

"I'm willing to pay the price," professed L'Ollonaise. "Turn me over to the law."

The Baron opened the satchel. There were tied bundles of American dollars inside. "Hoping for an acquittal, Herr L'Ollonaise? American juries do issue questionable verdicts from time to time. That is why I let it be known in certain discrete quarters that I am personally offering a bounty of 20,000 dollars if you are turned over to me alive."

"I told my father," volunteered Bill.

"And Arthur Gordon told me," imparted the Major.

"You can't turn me over to the Baron!" protested L'Ollonaise. "He'll torture me to death!"

"Arthur Gordon assured that you'll be treated fairly," noted the Major grimly.

"He spoke the truth," confirmed the Baron. "Please unlock the prisoner's shackles." Once the Major had unlocked the chains, the Baron removed the glove from his left hand, slapped the swindler's face. "Valentin L'Ollonaise, I challenge you to a duel. Provided you conform to the terms of the duel, your demise shall be quick."

"That's assuming you win," retorted L'Ollonaise.

"I am an accomplished duelist with 17 kills to my credit," boasted the Baron. "Your odds of survival are extremely remote. However, if you emerge victorious, you have my word that no one would obstruct your departure from this estate. Mr. Gordon, do you promise to follow my wishes if my demise transpires."

"Neither my men or myself will harm L'Ollonaise if you lose."

"What about the bounty killers?" asked L'Ollonaise.

"Jake and I will respect the Baron's terms," said the Major.

"Here is the bounty." The Baron handed the satchel to the Major.

The Major countered the money inside. "Our agreement, Jake, was to split the bounty evenly. I already advanced you 5,000 in Signo Amarillo. Here's the remaining 5,000."

Sartana took the cash. "Thanks, Major."

"You served as a soldier?" asked the Baron.

"I was a Major in the Confederate Army."

"As a fellow military officer, I humbly request that you act as referee in the duel."

"I would be honored to do so, Baron. Stand directly in front of Valentin L'Ollonaise. Turn around and walk twenty paces away from your opponent . . . Now turn around to face your adversary. Mr. Gordon, please draw your gun and point it in the direction of Mr. L'Ollonaise. Mr. Sartana, remove your gun belt. Mr. L'Ollonaise, my associate is going to hand you the belt. You will strap it slowly around your waist. If you try to draw the gun, Mr. Gordon will shoot you down like a dog." Once L'Ollonaise had

"Valentin L'Ollonaise, I challenge you to a duel."

fastened the belt around his waist, the Major pulled out one of the two pocket watches from his vest. "Mr. Gordon, holster your gun. Gentlemen, the watch in my hand plays a lullaby upon being opened. I shall play that melody. Once the music ceases, you will draw your weapons and fire."

As the music began, L'Ollonaise knew his doom was sealed. It was inconceivable that he would defeat the Baron. His soul became filled with hatred towards the bounty hunter who had bested him at every turn. He would probably be dead before having a chance to aim his gun at the Baron. Nevertheless, there was a more accessible target.

When the music was halfway over, L'Ollonaise swiftly drew his gun and shot the Major. Even before the bullet had slammed into the Major's torso, the Baron had drawn his weapon. His first bullet hit L'Ollonaise's right hand, the gun went hurling into the air. The revolver hadn't even hit the ground when another bullet penetrated L'Ollonaise's left hand. The third and fourth bullets smashed into the swindler's kneecaps. The bleeding L'Ollonaise fell face forward into the dirt.

Jake Sartana and Bill Gordon examined the Major.

"Is he dead?' asked the Baron.

"No," revealed Bill. "The bullet was blocked by another watch in his vest." Bill held up the timepiece which the bullet lodged inside it.

"I think one of my ribs is cracked," groaned the bounty hunter.

"Take him inside and attend to his wound," commanded the Baron. As the Major was carried away, the Austrian aristocrat advanced towards the sprawled L'Ollonaise. When the swindler raised his head, the muzzle of the Baron's gun pressed firmly against it.

"You would have simply perished from a bullet to the heart if you had followed the rules of the duel. Are you in pain, L'Ollonaise? My next bullet will end it by splattering your brains."

"Wait!" yelled a female voice. It came from the Baron's stepdaughter. Clutching her doll, Heidi ran towards the Baron.

L'Ollonaise breathed a sigh of relief. He had played with this young girl when she was barely a year old. Surely this young child would plead to spare his life. L'Ollonaise looked at her doll. Suddenly he noticed that the string connecting the doll to the wooden rod was tied around its neck.

"Grandpa use to hang traitors like this on his ship. I've never seen a lynching. Can't you hang him? Please."

"Spoken like a true granddaughter of Admiral Von Skimmel. Whereas your grandfather used a yardarm, we shall use that nearby tree. You shall have your hanging, Heidi."

The little girl danced with glee.

"Even a scoundrel like L'Ollonaise didn't deserve such a death," argued the Major a week later as he rode into El Paso alongside Jake Sartana. "It's one thing to hang a man, but you don't do it when he's bleeding to death."

"You can't fault the Baron," countered Sartana. "He promised to kill L'Ollonaise swiftly if he followed the rules. My former employer had only himself to blame. Anyway, what would you have done if you had been the Baron?"

"I would have sent a bullet into L'Ollonaise's lying mouth."

"That isn't the most pleasant way to die."

"At least it's swift. I intend to stay clear of doing business with the Baron in the future. He's got a mean streak that doesn't appeal to me."

"Too bad the watch with your sister's picture was smashed. I know you valued it highly."

"I still have the other one. It's identical."

Arriving at Gordon Munitions, the Major introduced Sartana to the proprietor.

"So you now have a partner," commented Arthur Gordon.

"Our alliance is only temporary," explained the Major. "We will go our separate ways once we leave El Paso. Are those rifles I ordered ready?"

"They sure are. Let me take you to my showroom." Gordon escorted his visitors to an exhibition hall where were showcased vast varieties of firearms inside glass cases. In one case were three rifles plus a revolver with an extremely long barrel and an attachable shoulder stock.

"May I examine them?' asked the Major.

Pulling out a ring of keys hanging from his belt, Arthur selected the one to unlock this particular case. Once it was opened, the Major reached for one of the rifles.

"A Winchester 1866 Yellow Boy," declared Sartana. "What's so special about that?"

"Gordon Munitions has modified it. There is a separate long barrel which can be attached to give the weapon a range of up to 600 feet. As a complimentary item, there is a leather bracelet that stores bullets for the rifle."

"By the way, Major," interrupted Arthur. "Did the derringer purchased on your last visit function satisfactorily?"

"It saved my life. Unfortunately, the four front barrels were shattered by a bullet."

"Leroy Bailey could easily repair such damage. If you give me the derringer, I'll send it to him in Mexico."

"If I had known that, I wouldn't have abandoned the derringer on the New Mexico trail. Bailey will just have to make me another one from scratch."

"You may have to wait up to two years. It's very difficult for Bailey to get the three barrels hidden in the handle to work properly."

"I can afford to wait. In the interim, I'll just use a regular derringer."

"Thank you for accepting the delay, Major. Can I interest you in anything, Jake?"

Sartana pointed to a very large organ in a corner. "I'm surprised to see such a musical instrument among all these weapons. I was taught how to play one when I was a choir boy."

"You don't happen to be a Baptist like me?"

"No, Mr. Gordon. I was raised a Catholic. Might I play that organ?"

Arthur Gordon's expression became extremely serious. "If I allowed you to play it, you would probably destroy everyone and everything in this room."

"You're saying it's a weapon?"

"Probably the most dangerous that my firm has ever made. Two of the outer pipes on each side can be lowered to fire cannon balls. The four central pipes can be lowered to shoot bullets more rapidly than a Gatling gun or a Mitrailleuse gun."

"Who dreamt up this compact arsenal?"

"Jake, I also own a subsidiary in France. I generally spent half the year there. In 1870, just before the outbreak of the Franco-Prussian War, a Frenchman contracted me to make such an organ based on his own designs. The man identified himself as Enrique Claudin. He was an enigmatic fellow who always wore a mask. Supposedly he had been disfigured while serving as a French soldier in Mexico. The masked man professed that the organ was intended to defend his home if the Prussians invaded France. When I realized how devastating a weapon Claudin had conceived, I had my Paris employees create a duplicate. Claudin took possession of his organ, and then all hell broke loose. Not only did the Prussians overrun France, but the left-wing Communards temporarily seized control of Paris. I fled France with this duplicate organ."

"What happened to Claudin?" asked Sartana.

"No one knows. He disappeared during the turmoil of the Paris Commune. Hoping to persuade him to design further weapons, I searched for him once France became stable. I even hired the Chupin Detective Agency. Not only couldn't they locate the masked man, they discovered that the French War Department had no record of any Enrique Claudin serving in the army during the occupation of Mexico. The man was a total fraud."

"That organ is an impractical weapon in its current form," concluded Sartana. "If you could find some way to copy the rapid firing gun barrels into a weapon the size of a Gatling gun, you would have a profitable piece of merchandise."

"A sort of mechanized gun. In his workshop in Mexico, Leroy Bailey is already laboring towards that goal. He hopes to have a working model within a few months."

"Is the organ for sale?"

"Yes. Bailey doesn't need to study it any further."

"What's the price?"

"10,000 dollars."

"I'll give you 5,000 for it."

"Jake, let's split the difference. 7,000 is my final price."

"It's a deal."

.The Major had watched the haggling over the organ with amusement. "Jake, you won't have much money left if you buy expensive items like that organ."

"I may need it. Just before I cast my lot with you in Signo Amarillo, I received a message about a man named Grandville Fuller."

"Fuller!" exclaimed Arthur. "He was convicted of murder six months ago. He's currently in a prison not too far from here. For some strange reason, the authorities keep delaying his execution."

"Struck me as odd too. Originally I was going to ignore the telegram, but now I'm in Texas. I may need a partner on this venture.[1] Interested, Major?"

"I'll pass. I have business in a different part of Texas."

---

1 See the movie *Light the Fuse . . .Sartana is Coming.*

The Major rode up to a small farm on the outskirts of Lost Knob, Texas. A brown-haired woman stood on a porch next to a young teenager. "Now that you've done your chores, Junior, you can play baseball with your friends." The adolescent happily ran off.

"Are you Mrs. Sabbath?" asked the Major on his horse.

"Yes. What brings you here?"

"It's a matter that needs to be discussed in private." Dismounting from his horse, the Major tied up his horse to a hitching post. He unhooked a small satchel from his saddle. "May I talk to you inside?"

Mrs. Sabbath entered the house. Carrying the satchel, the Major followed her.

After identifying himself, the Major explained the reason for his visit. "I need to talk to you about your husband."

"IF you're carrying a message from Christian, you wasted a trip. I want nothing to do with him."

"I barely knew your husband, Ma'am."

"Knew? You're talking about Christian in the past tense. Is he dead?"

"It is my unfortunate duty to inform you that your husband is deceased."

Mrs. Sabbath lowered her head. Tears formed in her eyes.

"I warned Christian that this would happen when he insisted on moving to Mexico. The Juaristas hailed him as a hero. They even called him by a Spanish variant of our surname. I warned Christian that if he moved there, I would leave him. When he sold our mansion in Kingsville, I took our son to this farm. My grandfather died at the Alamo to be free of Mexican rule. It made no sense to move there."

"Mexico's a constitutional democracy. The days of the dictatorial Santa Anna are long past. The current President, Sebastián Lerdo, is a just man. "

"But he was nearly overthrown by a revolt on the day he took office. Sooner or later, some modern day Santa Anna will dispose of Lerdo. Is that how Christian died? Fighting Lerdo's enemies?"

"Yes, your husband died defending Benito Juarez's legitimate successor from the enemies of democracy. He was a true hero. As he was dying from bullet wounds, Christian entrusted me with money that he had legitimately earned during his years in Mexico. His last request was that I bring it to you."

The Major handed Mrs. Sabbath the satchel. She opened it.

"There must be thousands of dollars here!"

"15,000 to be exact." Minus the money given to Sartana at the Baron's ranch, it was all the bounty that the Major had received for delivering L'Ollonaise alive."

"How did you find me? Christian didn't know where I was living."

"Christian's friend, Mr. Gordon, was kind enough to locate you for me."

"You can't mean Arthur Gordon the bigamist?"

"His first name is Arthur, but he only has one wife, Xaviera, to my knowledge."

"He's the same man. His second wife lives in France."

The Major assumed that Mrs. Sabbath was repeating some scurrilous rumor circulated by Gordon's enemies.

The widow looked skeptically at all the cash in the satchel. "I can't accept this money."

"Mrs. Sabbath, the money is legally yours; whether you keep it or give it to charity is none of my affair. However, I couldn't help but notice that you have a son."

"Christian Adam Sabbath Junior."

"Then I advise that you take him into consideration regarding any decision that you make."

"Good advice. Surely you should take some of this money as a fee for bringing it here."

"I must decline your generosity. When I met your husband in Mexico, I was engaged in a business affair that proved injurious to us both. I owe your late husband a grievous debt. The only way that the debt can be erased is for you to take total possession of the satchel's contents. You will need to sign a receipt."

When the Major rode away from the house, he noticed Christian Junior organizing a group of other boys.

"Chris, we can't play baseball against those kids from Skurlock," protested another boy. "We don't have enough players."

"We just won't use a shortstop and one outfielder. Seven is enough to overcome all odds."

"You're hiring me to accompany you and a corpse to Utah?" asked the Major in 1876. He was seated in Arthur Gordon's office in El Paso.

"Quite correct," answered Arthur Gordon. "The dearly departed died in Mexico. I employed Jake Sartana and another fellow to transport the body into Texas. Jake had to leave because he has another business venture to pursue. The body has to be buried in Fillmore, Utah."

"Who is the deceased?"

"An old friend of mine. His name was Mitchell Stangerson."

"Stangerson! He committed over a dozen murders in the 1850's!"

"That's why he was hiding in Mexico. I won't condone his killings, but he once saved my life."

"Why do his remains need an armed escort?"

"Relatives of his victims may seek to defile his corpse."

"You're carrying the coffin all the way to Utah by wagon. Wouldn't it be easier to travel part of the way by train?"

"A train would be the easiest place for someone to snatch the body."

The Major suspected that Arthur Gordon wasn't being entirely truthful with him. Nevertheless, he decided to accept the job.

"Arthur, who's the other man travelling with us?"

"His name is Djanko."

"Jango? What is he? Some sort of Indian?"

"No, he's Croatian, His name isn't Jango. It's Djanko. It's spelt D-J-A-N-K-O."

"Texas is pretty far from Croatia."

"A relative was involved in the botched assassination of a bigwig in Europe. Djanko's family felt it prudent to come to America."

"When do I meet this Djanko?"

"He's waiting outside." Getting up from his desk, Arthur opened the door to an outside corridor. "Please come in."

A man with bright blue eyes entered, He was dressed in a blue hat and Inverness coat of a Union army sergeant.

"My name is Ignacz Djanko," the newcomer said with a thick accent.

The Major rose from his chair. "I see from your attire that you served with the Union forces in the War Between the States,"

"I don't approve of slavery. Is that a problem?"

"That dispute is ancient history." The Major extended his hand. Djanko grasped it.

The Major took a gold case out of his inside jacket pocket. He opened it to display a set of very thin cigars. "Anyone care for a smoke?"

"You used to smoke a pipe," recalled Arthur. "When did you switch to cigars?"

"Two years ago. A rival bounty hunter whom I met in El Paso introduced me to this brand. It's made by the J. V. Harden Tobacco Company."

The night before they were scheduled to leave, the Major inspected their grisly cargo inside the wagon. Opening the coffin, he saw the cadaver of an elderly man. Ten minutes more of investigation divulged why Arthur Gordon needed to transport the body by wagon.

Arthur drove the wagon while Djanko and the Major, armed with rifles, rode parallel on each side of the vehicle. On their way to the border between Texas and New Mexico, the party proceeded to navigate a narrow canyon called Bryant's Gap. As the wagon entered the passageway, a party of sharpshooters impatiently waited along the top of the canyon.

"Any moment now, our quarry will be in range," predicted the woman to the six men lurking alongside her among the rocks.

The speaker was a shapely brunette. Her hair was tied in a ponytail She wore a frilled white blouse underneath a black vest. A Cordobes hat hung on her back. Her wide black pants looked like a skirt to a casual observer. Black gloves and boots graced respectively her hands and feet. She wore a ring with a black onyx stone on the middle finger on her left hand.

The men with her all wore the same black flock coats and derby hats that McIntock and his comrades had worn four years earlier.

A series of rifle shots erupted behind the party of ambushers. The men soon went tumbling into the gorge as the bullets of the Major's enhanced Yellow Boy rifle penetrated their bodies. The woman found herself surrounded by corpses. Her black eyes glared with hate as she saw the Major shooting from the bottom of the canyon.

"That fool! He must have a code that prevents him from shooting a woman!"

Raising her rifle, the woman quickly fired. The bullet never reached its target. It landed harmlessly into the dirt.

One of the Major's bullets hit the woman's hat. It went flying into the air before it landed at the bottom of the canyon.

"You're within range of my rifle," yelled the Major, "but I'm outside yours! Unless you want to join your friends in Hell, I suggest you throw down your rifle and climb down."

The woman did as she was instructed. When she reached the bottom, the Major had further demands.

"Keep your hands in the air as you walk towards us." The woman stopped upon reaching the Major. Seated on his horse, the ex-soldier looked sternly at his prisoner.

"You should have chosen a less obvious locale for your ambush. Bryant's Gap has been notorious as a death trap since outlaws killed a company of Texas Rangers here years ago. For that reason, I scanned the ridges closely with a telescope. Why are you trying to kill Arthur Gordon?"

"I don't give a damn about Gordon! It's you I'm after! My name is Delilah L'Ollonaise! Valentin was my cousin! He disappeared four years ago! You must have killed him!"

"How did you learn about my travelling with Gordon?"

"The Gentlemen of the Night know about your purchases from Gordon Munitions. We had their El Paso office under surveillance for months." Delilah moaned. "It's very hot. Can I retrieve my hat?"

"Being a gentleman, I'll do it for you," answered the Major.

Delilah's hat was lying upside down on the ground. Getting down from his saddle, the Major handed the reins to Djanko as he strolled towards the hat. Retrieving the Cordobes hat, he found a hidden pocket inside the hat. He pulled out a circular object with a small muzzle.

"Hey!" said Arthur seated on the wagon. "Let me get a closer look at that!"

Holding the device high in his raised hand, the Major moved closer to the munitions dealer. "Arthur, I've seen this in gun stores since the war. I've always wondered what it was."

"It's a palm gun! Leroy Bailey invented it before he went to work for Gordon Munitions. It carries up to ten bullets in a revolving magazine. You just fire it by squeezing."[2]

The Major grinned. "You're really full of tricks, Delilah! I'm confiscating this!"

"You can't do that!" protested Delilah. "That gun cost me 12 dollars!"

"Buy a replacement at your local gun shop." The Major deposited the squeeze gun inside his vest pocket. He then placed Delilah's hat on her head. "Lower your hands. Are you a Catholic?"

"I haven't been in Church for years!"

"I'll take that as a qualified yes. You must have gone to Confession at some point in your life. You must be familiar with the concept of Penance. I'm going to impose a Penance on you. That ring must have been originally made for a man. It'd too big for any of your fingers. You need to wear a

2 A virtually identical French weapon, the Protector, was created in 1882 by Jacques Turbiaux.

glove in order to make the ring fit. Your Penance is to give up that ring. Remove it."

As his right hand continued to point the rifle at Delilah, the Major extended his left hand forward. "Put it on the fourth finger. Good girl! Doesn't it look pretty on my hand."

"Please give that ring back to me! It was a gift from Madame Delphine!"

"Who's Madame Delphine? Your brothel keeper?"

"How dare you! Your own mother was a whore!"

"Quite true, but she serviced a far superior clientele than you do. Where did you and your men tether your horses?"

"At the exit of Bryant's Gap."

"Get in the back of the wagon and sit on the coffin," instructed the Major. "We're taking you to your horses."

"Who's in the coffin?" asked Delilah.

"Someone named Djanko," joked the bearer of that name.

Once Delilah was in the wagon, the party left Bryant's Gap. They found seven horses tied to a clump of trees. The Major pointed to a white stallion. "This horse is the most magnificent. I assume it's yours."

Delilah nodded.

Still on horseback, the Major untied Delilah's horse. "Here's where we part company, Delilah. Step out of the wagon."

"So! There is an ounce of chivalry inside you. You're going to let me mount my horse and ride away."

The Major removed a canteen attached to the white horse's saddle and tossed it to Delilah. She instinctively caught it.

"Why are you giving me this? You want me to take a drink?"

"I want you to ration the water inside so you don't die from thirst. You have to walk miles to reach the nearest town." The Major slapped the rump of Delilah's horse. The steed immediately galloped away. Placing the rifle in his left hand, the Major removed the squeeze gun from his pocket and fired. His shots severed the reins tying the horses to the trees. Panicked by the gunshots, the animals ran away.

"Farewell, Delilah!" The Major and his friends departed.

"Major, I swear in the name of my Master, the Lord of the Night, that you shall be repaid for the humiliations heaped upon me with a slow and brutal death!" screamed Delilah.

"It looks like you made an enemy," observed Djanko.

"If only all my enemies were as pretty as her," replied the Major.

Upon reaching Fillmore, the Major received his fee from Arthur. Djanko remained with their employer supposedly to assist with the arranging of Stangerson's funeral.

With his new funds, the Major went into a local saloon where he spied an old acquaintance."Phil Holden! I haven't seen you since Signo Amarillo!"

"I remember you. You called yourself Douglass, but Sheriff Ramsey later told me your real name. I changed my profession because of you."

"You're no longer a gambler?"

"I still gamble, but I'm always getting cleaned out. Seeing how easy it was for you to make a bundle on L'Ollonaise, I decided to become a bounty hunter. People call me Hot Lead."

"Looks like you almost really lived up to your nickname." The Major's penetrating eyes focused on Holden's right arm. It was in a sling,

Holden smiled. "That's only a flesh wound. When I got it, I felt it was time to visit my wife and child here."

"You're a father? Boy or a girl?"

"A boy. He's as handsome as me."

The Major laughed. Holden was extremely ugly. The only other man who equaled Holden's repulsiveness was a hunchbacked outlaw whom the Major had slain with a regular derringer two years ago. Shortly after that fatal shooting, Arthur Gordon had replaced the four-barreled derringer damaged in New Mexico.

"Who shot you?"

"Marrying Jack. He's got a bounty of 10,000 dollars on him over in Snow Hill County. He made the mistake of only wounding me. Once I'm fully healed, I'm going to collect that bounty. I need the money. I promised my son a pony for his birthday, but I lost all my cash to that cardsharp seated over there."

A poker game just concluded. Two disgruntled men were leaving the table. Basking in his triumph was a handsome man with a handlebar mustache.

"Well, well . . . If it isn't my old commanding officer. Care for a game, Major?"

"I'll take you up on that offer, Lieutenant Tervis!"

"Mind if I sit down and watch?" asked Holden. Neither of the two ex-Confederate officers objected.

When the game began, Tervis had 20,000 dollars. An hour later, he owed the Major 5,000 dollars."It going to take a while to raise the money that I owe you."

"How much time do you need. Lieutenant?"

"About a month, but I can give you collateral in the interim."

"What collateral?"

Tervis reached into his jacket and pulled out a star-shaped object. "The medal I won in the war."

"I'll take it. I have to leave Fillmore for a month. When I return, I'll expect you to be here with the 5,000."

Tervis rose and saluted. "You can rely on me, Major."

Holden smiled as Tervis departed the saloon. "You know he'll be far away from Fillmore 30 days from now."

"If he breaks his word, I'll just impose a Penance."

"What Penance will you impose?"

"I'll shoot off one of his fingers."

"I'm glad that Jake Sartana is more forgiving than you are. Major."

"What makes you say that?"

"For the last three years, I've owed him a poker debt for the same amount. 5,000 dollars."

"By the way, here's 200 dollars. Buy your boy a pony."

"I don't take charity."

"It isn't charity. It's a finder's fee."

"Finder's fee?"

"Holden, if you're going to be a success in our profession, you have to learn Rule Number Eight of the Bounty Hunter Code."

"What Rule is that?"

"Never tell a competitor about a bounty. I'm now headed for Snow Hill County to kill Marrying Jack."

Located north of Fillmore, Snow Hill County was wedged between Juab and Millard counties.[3] Upon his arrival in Snow Hill, the Major went to the county courthouse.

"Marrying Jack is a seditious rebel," explained the Justice of the Peace. The magistrate had a lean and hungry look like Cassius in Shakespeare's Julius *Caesar*. "Everyone who goes up against him has either been wounded or killed. You know what he and his gang call me. Judge Cutthroat. I'm just trying to enforce Federal Law."

---

3 You won't find Snow Hill County on any modern map of Utah. The county was dissolved by the Utah State Legislature in 1898.

"...here's 200 dollars, buy your boy a pony."

"What Federal Law does Marrying Jack object to?"

"The anti-polygamy laws, Major. During the Civil War, Lincoln made a deal with Brigham Young. The Mormons would support the Union in exchange for non-enforcement of the anti-polygamy laws. Now that there's been peace for more than a decade, I and other magistrates here intend to make Utah a law-abiding community like the rest of these United States."

"Aren't the Mormons arguing that freedom of religion entitles them to practice polygamy?"

"Indeed, they are. Marrying Jack is claiming that the matter should wait until the Supreme Court issues a ruling.[4] In the interim, Jack claims that everyone should let matters rest."

"What's wrong with that?"

"Nothing, if Marrying Jack was playing fair. He's been stockpiling guns and organizing his own private militia. It's only a matter of time before the Supreme Court rules against the Mormons. When that decision comes down, Jack will lead his followers in open rebellion."

"Isn't there a Sheriff who should arrest Marrying Jack?"

"The last Sheriff died a hero stopping a stagecoach robbery. The territorial governor hasn't had time to appoint a new one. In order to fill the gap left by the Sheriff's death, I've had no recourse but to enforce the law with bounty hunters."

"Even if I remove Marrying Jack for you, Judge, his outlaw army will still remain."

"Regardless of your success, I intend to implement countermeasures like those used against Bennet's Raiders."

"You intend to organize a huge posse and attack the outlaws in their base."

"Precisely. If you eliminate Marrying Jack, the outlaws will be leaderless. My planned assault will be a guaranteed success."

"Where does Marrying Jack reside?"

The Judge pulled out a map of Snow Hill County. There was an area outlined as "The Mormon Redoubt." The houses of several people were identified. One residence was labeled "Marrying Jack's."

"You have to be careful travelling into the Redoubt, Major. Marrying Jack has posted sentries on all the main roads."

4 In 1878 (two years after this conversation), the Supreme Court decided that polygamy could not be justified by freedom of religion. Polygamy was abandoned by the Church of Latter-Day Saints in the Woodruff Manifesto of 1890.

The Major had often gone on reconnaissance missions for the Confederate army. He was an expert at finding devious routes to a destination. Through dexterous maneuvers, the bounty hunter bypassed the sentries and located Marrying Jack's residence.

Through a pocket telescope, the Major spied on the house from a distance. Marrying Jack didn't seem to be at home. There was a young woman and a male child. The Major judged the boy to be about ten years old. A man rode up on a horse. After dismounting the man kissed the woman and hugged the boy.

It was easy to identify Marrying Jack from his wanted poster. He was a muscular man with dark hair and a beard. Jack told his wife that he was going to milk the cows. With a pail in hand, he strolled towards the barn where the animals were kept. Through his telescope, the Major pointedly noticed the holstered revolver hanging from Jack's belt. It was against the Major's private code to kill an outlaw in front of his wife and child. The bounty hunter would confront Marrying Jack in the barn.

When the Major entered the barn, he had his four-barreled derringer drawn. Seated on a stool in front of a cow, Jack's back was turned away from the bounty hunter. The Major treaded so silently that the wanted man was totally unaware that an intruder had entered the barn.

"If you wish to avoid a bullet in the back, you'll raise both your hands in the air," suggested the Major. Marrying Jack silently complied. "Good! Now turn around and face me."

Looking firmly at his captor's face, Jack's eyes flashed with anger. "It takes real courage to ambush a man milking a cow."

"Marrying Jack, the territory of Utah has issued a bounty for you dead or alive. There's two ways we can do this. The easy way or the hard way."

"What's the easy way?"

"You let me take you as my prisoner to the Justice of the Peace."

"Trust the tender mercies of Judge Cutthroat? I might as well commit suicide. What's the hard way? You're going to have to take me in as a corpse. What are you waiting for? Pull the trigger!"

"You misjudge me, sir! I'm no executioner! I give each and every man an even chance. I'm putting this derringer under my belt. Lower your hands. At the count of five, we draw. Agreed?"

"Agreed! Bounty killer!"

Years ago, the Major had trained a man called Specs to be a bounty hunter, The Major had created an unofficial Bounty Hunter Code to train Specs. Rule Number Two was "Before you draw, watch a man's hands."

As the Major lodged the derringer under his belt, his steely eyes shifted towards his adversary's hands. "One!" Jack's fingers crept minutely toward the Colt Peacemaker in his holster. "Two!" The Major could see the ring on the fourth finger of Jack's right hand, It was boldly emblazoned with an ebony letter G. *"Intermission!"*

"Damnation!" yelled Jack. "Who ever heard of an 'Intermission' in a gunfight!"

"I want to discuss that ring on your finger! What does the G stand for?"

"Gordon. My real name is John Gordon."

"Any relation to Arthur and Bill Gordon?"

"Arthur's my Pa. Bill's my brother, but everyone calls him Frank."

"Mr. Gordon, I owe you a distinct apology."

"I should have guessed that Arthur is a Mormon," stated the Major as he drank a glass of whiskey inside John Gordon's house. "A woman in Texas referred to him as a bigamist."

"My father married three times," revealed John. "Besides my mother, Pa wedded a Frenchwoman whom he met in Europe. She knew Pa was a Mormon with another wife when they married. Pa also took another bride in Utah."

"How many kids does your father have?"

" Between the three wives, five sons."

"Your father always says he's a Baptist."

"He was raised a Baptist, but then converted to Mormonism. In 1861, he left the Church of Latter Day Saints to become a Baptist again."

"What prompted that decision?

"Pa was an ardent supporter of the Confederacy. He never forgave Brigham Young for striking a bargain with Lincoln. More importantly, there was Pa's role in the Stangerson Affair."

"I was wondering about that. I've only heard garbled accounts of that controversy. What exactly is the truth about Stangerson?

"Mitchell Stangerson, Horst Drebber, and their two sons formed a criminal gang called the Council of Four. Through murder and extortion, they forced women into marriage. Their crimes were exposed in 1860 when the Council of Four caused the death of John Ferrier and his daughter. The Ferriers were close friends of Brigham Young, who swore to bring their killers to justice. Before the Council of Four could be apprehended, they fled the territory. Mitchell Stangerson once saved my father's life. Pa repaid that debt by helping Mitchell and his son escape the gallows. Brigham Young was threatening to excommunicate my father for his role in the Stangersons' flight. Pa forestalled this move by voluntarily resigning from the Church of Latter Day Saints. My mother and my two brothers followed Pa in his return to the Baptist Church. Only I remained true to the Mormon faith."

"I've heard that the Council of Four was synonymous with the Avenging Angels."

"That's pure hogwash, Major. The Avenging Angels were disbanded in Missouri during1838, and their leader was excommunicated by the Church of Latter Day Saints. The Avenging Angels never operated in Utah. There are all sorts of falsehoods circulating about the Stangerson Affair. Some people even claim that Brigham Young was a member of the Council of Four. Those libelous stories will die a natural death unless some dang fool records them in a book."[5]

"Why does Judge Cutthroat want you dead?"

"The Judge is engaging in an enormous land swindle. Taking advantage of the vacancy in the Sheriff's office, Cutthroat is issuing warrants for law-abiding Mormons on trumped up charges. Once bounty killers have slain the Mormon settlers, the Judge finds some legal pretext, such as unpaid taxes, to seize their land. All his crimes are masked by anti-Mormon prejudice. He gave me the nickname of Marrying Jack even though I only have one wife. I've organized a Mormon militia to resist the Judge."

"What are you going to do if the governor appoints a new Sheriff?"

"I'll turn myself over to him and give him proof of the Judge's crimes."

"There won't be time for that. John. Judge Cutthroat is organizing his own private army of anti-Mormon fanatics. His plan is to use that force to massacre all the Mormons in Snow Hill County."

"My militia will just have to fight as best we can."

"Your father can help."

"What can he do? He's in Texas."

---

5 John Gordon's fear was justified. A "dang fool" did falsely record the events of the Stangerson Affair. His name was John H. Watson, the biographer of Sherlock Holmes. Two members of the Stangerson-Drebber gang fled to London in 1881, There they were murdered by Jefferson Hope, a close friend of the Ferriers. When Hope was arrested, he told a garbled account of the Stangerson Affair distorted by anti-Mormon prejudice. Without doing the proper historical research. Watson repeated this inaccurate account in *A Study in Scarlet* (1887). Visiting Utah in 1923. Watson's Literary Agent, Sir Arthur Conan Doyle, admitted that *A Study in Scarlet* was unintentionally filled with historical inaccuracies about the Mormon experience in Utah.

"Actually he's in Fillmore. Your father has something that will defeat Judge Cutthroat."

"If you want to help, I think it would be wiser to stay with me until the new Sheriff arrives. I could use someone with experience in dealing with professional lawmen."

"My plan is better. Sheriffs are hampered by rules and regulations. Vermin like Judge Cutthroat need to be removed with swift action. I'm leaving for Fillmore."

There was a knock on the door of Arthur Gordon's hotel room. "Mr. Gordon, it is Count Stanislaus Kowalski of Poland. Your son Bill recommended me to you."

Arthur Gordon opened the door. Standing in the doorway, the Count was a burly man with a huge mustache that would have rivaled Otto von Bismarck's. The Count's reference to Arthur's son as Bill rather than Frank proved that he had genuinely been referred by the munitions dealer's offspring.

Accompanying the noblemen was a slim man with dark eyes. In contrast to the middle-aged Count, his companion was only twenty years old. "I am the Count's secretary. My name is Anton Niklas Petersen. I'm Swedish."

"Forgive me gentlemen," said Arthur, "but you claims of nationality don't match your accents. Both of you speak English with distinct Italian accents."

"Persecution by the Russian Tsars has forced both our families to live in exile in Naples. The majority of our lifetimes have been spent in Italy."

"Forgive me again, gentleman, but only half of that story makes sense. Russia controls the majority of Poland, but Sweden is completely independent."

"However, Mr. Gordon, the Russian Empire owns Finland," argued the secretary. "I come from the Swedish minority that lives in Finland."

"Thank you for clearing that up, Mr. Petersen. The gentleman in blue is my bodyguard, Ignacz Djanko."

The Count's eyes widened. "Djanko? A Croatian name?"

"Correct," acknowledged Djanko.

"Your manner of dress suggests an association with the Union cause during the recent conflict," noted the Count.

"I served under Sherman," revealed Djanko.

"A truly remarkable general!" exclaimed the Count. "Besides being a strategic genius, his commentary on the nature of war is extremely insightful."

"As an ex-citizen of the Confederacy, I frankly view Sherman as a murdering bastard," interjected Arthur.

"Considering your feelings about Sherman, why do you employ one of his former soldiers?"

"Djanko's past is irrelevant when weighed against his proficiency with a pistol. In fact, I believe him to be the fastest shootist in the West."

"Fascinating. Let's get to the matter at hand. When I was a guest at the Baron's ranch, your son told me about a certain weapon that you are trying to find a buyer for. I expressed an interest in acquiring this device for a new rebellion in Poland."

"You have my sympathies, Count. I remember the Tsar's brutal suppression of the revolt in 1863. Lincoln supported Alexander II's countermeasures in Poland in exchange for Russian assistance during the War Between the States."

"One thing puzzles me, Mr. Gordon, why are we in Utah? Wouldn't it have been easier to meet in Texas?"

"When I inform you of the history of the weapon, you'll understand the need to handle this transaction as far from Texas as possible. Are you familiar with the Rio Grande Massacre of 1873?"

"Is it related to the Rio Bravo Massacre in the same year?"

"We're talking about the same thing, Count. The river called Rio Grande is known as Rio Bravo in Mexico."

"How is your product connected to that atrocity?"

"In 1873, my company's chief gunsmith, Leroy Bailey, perfected a rapid fire weapon that was a vast improvement on the Gatling gun. Whereas a Gatling gun is fed loose ammunition through a hopper, a Bailey gun uses a cartridge belt. A Gatling gun can only be fired by turning a crank. A Bailey gun is a true automatic weapon employing a recoil system to eject each spent cartridge and insert a fresh replacement. A Gatling gun is so large and bulky that it is often mounted on wheels like a cannon. A Bailey gun is light enough that a muscular man like Djanko can carry it while firing. I tried to sell this weapon to the American Army, but it refused to even attend a demonstration."

"How could the Army be so shortsighted?" asked the Count.

"I am despised by many high-ranking officers because of my Confederate past. I suspect that both President Grant and General Sherman are strongly opposed to any financial dealings with my firm. Looking for a substitute client, I sent envoys to President Lerdo of Mexico. At the time, Lerdo just had survived an unsuccessful revolt by Porfirio Díaz in the prior year. "

"I am well aware of the political situation in Mexico," said the Count. "Lerdo foolishly pardoned Diaz after that failed insurrection. Diaz has repaid Lerdo's clemency by launching more uprisings. It's only a matter of time before one of them succeeds."[6]

"Lerdo needed armaments to consolidate his rule. Rather than purchase them from me, he made a secret deal with President Grant. In exchange for Mexican gold, the American army woulddeliver weapons to troops loyal to Lerdo in a series of secret meetings along the Rio Grande. Since Lerdo rebuffed my entreaties, I intended to sell my Bailey gun to his rival, Diaz. A man claiming to represent Diaz purchased one such weapon from me. Unfortunately, the man was an impostor. He was actually the leader of a group of bandits operating out of the Mexican border town of San Miguel. Somehow the San Miguel bandits learned of the secret Rio Grande meetings. After using the Bailey gun to annihilate a group of American soldiers escorting the military weapons to the rendezvous, the bandits impersonated the soldiers in order to slaughter the Mexican troopers guarding the gold."

"Weren't all the bandits later killed by the Mexican Army?"

"No, Count, they were all slain by the Drifter with Many Names."

"Who is that?"

"A very lethal American bounty hunter. He's called the Drifter with Many Names because of his shifting aliases. At the time of the Rio Grande Massacre, he was known as Joe Limbo. During the Civil War, a Mexican bandit gave the bounty hunter the nickname of Rubio."

"Rubio? Does the Man of Many Names have blond hair?"

"Actually his hair is dark brown. Recently this bounty hunter uses the name Lefty because he now wears a gauntlet on his left hand. After the Drifter with Many Names left San Miguel. Mexican troops occupied the town. They found all the bandits dead and buried, but no trace of the Bailey gun was ever found. No one knows what happened to it. Maybe the Drifter took it."

"Did the American government ever connect you to the San Miguel bandits?"

"A cavalry officer named Chadwell conducted an investigation into

6 Some months after this conversation, Diaz overthrew Lerdo in November 1876.

the Rio Grande Massacre. He concluded that the American and Mexican soldiers were killed by an unknown weapon superior to a Gatling gun. Checking War Department records, Chadwell found my letters offering my Bailey gun for sale. When he interviewed me, I claimed that the Bailey gun proved unreliable due to overheating. Therefore, I canceled production. Chadwell didn't believe me, but he couldn't prove that I was lying. If the truth was known, then my enemies in the War Department would unjustly charge me with being an accomplice to the Rio Grande murderers. Ever since that time, the Army has been on the alert for anyone peddling an unusual rapid fire weapon in Texas. I cached my remaining guns in Mexico."

"Therefore, selling a Bailey gun in Texas would be foolhardy. By contrast, Utah is a safe distance from the site of the Rio Grande Massacre."

"Precisely, Count. When a friend of mine from Utah died in Mexico, I used the transportation of his corpse as a pretext to smuggle a Bailey gun into the United States."

The negotiations were interrupted by a series of loud knocks on the door. "Arthur, it's the Major! Your son John needs your help! There's trouble in Snow Hill County!"

Djanko opened the door. The Major rushed inside. He quickly noticed the Count and his young secretary.

"Can these men be trusted?"

Arthur Gordon nodded his head, "My son Bill vouches for them. You can speak freely in front of them."

The Major quickly outlined the dire situation in Snow Hill County. "The only thing that can even the odds is that mechanical gun that traveled alongside Stangerson's corpse."

The munitions dealer was stunned. "I never told you about that?"

"I did some detective work. I didn't protest your refusal to fully confide in me because I value your friendship."

Arthur offered no apologies."Djanko, hitch up the wagon! We're going to Snow Hill County."

"Mr. Gordon," said the Count. "The family is very important in my native land. My secretary and I would be honored to ride with you to help your son."

"Can both of you handle a gun?"

"Guns?" questioned Petersen. "His Excellency and I don't use guns." Turning over his tie, the young man revealed a stiletto hidden underneath. "We use knives."

"I am similarly armed," confirmed the Count.

"Ride with us," decided Arthur.

At a stable inside Fillmore, Djanko and the Major prepared the wagon together.

"This time, Major, we'll carry an empty coffin. The casket containing Mitchell Stangerson is buried in the earth."

"Who are the two men travelling with us?"

"Potential buyers for Bailey's invention. The older man pretends to be a Polish Count planning to liberate Poland from the Tsar. The younger man is supposedly his Swedish secretary.

They are no more Polish or Swedish than I am. They're both Italians. Did you notice the rings they're wearing?"

"The rings are carved in the shape of coiled snakes."

"Such rings are worn by the Camorra, the Italian crime syndicate. It's also called the *Veste Nere*."

"*Veste Nere*?"

"It means Black Coats."

"That's another name for the Gentlemen of the Night! They're associates of Valentin and Delilah L'Ollonaise!"

"Not necessarily. When I was a boy in Europe, I heard all about the Black Coats. The Gentlemen and the Camorra are rival branches of that association of crooks. The Irish leader of the Gentlemen is rumored to bitterly hate the Camorra chieftain. Possibly the Camorra wishes to use the Bailey gun in their blood feud with their London competitors."

The Major wondered if the treacherous Delilah lied to him at Bryant's Gap. Her real motive for the ambush may have been to prevent Gordon from selling a Bailey Gun to the Camorra.

"Does Arthur know that he's really dealing with the Camorra?"

"He probably suspects the truth, but the true nature of his buyers won't bother him. Arms dealers like him only care about profits. They'll sell to anyone. Arthur is only motivated by money."

"Is that what motivates you, Djanko? Money?"

"No, vengeance. A woman very precious to me was killed by a band of outlaws. The gang consists of over forty men. Arthur has promised me a

"This time, we'll carry an empty coffin."

Bailey gun if I serve him faithfully for two years. Once I have that weapon, I'm going to wreck havoc on my beloved's murderers."

During the journey to Snow Hill County, Djanko drove the wagon with the coffin inside. The vehicle was drawn by two horses. Arthur Gordon, the Major, the Count and Petersen all traveled on horseback,

"I've heard of you, Major, from some friends of mine," noted the Count. "They call you Gunsight Eyes."

"Gunsight Eyes? That's a ridiculous nickname. Who are your friends?"

"Bill Gordon, the Baron, and other employees of Brockston-Morton. They told me about your dealings with a man named L'Ollonaise."

"Your tone suggests you knew him."

"Unfortunately, I had some business dealings with him. Like the rest of his family, he was a man without honor. You did me a favor by delivering him to the Baron for judgment. I only wish that all his kinsmen could feel the embrace of a hangman's rope."

The Major noticed a black bag hanging from the saddle of the Count's secretary.

"What's in the bag, Petersen?"

"Surgical instruments. I'm studying to be a doctor."

"Mind if I call you Doc?"

"Hmm... Doc Nik... Doc Niklas Petersen... I like it."

When the party finally were about to enter Snow Hill County, they were stopped by a group of six men armed with rifles.

"Are you Christians?" demanded the leader of the sentries.

"We are indeed," replied the Major. "Why does our religion matter?"

"There's a gang of Mormon outlaws nearby. Our posse's going to flush them out."

The Major spied a party of mounted men about a mile away. He judged the group to be at least fifty men.

"Why is there a coffin in the wagon?"

"It's empty," claimed the Major. "We're from Fillmore. A relative of ours died in Juab County. We need to pass through Snow Hill County to bring the body home for burial."

"Check the wagon, Barney," said the leader to one of his men.

Climbing into the wagon, Barney removed the lid of the coffin. "It's empty, Sam."

"Two of my men shall escort you through Snow Hill County, but you're going to have to surrender all your guns," proclaimed Sam. "They shall be returned once you exit the County."

Unbuckling his gun belt, Arthur handed it to the sentry. Perched on the front seat of the wagon, Djanko similarly relinquished his gun. Both the Count and Petersen pulled the flaps of their unbuttoned coats wide open. "Neither my secretary nor I carry a gun."

The Major opened his coat. "I have a derringer tucked inside my left pants pocket."

"Remove it slowly," ordered Sam. "Hand it to me butt first."

Pulling the gun out of his pocket, the Major relinquished it to Sam..

Sam noticed an object sticking out of a pocket on the Major's vest. "What's that weird thing?"

"A Confederate medal."

"I've never seen one of those. Show it to me."

The Major took the medal out of his vest pocket. However, underneath the watch was Delilah's palm pistol.

Barney pointed to Arthur. "He's wearing a ring like Marrying Jack's! They're Mormons!"

The Major pressed the medal against the squeeze gun. He fired four times. Sam and two of the sentries fell to the ground dead. The gun then jammed. Its delicate mechanism had been damaged when it hit the bottom of Bryant's Gap while inside Delilah's hat. The Major was at the mercy of the other two gunmen, but the Count and Petersen intervened. Pulling the hidden knives from under their ties with lightning speed, they threw their knives at the two remaining sentries. Petersen's slammed into the forehead of his target while the Count's pierced the other's heart.

The Major dropped the broken palm gun. "I'll have to spend 12 bucks on a replacement."

"The posse heard the gunshots!" yelled Arthur. "They'll be here in no time! Count, you and Petersen tie up the horses to those trees!" Arthur pointed to the wagon. "Major, help me unhitch the horses! Djanko, get the Bailey Gun!"

Once the bolt was removed to the harness attached to the wagon, Arthur and the Major drew the horses away from the vehicle. "We need to keep these two horses from panicking and bolting once the shooting starts," declared Arthur,

Standing inside the wagon, Djanko shoved the empty coffin with all might. Sliding swiftly on the wooden floor, the oblong box shot out of the wagon and struck the rocky ground. The removal of the coffin revealed a loose plank in the wagon's wooden floor. Lifting the plank, Djanko exposed a secret compartment. The Bailey gun was inside.

Lifting the mechanized gun, Djanko stood tall atop the wagon. The cartridge belt of the Bailey gun hung down and ended in a pile at the gunfighter's feet. The posse was charging the wagons as the Light Brigade charged the Russian artillery. A rifle bullet whisked by Djanko's ear. "Die!" he screamed defiantly and squeezed the trigger.

A crescendo of bullets erupted through the air. Riddled with lead, riders fell from their saddles. Dying horses slammed into the gun. Multiple riders untangled themselves from their lifeless steed and tried to run to safety. The deadly pellets of Djanko's gun tore into their bodies. Within, a matter of minutes, the gunfighter gazed triumphantly on the mass of cadavers before him. The Bailey gun ceased fire. The stench of death was carried into Djanko's nostrils by the wind.

Once the carnage had ended, the Major addressed his companions. "I'm going to search the dead for Judge Cutthroat's body. If I don't find it, this battle is far from over."

"Some of Cutthroat's followers may still be alive," observed Petersen. "I might be able to help them survive long enough to be questioned."

"Come along then," said the Major.

It wasn't long before the duo found a critically wounded man moaning on the ground.

"Where's Judge Cutthroat?" asked the Major.

"Go to Hell," uttered the man defiantly.

"Major, please let me try," suggested Petersen. "I know a technique developed by Anton Mesmer." The counterfeit Swede knelt beside the wounded man. "I am a doctor. I shall not deceive you. There is nothing I can do to save your life, but I can remove the pain. You shall die peacefully in your sleep."

"Help me!"

"What is your name?'

"Dick."

Petersen placed his hand in front of the man's face. "Look at the eyes in the snake ring, Dick. Watch the snake's eyes as my hand moves back and forth. You are sleepy. Very sleepy. You cannot keep your eyes open."

Dick closed his eyes.

"You do not feel any pain, Dick. You are going to answer my questions. Where is Judge Cutthroat?"

"He's gone to Marrying Jack's house?"

"Why did he go there?"

"To kill Jack."

"How does the Judge plan to kill Jack?"

"While the Judge watches, two of his men are going to pose as the newly appointed Sherriff and his deputy. The impostors will ask Jack to surrender to them. If Jack agrees, he's be shot in the back."

"Have you ever made love to a beautiful woman?"

"Yes. At the whorehouse. Her name's Regina."

"Think of Regina. She has become the Shadow of Death. Embrace her and she will transport you to a land of miracles."

Dick gave a deep sigh. This was his last breath.

"We must go to John Gordon's house immediately!" insisted the Major.

"I don't understand," admitted Petersen. "Why did the Judge attack John Gordon alone before unleashing his posse on the Mormon Redoubt."

"It's sound military strategy. Kill the leader of the enemy forces first. While your adversary is rendered leaderless and confused, launch the main assault."

As the Major and his allies approached the Gordon farm, the bounty hunter instinctively sensed that something was wrong; a bleak silence pervaded throughout the surrounding area.

The Major was the first to enter the house. John Gordon was lying on the floor of the living room. The Major discerned rather quickly that Arthur son's had been shot once in the back and twice in the front.

"I'm sorry, Arthur. Your son is dead."

"His killers shall face God's wrath!" shrieked the grieving father.

Djanko found the body of John's wife sprawled at the bottom of the stairs. She had been fatally shot in the chest. There was a star-shaped badge next to her corpse. It must have been discarded by the bogus Sheriff after his grisly work had been done.

"There's a boy over here," shouted Petersen from inside the adjacent kitchen. "He still lives!"

"My grandson! Louie!" Arthur rushed inside. He spied Petersen kneeling next to Louie's motionless form. The bogus Swede was pressing a cloth against the child's neck.

"Has he been shot?"

"No, but some butcher cut his throat. Luckily the jugular vein was missed. I have to stop the bleeding."

Louie was eventually carried to an upstairs bedroom. Throughout the night, the newly christened "'Doc" Petersen fought to save the young boy's life. Occupying the house, the others took different turns as sentries guarding the residence.

In the morning, Petersen made an announcement. "Louie will live, but his vocal cords have been irretrievably damaged. He shall be a mute for the rest of his life. The boy is sleeping now."

Arthur Gordon strapped on his gun belt.

"What are you doing?" challenged the Major.

"'I'm going to pay Judge Cutthroat a visit at the local courthouse."

"That's a bad idea."

"Why?"

"How well does your grandson know you?"

"'Even though I travel extensively, I've always made it a point to visit John's family at least once a year. Louie knows I love him dearly."

"Your grandson not only has been maimed for life, but he's also witnessed the murder of his parents. When Louie wakes up, he needs to see the face of someone whom he trusts. Otherwise, this entire ordeal could drive him mad."

"You're right. I'm going to steal a page from the Baron's book. You're a competent bounty hunter. I'm putting my own private bounty on Judge Cutthroat. 20,000 dollars. It's yours to collect, Major."

"You can keep your money, Arthur. I'll do this job for free."

"Can you use a helping hand?" asked Djanko. "I'll also work for free."

"Your assistance will be invaluable, but someone needs to guard this house with the Bailey Gun while Doc and Arthur care for Louie."

"That can easily be me," indicated the Count. "That weapon is so simple to fire; even a child could do it."

Mounting their horses, the Major and Djanko departed on their mission of retribution.

When they entered the county seat, the two gunfighters were surprised to discover the town occupied by Federal troops. After hitching up their horses, they proceeded on foot towards the courthouse. The Major and his companion passed by a group of soldiers unloading a wagon. They were being supervised by an African-American sergeant.

"Boomerang Smith!" said Djanko.

"You're a sight for sore eyes, Djanko," replied the sergeant.

"Why are these troops here?"

"The territorial governor declared martial law. We just rode in this morning with the new Sherriff. For old times' sakes, Djanko, I don't want to know if you've been involved in the violent feud between Mormons and Christians here. If you have, go to the courthouse to hear the terms of the governor's conditional amnesty."

"Thanks, Boomerang." Djanko looked angry as he and the Major headed away from the sergeant.

"What's wrong?" asked the Major.

"I served with Boomerang under Sherman. He's still a sergeant. It's so unfair. If that man was white, he's been at least a captain by now. During the war, he developed explosive sticks that were essentially dynamite."

"That would have been years before Nobel supposedly invented it in '67."

"Smith didn't bother to patent his explosive. He donated it to the War Department to use in the crusade against slavery, but they only utilized it in a few instances. The most notable instance was the destruction of a bridge in New Mexico."

There was a large crowd gathered on front of the courthouse. On the porch were gathered a party consisting of eight soldiers and two civilians. One of the civilians was Judge Cutthroat. The Major couldn't discern the face of the other man who must be the new Sheriff.

Captain Younger of the U. S. Army was speaking. "I shall repeat the terms of the governor's amnesty. For the next seventy-two hours, there will be no arrests for any crimes committed prior to this date. Within that time frame, anyone surrendering his guns to the Sheriff will be granted an amnesty for any crimes committed in the past. Those receiving the amnesty will have any outstanding charges or bounties revoked, nor can any charges for past actions be brought against them."

"May I say a few words?" requested Judge Cutthroat.

"You may." The Captain stepped aside.

"Citizens of Snow Hill County," commenced the Judge, "there has been too much bloodshed between Christians and Mormons. Mistakes have been made by both sides. Men of all religions should learn to live together."

He unbuckled his gun belt. "I accept the generous terms of the governor. I surrender my gun to the new Sheriff entrusted with bringing peace to Snow Hill County, Priam Ramsey."

As the lawman stepped forward, the Major immediately recognized the man who had served as the Sheriff of Signo Amarillo four years earlier,

"Djanko, we need to go back to the Gordon farm," said the Major.

"That slimy bastard!" shouted Arthur Gordon in his dead son's house. "Judge Cutthroat must have known about the governor's amnesty in advance. He intended one last massacre of Mormons before the federal troops arrived. Now he's been granted an amnesty for all the murders he's responsible for. My son's soul cries for justice."

"What do you intend to do?" asked the Major.

"If we kill Judge Cutthroat now, the entire might of the U.S. Army will come crashing down upon our heads. The best thing to do is retreat but vengeance can be patient. Besides myself, my son is survived by his brothers and my grandson. If it takes decades, a member of the Gordon clan will one day force Judge Cutthroat to face retribution."

"I commend you, sir, on understanding the obligations of a family vendetta," said the Count.

"Count, if not for you and your secretary, my grandson would be dead. I shall take that into account when we conclude our negotiations back in Fillmore. Doc, is it safe to move my grandson?"

"Yes."

"Then there is only one thing keeping us here. We need to bury my son and his wife."

The Gordons were interred next to the barn. The Bailey gun was placed in the secret compartment of the wagon. A bed was prepared for Louie Gordon inside the wagon; he would be attended by Petersen while Django drove the vehicle during the long journey home.[7]

While preparations were being made to leave, the Major found John Gordon's journal. The bounty hunter read the last entry.

"I received word that the governor has appointed a lawman from New Mexico the Sheriff of Snow Hill County. His name is Ramsey, and his

---

7 In "The Last Vendetta" from *Sisters of the Shadows* (Black Coat Press, 2013), I claimed that Djanko and Gordon had first met along the Pecos River in 1878. I now know that was a mistake. They had actually met at least two years earlier. At the Pecos River in 1878, Arthur gave Djanko the Bailey gun to slay his lover's killers.

reputation is above reproach. If he demands that I turn myself in, I shall put my safety in his hands."

"Let's move out!" yelled Arthur Gordon.

"I'm not going with you, Arthur," revealed the Major. "I have unfinished business here."

"Don't be a fool, Major! Killing Judge Cutthroat would be suicide!"

"My business isn't with the Judge. It's with the Sheriff."

"Four year ago in Signo Amarillo," recalled Sheriff Priam Ramsey in his new office, "I turned over Ballantrae to you for extradition to Texas. One year after the Sunlight Saloon incident, Samson McDade resigned as my Deputy to join the revived Texas Rangers.[8] In fact, my son is currently serving under him. McDade wrote me that Ballantrae was never handed over for trial. What happened to him?"

"I turned him over to vigilante justice. He was lynched."

"You realize, Major, that you're confessing to the crime of murder."

"Yes, I'm willing to be extradited to Texas for trial."

"Where is Ballantrae buried?"

"I can't tell you that."

"You must be protecting the vigilantes who hanged him. Without a body, your confession is worthless. There's no proof that Ballantrae is dead. The legal doctrine of *corpus delicti* prevents you from being tried."

"I'm not a lawyer."

"Quite true. Your profession has never understood legal rules. I always suspected that your interest in Ballantrae was more than merely monetary. What was the history between you two?"

The Major gave an honest account of how Ballantrae tricked him into slaying Christian Sabbath.

"You lived with the guilt of Sabbath's death for four years. Why does it disturb you now?"

"Before I answer that question, I need to know your opinion of the man whom the Mormons have dubbed Judge Cutthroat."

"He's a murdering polecat who deserves to be hanged! Unfortunately, the territorial governor thinks imposing peace on Snow Hill County is better than bringing justice. He hopes to be the Vice-Presidential candidate

---

8 The Rangers were dissolved in 1865 during the Reconstruction Era. They were reconstituted eight years later.

nominated at the Cincinnati Convention next month. As a former Deputy of mine, Giddy Burnett, always says, a politician would pardon his father's murderer to gain higher office."

"Like Ballantrae, the Judge manipulated me into pursuing an innocent man. I nearly killed him."

"What happened to the man?"

"He was killed by the Judge's underlings just before your arrival. I left Snow Hill County to get help, but I failed to return in time to save the innocent man."

"And you feel responsible for this man's death."

"I shouldn't have left him. He was fatally tricked by a man posing as you. If I had stayed, I would have exposed the impostor and prevented a horrible tragedy. The innocent man and his wife are dead. Their child is maimed for life. It's all my fault. I feel unworthy of my father's name."

"Are you a Catholic, Major?"

"No. Why are you asking me that?"

"Because you seem to be under the delusion that my office is a confessional, and I'm a priest. If you're looking for absolution or forgiveness, you won't be getting it from me!"

"Can you at least impose a Penance?"

"A Penance? All right, I'll impose a Penance. You call yourself a bounty hunter, but God-fearing folk have a better name for your profession. Bounty killer! To lawmen like me, you're one step away from being an outlaw! If you're going to pursue this dark path, you better not hunt an innocent man again! You admitted that you disgraced the family name. Your Penance is to change your name! You are condemned to forever remember the lethal mistake you made in Mexico! Take the name of the man whose blood is on your hands! From this day forward, thy name is Sabbath!"

Three months later, a man in an Inverness cape entered an inn in Delta Valley, California. Taking out a gold case with a big black "S" emblazoned on it, he removed a thin cigar. After lighting it, he signed the register as "D. M. Sabbath." In the years to come, this signature would become feared by outlaws throughout the West.

THE END

RICK LAI - is an authority on pulp fiction and the Wold Newton Universe concepts of Philip José Farmer. For the pulp fanzines of the 1980'a and 90's, he originally wrote pseudo-historical articles in which pulp heroes and villains interacted with one another in a huge Farmeresque crossover universe. The various articles were eventually revised and collected in a series of books published by Altus Press: *Rick Lai's Secret Histories: Daring Adventurers, Rick Lai's Secret Histories: Criminal Masterminds, Chronology of Shadows: A Timeline of The Shadow's Exploits* and *The Revised Complete Chronology of Bronze.*

Rick's first published piece of fiction was "The Last Vendetta," published in *Tales of the Shadowmen #1:The Modern Babylon* (Black Coat Press, 2005). The story concerned a 1900 convention of master criminals at which were auctioned various weapons from Victorian mysteries, spaghetti westerns, and Hong Kong Kung Fu movies. The central character from that story was Arthur Gordon, an underused character from Emile Gaboriau's *Baron Trigault's Vengeance.* Various references in "The Last Vendetta" led to the writing of "Thy Name is Sabbath."

Rick is currently writing a series about the Revenant, a female vigilante trained by Gaston Leroux's the Phantom of the Opera. Short stories in this series include Rick's fiction has been collected in *Shadows of the Opera, Shadows of the Opera; Retribution in Blood* and *Sisters of the Shadows: The Cagliostro Curse* (which also reprints "The Last Vendetta" slightly revised). He has also translated Arthur Bernède's *Judex* and *The Return of Judex,* novels about a French pulp hero, into English for Black Coat Press. Rick also regularly appears on the Lovecraft Ezine internet chats.

CITY OF ENEMIES
BY ERIK FRANKLIN

"You're an idiot." Major Sabbath said with great irritation to his captive. He felt sweat trickling down his forehead and into his beady brown eyes. Between the Major and his captive, the canteen was drained dry hours ago. Sabbath was beginning to feel his throat grow parched, his tongue growing thicker and he had to keep forcing himself to stop from licking the sweat accumulating on his mustache. That would only dehydrate him more.

"I know..." Elliot Castle groaned as he trudged through the Texas desert with the Major's Derringer pistol pointed at his back. He was several paces ahead of his captor, his hands shackled in front of him. The thief was too far away to try and lunge at Sabbath and too close to make a break for it, any bullet fired by the bounty hunter would hit its mark instantly.

"Imbecile!" Sabbath snapped at the young man. Elliot turned to the legendary bounty hunter with an expression of indignation on his face.

"Now that is quite enough of that, Major Sabbath! There's no cause to..." he started defiantly, his native Texan accent punctuating certain words for emphasis. Apparently, despite his current circumstance, he fancied himself a Southern gentleman, speaking to Sabbath as if he were at a high society tea. Sabbath, however, saw him exactly as he was: a bank robber on the run from the law. He had tried to bribe the bounty hunter but a warning shot from Sabbath had dissuaded Elliot from attempting it again.

"No cause? You shoot my horse... the only horse for miles... and now we have to walk through the desert for god knows how long to get to the nearest town? I get to call you whatever I damned well please."

Elliot Castle was becoming a familiar name among the outlaws of Texas. He had singlehandedly pulled off some of the most daring, the boldest and bravest bank robberies that the state had ever known. His adventures graced the local newspapers, some national ones, and he even had a dime novel (with highly exaggerated action sequences) written about him. The bank had placed a large bounty on his head and Elliot was forced into hiding for the time being. Despite his various aliases and disguises, he had a habit of spending a great deal of money wherever he went. That caught the attention of Major Sabbath and he followed the paper trail until it led him to Dallas, Texas... and Elliot.

Tracking the thief was easy. Elliot was a city creature who did little in the way of disguising his tracks out in the wild. Sabbath had tracked the young bank robber to an abandoned cabin out in the middle of the desert. The bounty hunter planned to hogtie Elliot behind his saddle and take him back to town alive. However, Major Sabbath had not planned that Elliot's overwhelming bravado was matched only by his poor skills as a marksman. Elliot, lying in wait for the Major, had sprung a trap! However, his attempt to kill the Major had ended up killing Sabbath's horse instead, and after a savage beating the bounty hunter forced Elliot to march to the nearest town at gunpoint.

The two had spent the last several hours crossing the desert with no shelter from the sun. Elliot would occasionally look back to see if the older man was tiring, but every glance was met by the intense gaze of Major Sabbath's snake-like eyes. His dark, hawk-like face focusing solely on the bank robber. The bounty hunter glanced down at his black coat. A layer of fine, tan sand was beginning to cover the material.

"Pick up your feet when you walk, you're getting dust on my coat." the Major ordered.

"Sorry." Elliot complied as he took more elaborate steps. "You know, they say that it's not healthy to wear black in the heat. It makes you perspire excessively because dark material absorbs the sun or something like that. Don't you think you should rest, Major?" the young man said, trying his best to seem concerned.

Sabbath studied the young man's face. Elliot Castle was attempting a beard, but had to settle for a perpetual five-o'clock shadow. He was of an average height and thin build, not very imposing for a bank robber, Sabbath thought. Elliot's blonde hair was covered with sand and dirt, and his dandy clothes (now in need of a good scrubbing) resembled those of a high-stakes gambler, most likely purchased with the money he stole. Elliot was trying his damnedest to subliminally influence Sabbath by suggesting that the Major was becoming weak. His charm may have worked on anyone else, but Sabbath stood unimpressed by this false show of compassion.

"You know what else is bad for your health Elliot?" Sabbath asked "A bullet to the head."

"Yeah, but then I'd be worth a lot less to you, Major. What was it? Full price alive, half the bounty dead?" Elliot said with a wry smile, knowing he had the upper hand over Sabbath in this regard. To Elliot's great surprise, he heard the cocking of the hammer on the Derringer pistol.

"I could always shoot you in the leg," Sabbath warned, and then a sour expression appeared on his face. "No, that wouldn't do, because then I suppose I'd hear you howling like a wounded calf all the way to Blackheart."

"Blackheart?" said Elliot with genuine surprise. "You're taking me to Blackheart?"

"According to my map it's the nearest town. I'll drop you off at the sheriff's office and wire for your bounty. You can keep quiet until then."

"Trust me, Major, there ain't nothing for you in Blackheart! You might as well turn back now, I ain't fooling!" Elliot said giggling like a coyote. Sabbath was growing annoyed by the young man's perpetual arrogance.

Sabbath decided to ignore Elliot's suggestion. Of course *he* was the one who did not wish to go to Blackheart. One thousand dollars was a hefty price, and when a sum like that was on one's head, it was certain it would be dangling at the end of a rope once delivered into the arms of the law. Cruel though it may seem, Sabbath had long since given up caring about the plight of lawbreakers. He saw them as men who were looking for an easy life, but they had to live with the consequences of men like him coming after them. Not for one minute did he buy their philosophy that murder and mayhem were justified when one's goal was "to live free".

"Major, you really don't know much about Blackheart, do you?" the young thief said, interrupting Sabbath's thoughts.

"Are you going to keep talking the rest of the way?" Sabbath said with irritation.

"Well, I can't help it, Major! I'm a social person. I just like to…"

The dull smack of Major's Sabbath's Derringer against the back of Elliot's skull silenced his inane banter. True, the wanted poster specified that Elliot Castle needed to be kept alive for one thousand dollars, but it never specified in what condition he needed to be kept in. Sabbath hoisted the man over his shoulder and kept walking. He could feel the young man's steady, unconscious breathing.

Major Sabbath knew that carrying him in this manner would delay his arrival in Blackheart by a couple of hours. He was already feeling the weight of the rifle slung across his back and Elliot was about to add to it. True, he would be as fatigued as Elliot was intimating, but was willing to accept that bargain because it meant an end to Elliot's rambling.

The sun had set by the time Major Sabbath had reached Blackheart. Elliot Castle began to stir, gently feeling the rising bump on the back of his head.

"I do declare that was completely uncalled for, Major Sabbath!"

"That's a matter of opinion." Sabbath replied coolly. He dropped Elliot from his shoulder and the two started walking through the town.

"And you call yourself an officer of the law!" Elliot sneered with disdain.

"I never said I was any such thing. If that lump on the back of your head wants a little brother, I suggest you keep talking."

The young bank robber maintained his silence. Side by side with Elliot, Sabbath fondly recalled how he had enjoyed the past few hours of golden silence. He welcomed the cool evening air of the desert and felt the gentle breeze wick the moisture from his face.

Blackheart was not exactly a booming city, but it was not a one horse town either. Sabbath had observed the glow of the oil lamps from the city's saloon, where the sound of the rowdy patrons spilled out into the street. No shops were open. The bounty hunter observed several bullet holes in the walls of the buildings around him. A quick glance up and down main street revealed broken, boarded up windows. Evidentially, the law did not have a firm grip on Blackheart, as yet. This did not matter to Sabbath. Even if there was not a proper Marshal's office in town, he was a patient man who could wait for his reward money to arrive. The town seemed unremarkable at first glance, and he thought he might spend some time at the hotel until the money showed up.

Sabbath glanced over to his left and was intrigued by what he saw. A group of people, no more than a dozen, were somberly marching towards a building at the corner of town. Sabbath could barely read the painted "Schoolhouse" sign in the darkness. The Major watched them, and though he could not see their faces, they moved as if they were in a funeral procession. Perhaps he would investigate this later, but he had more pressing matters at the moment.

"Let's get this over with and go find the sheriff's office." Sabbath grumbled at Elliot, but he noticed the young man snickering to himself. "What's so funny?" Sabbath demanded.

"Nothing, Major Sabbath... nothing at all," he said unconvincingly "lead the way!"

Something was not right. Every instinct Sabbath had told him to keep his guard up. Why would Elliot find it so amusing to be marched to the Sheriff's office? Maybe the heat had scrambled his brains, but Sabbath doubted that this was true. He kept his eyes peeled as he searched for the sheriff's office. He could see numerous wanted posters nailed to the town's buildings, but was unable to read them in the dark. The small city, though recently built, displayed signs of battle damage that was not customary for this young frontier city. Maybe he would speak to the sheriff about it and see if the townsfolk would be willing to pay him to deal with their problems. Outlaws hiding out in the desert, he thought. They probably rode in to town periodically to steal supplies and stir up trouble for sport.

Sabbath had finally located the sheriff's office. It was unremarkable, save for the prerequisite bullet holes that now seem the standard with each building in this city. The sheriff's sign was shot up pretty badly, and indicated to Sabbath that the law is, or had been considered useless to the town. A stable was located next to the sheriff's office. The bounty hunter spotted a strong looking black mare in the prime of its life. The Major made a mental note that come morning; he would offer to buy the horse. He ought to force Elliot to pay.

Sabbath rapped on the door of the sheriff's office, holding Elliot firmly by the arm. They were greeted by a booming, hearty voice. "Come in, come in!" which was followed by gregarious laughter.

Walking into the sheriff's office, Sabbath noticed immediately that the jail cells were empty. Odd, for a town that was, to Sabbath's estimation, rife with crime. The furniture showed the wear and tear of many years use, and the walls were covered with wanted posters; some of them had faces crudely crossed out. An oil lamp hanging from the ceiling was the only source of light, but the glass had not been cleaned for months, casting a murky, sickly yellow light.

The large, robust figure of the sheriff rose up from behind his desk and walked towards them. Sabbath was of an average height, and disliked having to look up to the man. The sheriff's clothing was tight fitting, straining to conceal his powerful frame. He wore a dumb, contented expression on his face as he chewed on a stock of straw. Sabbath thought he looked familiar, though he had never been to this part of Texas.

"You bringin' somebody in here, partner?" he spoke in a loud, resounding voice that gave Sabbath an instant headache. Hopefully this meeting would be a quick one.

"Yes I am, and I'm also thirsty. Would you mind if I took a drink?" Sabbath asked, seeing a full pitcher of water close by. He forgot how thirsty he was until he saw the water pitcher.

"Help yourself partner!"

"Obliged!"

Major Sabbath poured himself a glass and sipped slowly.

"You didn't try and cross the desert on foot with this man, did yah?" asked the sheriff in astonishment.

"Yes, yes we did." said Elliot as he watched Sabbath drink.

"Thank you very much for the water. Now about my bounty... his name is Elliot Castle, and he's wanted in the state of Texas..." Sabbath began, but was silenced by a wave of the sheriff's hand.

"Aw, we know all about him here, mister. He's mighty famous around these parts." He said as he plopped back down into his chair, the wooden legs creaking in protest. He motioned to two deputies whom Sabbath had not seen. They came out of the shadows, moving nearer to the oil lamp.

"I don't recall Blackheart offering to put up any of the reward money. How's he famous?"

"Well... because he used to live here! Didn't you know that? I thought everybody knew that!" the sheriff said with another hearty laugh. Sabbath could hear the deputies giggle as well, but still could not see them clearly.

Sabbath decided to ignore the idiotic laughter and get on with business. Trouble or not, Sabbath had made up his mind that this town was becoming an annoyance. The sooner he was out of here the better. "I need to wire the nearest marshal and collect my reward." Sabbath said to the sheriff.

"Well, I'm afraid you can't do that partner, no siree," said the sheriff.

"Let me guess, the wires are down."

"Precisely, he is good isn't he? Well, I suppose that it's time to take care of business. Stand over there, Mr. Castle." The sheriff said indicating to Elliot. The sheriff steadily rose from his chair and casually withdrew his pistol. Sabbath was pleased and relieved that this adventure was drawing to a close. He looked forward to a long bath and eagerly awaited the chance to get the stench and sand of the desert off his body.

Elliot stood to the side and presented his cuffed wrists to the sheriff. The large man squeezed one eye shut as he aimed his gun at the chain. The bullet shattered the chain, freeing Elliot's hands.

"You crazy fool! You scared me half to death!" Elliot screamed wildly at the sheriff.

"I wanted to see if I still got it...I do! I guess you never really do lose your touch once ya got it!" the sheriff said, feeling immensely proud of himself.

"I *do* have the key with me," Sabbath said with bitter annoyance "and I'll have to ask you to reimburse me for the handcuffs. They aren't cheap, you know."

"Aw hell, that'll be the least of your problems, partner!" said the sheriff as he pulled a wanted poster from the wall. He read it carefully, glancing up to Sabbath from time to time. "Well, according to this here paper printed in this town, you are worth one-thousand big ones, partner. See the rest of these posters? The ones with the 'x's? We had to go out and hunt for these fine, upstanding gentlemen ourselves. You, Major Sabbath, just fell into our laps and we didn't have to lift a finger!"

"Excuse me?" Sabbath said, genuinely surprised. His hand went to his pistol as his muscles tensed. He was a cobra ready to strike.

"You know you are the first bounty man to wander blindly into Blackheart, and as far as I'm concerned, the cream of the crop!"

The two deputies walked towards Sabbath, their snarling faces now visible. Suddenly everything came together! The man on the left was named Diego Gutierrez, a Mexican assassin whom the authorities had failed to capture. He mysteriously vanished after murdering a Spanish dignitary almost a year ago. His cohort was Val Smith, a former enforcer for an illegal opium smuggling operation who was wanted for murder in at least six states. If these men were truly Diego and Val, Sabbath realized that the sheriff could be none other than their cohort Utah Grizwald, the infamous sadistic prison guard of the Civil War who went into hiding to escape prosecution for his crimes. The criminals were running the city!

"Utah Grizwald..." Sabbath began with a scowl.

"I'm surprised it took you so long to recognize me, partner!" he said with a boisterous laugh, a laugh that betrayed the cruelty of his true nature.

"The likeness on the wanted poster left something to be desired, and of course you went by another name for quite some time. Shame I didn't catch up with you earlier. These two, Diego and Val... they with you?"

"They are... and so is Elliot... and the rest of town!" Utah said, spreading his muscled arms wide to indicate the enormity of his tactical advantage. Sabbath heard a chair slide across the floor and butt up against the door. He instinctively surmised that Elliot was cutting off his closest escape route. Utah pointed at Sabbath "and I intend to collect the bounty on you! Get him boys!"

Diego leapt at Sabbath before he had a chance to shoot. The Mexican thug threw a wild haymaker at Sabbath, but the bounty hunter's straight left jab connected with his nose before he could reach the Major. Diego was out of the picture momentarily, but Val was closing in fast! With a powerful right hook, Sabbath sent Val's bloody teeth flying against the wall as he pivoted to face Elliot. The young punk had drawn a pistol, but Sabbath denied him the opportunity to use it. With blinding speed Sabbath kicked his leg up, catching Elliot's hand and knocking the pistol in the air. Sabbath flew at the thief, seized him by the collar and hurled him into Diego. The assassin, who lunged at Sabbath, was abruptly cut down by Elliot's body and the two crashed heavily to the floor.

"I'll teach you to punch me!" Val said through a bleeding mouth.

"I already know how." Sabbath said as he dodged a right swing from Val. The enforcer's fist made contact with one of the jail's iron bars, and a terrible crunch signaled broken fingers and a mangled hand. Grabbing him by the collar, Sabbath slammed Val's head against another jail bar. The bloody thug slid to the floor. Sabbath turned to Utah.

Utah was watching the battle unfold with amusement, like a spectator at a rodeo. He did not move during the entire brawl, nor did he feel the need to. Sabbath eyed him curiously, with a terrible feeling that Utah had planned something. Utah nodded to Diego and Elliot and Sabbath turned his attention to them. The two had untangled themselves from each other and got to their feet.

"This is for bashin' me over the head!" Elliot said as his fists flew at Sabbath. The bounty hunter put his hands up to block the incoming attacks, and saw Diego swinging a wooden chair! Sabbath was struck by the improvised weapon and crumpled to the floor, but quickly turned on his side to see Diego pounce on him, pinning him to the floor, and unsheath a fearsome knife. Sabbath knew this blade by reputation, for it was Diego's signature weapon. It left a distinctive serrated cut that distinguished his handiwork.

"One thousand dollars, you say?" Diego asked Utah.

"One thousand it is, dead or alive. Although..." Utah began to speak.

"Hold on! He put me through hell! I should be the one to gut him!" Elliot said, pushing past Utah and looking down menacingly at Sabbath.

"Will you stop trying to talk tough, ya upstart!" Utah chastised. "You ain't never killed a man in your whole life and nobody believes that you're gonna start now!"

"I could if you'd give me the chance!" Elliot protested.

"Killing is a man's sport, and you're just a boy!" Utah growled.

Diego turned his head to the bickering men and snapped at them. Sabbath was only half listening to their arguing, he was trying to prepare his escape. Diego had picked up the chair that was blocking the door and used it against him, so that route was now clear. Sabbath was never one to run from a fight, but knowing that he was outnumbered in this strange, unfamiliar city persuaded him that to prolong this battle would be futile. He would need to come back with a superior force of lawmen, and as soon as he got free from the Mexican's blade, Sabbath planned to steal the black horse next door and ride away.

"Killing's a man's sport and you're just a boy!"

His Derringer had been knocked away in the battle, but Sabbath spotted an opportunity to strike when the gleam of another blade caught his attention. Diego kept another knife, the handle resembled a throwing type, tucked in his belt. Sabbath's left hand was free, so with a great burst of speed he slipped the knife from Diego's belt and stabbed the outlaw deep in the stomach with all his might!

Diego moaned as Sabbath pushed him off. Racing towards the door, he dealt a swift backhand to Elliot as the young man attempted to restrain him. Jumping over Val's prostrate body, he was almost at the door when he felt two powerful hands grab his black coat. The next thing Sabbath knew, he was thrown into a jail cell like a sack of flour. The hay that was strewn on the floor of his cell provided little cushioning as he landed hard. He looked up to see Utah forcefully remove his black coat, stripping him of every weapon he owned. Moments later he heard his cell door slam shut and the clicking of a lock. Major Sabbath realized that he was trapped!

Sabbath was in a great deal of pain. He was feeling both the weariness of the battle and his long journey. The Major watched the bitter faces of the criminals stare back at him. Elliot spoke first, and Sabbath took small satisfaction that his backhand had given the thief a nasty black eye.

"What the hell, Utah! Why didn't ya help us!"

"If you ever get into a position of authority, son, then you're going to need to learn the art of delegation. Why bother working when you can tell somebody else to?" Utah said unapologetically as he placed another piece of straw into his smiling mouth.

Val had come to and stood up with great effort, leaning on one of the jail cell bars for support. He cast a sinister gaze in Sabbath's direction.

"I say we kill him here and now. Stupid lawman needs to die!"

"He ain't just a lawman you idiot! That is *the* Major Sabbath right here in our own town. Do you really want to just shoot him now?" Utah protested.

"Hell yes!" Val said, pulling out his six shooter, but Utah smacked his hand down with determination. A fierceness crept into his eyes and he barred his teeth. Val wisely backed down.

"Now, the way I see it, we all had a hand in bringing Major Sabbath here to justice, and one thousand dollars is a great deal of money! So we divide it by four..."

"Three," Sabbath corrected him, casually pointing to Diego's body, his blood staining the floorboards.

"Oh yeah, three... well I suppose that's good news for us in the long run. Anyway we approach the Mayor and divide our prize money. Then come morning, we hang him!" Utah said enthusiastically as if planning a hanging was celebrated like a grand birthday party. Utah looked down at the wanted poster and snickered. "Ain't that funny Elliot, according to this poster, he's worth the same bounty as you are!"

"I feel insulted," Sabbath said flatly. Utah started laughing, finding himself agreeing with the bounty hunter. Elliot pushed his face against the cage.

"Just shut up you stupid old fool!" Elliot snapped at Sabbath, before turning to Utah with another complaint. "I still don't understand why we have to wait until morning! Why not do it now?"

Utah rolled his eyes. "Because everyone in the city's gonna wanna see this one, and right now they're all too damn drunk to see anything standing in front of them. Can you imagine the fuss they'd make if they found out we killed Major Sabbath before they got a chance to see it?"

Elliot thought about this possible outcome, and nodded, agreeing with Utah quietly. With his smile back in place, Utah turned his attention to Sabbath.

"Well, see you in the morning! I gotta go talk to the Mayor about your hanging. Val, go to the doc and have him patch you up a bit, and send somebody to keep watch on the Major."

"What about him?" Elliot asked, pointing at Diego's corpse.

"Aw hell, leave 'em here. Undertaker said he was low on wood planks anyway. I'm too tired to clean this mess up now."

With that, Utah gathered up Major Sabbath's possessions and walked out of the sheriff's office with his fellow outlaws in tow. Sabbath leaned back in his cell and grimly considered his prospects. He was locked up tight, his weapons were in the hands of deadly outlaws, and come sunrise, he would be hanged!

Not knowing the layout of the town, Sabbath estimated that he had only a few minutes to attempt an escape. He had read about Val Smith from the newspapers, and if the accounts were to be believed, the outlaw's first and foremost thought was going to be of himself. Sabbath had the notion that Val would seek out the doctor before he went looking for someone to guard the jail. It was a hunch, but it was the only hope he would allow himself.

Nothing in the cell could be used to help him escape. He glanced quickly at the wanted posters that Utah had pointed out and noticed that they were all marshals and lawmen! Evidentially the city of Blackheart was quite demented, having the notion that capturing authority figures was a rewarding and honorable enterprise. "What else could you expect from a city ruled by outlaws?" he thought to himself.

He quickly glanced over at Diego's body. He recalled hearing that Diego had been an expert safecracker in addition to his other skills, and Sabbath was optimistic that Diego would keep his tools on him. Picking a jail lock was no different from a safe, so all Sabbath had to do was reach the body. Taking off his belt, he decided to use the buckle as a loop. With steady determination and impressive skill, Sabbath cast the belt and looped the buckle over Diego's spur! Sabbath gave it a quick test tug and was pleased to see that the buckle was securely attached.

Cautiously pulling Diego's body across the floor to within arm's reach, Sabbath rifled in the dead man's pockets for anything that could be useful. He found three throwing knives and Diego's signature blade. Utah had thought ahead, so he picked up Sabbath and Diego's pistols on his way out. There was no chance of Sabbath getting a gun here. After a few more moments of searching Diego's pockets, he found what he was looking for! It was a thin rod of metal, and the scratches on its tip revealed its purpose... it was a lockpick! Sabbath gripped the lockpick with a smile as he moved to the lock.

Working diligently, Sabbath felt the tumblers on the lock move. Placing his ear close to the lock, the Major could hear the mechanism shifting. It took him longer than he had anticipated, but eventually the door swung open and he was free once more. Before he could consider his next move, he heard the sound of footsteps approaching the door. Val must have found someone to stand watch!

Improvising, Sabbath dragged Diego's body into the empty cell, pulling the hat down over the face so it would not be recognized at a glance. The guard would have been suspicious if he saw an empty cell, but he would certainly have recognized Diego. All Sabbath needed was a moment for the replacement guard to investigate the situation before he dealt with him. Crouching in the shadows, he saw the outlaw wander in. He was decidedly drunk and the odor of cheap whiskey reached Sabbath's nose. All the better that his senses were dulled. The man staggered from the front door as he drunkenly improvised an irritating, garbled song.

"Major Sabbath! O' Major Sabbath! I'm a gonna watch you Sabbath! Watch you before you die!"

He clumsily shut the door. Perfect. Sabbath waited until he got closer to the cell, his hand gripping Diego's knife firmly. The inebriated outlaw stumbled towards Sabbath's cell continuing his song until he got a closer look at the body. He tipped the hat upwards and reeled backwards in drunken surprise.

"Sabbath... Hey, you ain't... that ain't you Sabbath! You Diego! Now what the hell are you doing in there Diego? Ain't no time for a..."

Clearly this drunk was not a threat. When Sabbath returned with a whole force of bounty hunters, he might as well earn double the money by keeping this one alive. With a sweeping kick Sabbath tripped the outlaw, causing the drunk to fall to the floor. The impact was too much for the man, and he passed out. Sabbath checked the man's pockets for anything useful. With the exception of the outlaw's pistol, the Major found nothing of use.

Sabbath dragged him into the cell with Diego and closed the door, blocking it with another chair since he could not find the key to lock the cell. It would take hours for the man to sleep it off, and Sabbath planned to be long gone. Before he left the sheriff's office, Sabbath took a look at the map hanging on the wall. Blackheart was hours from civilization in any direction, and the desert was full of poisonous snakes, scorpions, and deathly heat. He needed a horse.

Sneaking outside and hiding in the shadows, Sabbath cursed under his breath. The stable was now empty. The horses were being ridden by a few drunken outlaws who were charging up and down the street, yelling and howling in anticipation of Major Sabbath's hanging. Sabbath weighed his options before acting. He could have shot one of the riders, stolen his horse, and made a break for it... but the odds were against him. There were too many outlaws roaming around and he recognized some of them. The majority were infamous gunslingers, and drunk or not, he had a feeling at least one of them could get lucky and shoot him in the back as he was trying to escape. And that was never how Sabbath intended to die.

There could be another horse stabled nearby or another exit from Blackheart other than through the front gate. Trying his luck, Sabbath clung to the shadows as he stealthily made his way from building to building. Most of the structures were occupied; he could hear the voices of people inside. Peering through the windows was like a who's who of wanted posters. Sabbath could make a fortune if he managed to capture them all. He spied lights on in one of the more opulent looking buildings in town and decided to take a peek.

The building was two stories tall and was crafted with fine woods and the occasional carving. Based on his experience, Major Sabbath figured this is (or was) the home of the mayor. Crouching beneath a window sill, Sabbath heard the booming voice of Utah talking to a man whose voice he did not recognize.

"Well I'm telling yah if we don't give him a public hanging then everyone's going to be furious with us! There will be an insurrection I tell yah! A plain old fashioned mutiny!"

"You exaggerate greatly," said the other man, as he spoke with an icy, calm voice. He sounded like an Easterner, possibly university educated. "Do you really believe that depriving the town of Major Sabbath's hanging with bring all manner of hell upon us?"

"Yes, yes sir I do." Utah said honestly. Sabbath had managed to peer above the sill and beheld Utah, hat in his hands, talking to the other man. The man was wearing a fine white suit (too fine for life in the Texas desert), was well groomed, and looked to be in his forties. His nose resembled a bird's beak, and his grey eyes looked displeased at his underling. Sabbath did not recall seeing a wanted poster for him specifically, but if he was the leader of this community, then he must have a great deal of clout in the outlaw world. Anyone that caused a man as cruel and vicious as Utah Grizwald to bend would be worth investigating.

"Perhaps you do not have enough control over your men. Perhaps I should appoint someone more qualified, more respected, for the job of sheriff?" the man said slyly. The man clearly enjoyed watching Utah squirm.

"No, no Mr. Steerwell, I can do my job just fine!"

Steerwell... Steerwell... no, nothing came to Major Sabbath, but that did not matter. Over in the corner of Steerwell's office, Sabbath spied his belongings. Seeing that he was well hidden from onlookers and the window was in shadow, Sabbath decided he would wait until the two men left the room before he climbed in and recovered his weapons and coat. Hopefully their conversation would reveal more about Blackheart.

"The only reason that we've been able to keep this town free from the law is by killing the law and anyone else we do not personally invite to be counted among us. Dead men tell no tales, remember?"

"Yes sir. I do." Utah said nervously, his fingers twisting the edge of his hat.

"No one from the outside wanders in and lives. Ever!" Steerwell emphasized the last word by smashing his fist on his intricately carved wooden desk. The office itself was opulent, with rich red damask wallpaper contrasting beautifully with the deep mahogany wood furniture. Many law books were stacked neatly on ornate book shelves and certificates framed in gold-leaf decorated the walls. Steerwell poured some wine into a cut crystal glass as he leaned back in his padded leather chair.

"Now then, Utah, given that this has been the elected policy of this town: killing the uninvited with expediency lest they attempt an escape, what do you think is the best course of action?"

"We... uh... we kill him in his cell and then hang his body for public display?" the large man stuttered, shrugging his brawny shoulders. His response brought a bemused look to Steerwell's face as he took a sip from the glass.

"You are sure hung up, forgive the pun, on the idea of a public display, aren't you Utah?"

"Well, it's just that many of the boys have been living in fear of Major Sabbath ever since he started huntin' us down! He's a terrible mean man once you get on the wrong side of him! You should have seen what he did to poor old Val, Elliot and Diego! He fights like a wild bobcat with a..."

"Yes, yes, you described the battle quite vividly to me already. I'm not as impressed by tales of carnage as you seem to be. Now I'm guessing that you want the reward money for his capture?"

"If I may be so bold, sir..."

Steerwell rolled his eyes as he twisted the dial to unlock the wall mounted safe. Sabbath's eyes bulged, the metal box was filled to capacity with stacks of paper money! Steerwell consulted a records book, withdrew a few stacks and counted them carefully.

Steerwell was amused by Utah's gaping mouth "This is just a sample, Utah... and please close your mouth" Steerwell said tauntingly "I know why you and your associates obey my every whim, you're waiting to find out where I've hidden my fortune..." the Mayor looked at Utah with an accusatory gaze. The large man's hesitation indicated that Steerwell's supposition was true. "I'll keep rationing the money as promised, and maybe, perhaps when I'm on my deathbed... I'll give you the map."

"Well, you know Mr. Steerwell, I know that you were the one who planned the train job... but me and the boys pulled it off. We all agreed that you would stash the money 'till things quieted down... but it's about as quiet as it's gonna get! And since your plan for Blackheart is working out just fine... I think it's only fair that I should know too?" Utah ventured. "You know, kind of like a partnership?"

"Yes, it would be fair. But if I would tell you, why keep me around? I have no incentive to reveal the location to you. But getting back to the business at hand... I assume that Major Sabbath is under guard?" Steerwell said, his voice had a slight edge to it. Any answer other than "yes" would be unacceptable. Steerwell was not a physically imposing man, Utah could have broken him in half if he so desired, yet it was clear the brute was under Steerwell's thumb.

Sabbath nodded to himself. It was the promise of money that kept these outlaws under his control; they were forced to keep him around. If Steerwell were to ever lose the map, then all would be lost for him.

"Yes sir, Val said he'd get one of our best men to keep watch while he was getting fixed up! But I gave that Major Sabbath a good wallop, so he ain't gonna be doin' much fightin' or escapin'!"

"That'll do for the moment, I suppose." Steerwell relented. "Here is your money as promised, all carefully counted by yours truly. Divide it amongst yourselves as you see fit. But before you take care of that business, you need to deal with Major Sabbath per our agreement."

"Will do, sir. Will do. But..." Utah started, still feeling uneasy.

"I will deal with any unpleasantness that may develop amongst the populace. Now you get a move on!" Steerwell said, waving Utah away the way one does to a petulant child. Utah nodded, almost bowing as he carefully maneuvered his way out of the office, making sure not to bump into any of Steerwell's possessions.

Sabbath leaned back against the wall, slumping down. Utah was heading straight for the jail, and Sabbath had only minutes in which to act! Utah would find the drunken guard in the cell and start hollering about Sabbath's escape. The Major had to stop Utah before he got to the jail, but that presented another set of problems.

But how? Utah's immense strength overwhelmed his, and the surest way to kill the man was to shoot him, but that would grab the attention of the entire city. He would have considered stabbing him, but the large man was sure to walk fearlessly down the middle of the street, and Sabbath would have been detected. Feeling around his person, Sabbath found one of Diego's throwing knives tucked into his belt. Pulling it out, Sabbath felt along the edge of the blade, and thought that maybe it was his only option. Of course, Utah was a mountain of a man, and Sabbath doubted if he could hurl the knife with enough force or accuracy for the blade to penetrate a vital organ... but he had to do something!

Utah barged out of the front door into the night and walked down the street with no particular haste. Sabbath was growing nervous, looking for some way to dispatch this foe. Then he spotted it! A way to kill Utah and raise no alarm. The big man was walking close to the buildings, the light from the oil lamps enabled him to see. Sabbath saw that down the path, a large barrel was balanced precariously on the edge of an outdoor stairway. The stairs looked rickety enough, and Sabbath figured that no one would question it if one day they would give way and the barrel would drop.

Sabbath raced from shadow to shadow, hugging the corners of buildings, keeping silent while Utah swaggered down the street. He would see him stop and make some small talk with the occasional outlaw he encountered, buying Sabbath more time. Sabbath got into position as he waited for Utah to approach. There were only seconds before Utah came into sight and Sabbath's heart was racing... what if he missed? What if Utah spotted him? What if the barrel was empty? A slight push against the barrel convinced him that it was filled and indeed very heavy. At least that solved one problem.

Utah stepped into the desired position and Sabbath pushed against the barrel with all of his might. The rotten wooden railing broke apart as the barrel fell swiftly towards the sheriff. Looking up at where the noise came from, Utah had a look of shock before the barrel struck him! It broke apart, sending the contents everywhere and dropping Utah to the ground, snapping his neck. Sabbath kicked out the floor of the stairwell to add credibility to the supposition that the wood gave way. Sabbath could not stick around to watch the ensuing investigation; he headed towards Steerwell's home. He did allow himself one quick glance back to see Utah lying motionless, and thought he saw a trickle of blood running from his mouth. The occupants of the upstairs room came out to investigate the commotion and immediately guessed that, as Sabbath had planned, the structure simply collapsed. There was much yelling and accusations about the perilous placement of the barrel, but Sabbath did not stop to listen.

He slid back below Steerwell's window and peered inside. The room was empty, but the window had been shut. Now was not the time to pontificate his next course of action, Sabbath had to rely on instinct! He jammed one of the thin throwing knives into the window seal and pulled down on it. The improvised lever opened up the window and he was able to climb inside. Sabbath had to act fast, for he had no idea if anyone else was going to come into the room. He gathered his belongings and, in a moment of forethought, took an overhead map of Blackheart that he saw lying on a filing cabinet. This would help him to better plan his escape. On the wall, he paused to read a law degree certificate from Harvard made out to Louis P. Steerwell which confirmed his suspicions.

"Utah is dead? How!" he heard Steerwell shout. The voice was coming closer! The footsteps of two men at least! Sabbath ran across the room and dove out through the small opening, rolling over his shoulder on landing. With quick thinking, he sprang back up and closed the window only seconds before Steerwell and another outlaw walked into the room.

Sabbath breathed a sigh of relief, hidden in the night shadows, as he thought about his next move.

A quick glance at the map gave Sabbath an idea. Among the many buildings in the city, there would be one place that the outlaws would not think much about going to. There was nothing to hold their interest in the building, it was the church. Figuring that he would be safe there, he stealthily made his way to what he presumed was an abandoned building.

The church was exactly as he expected it to be: ruined and beginning to decay. When the outlaws stormed into town, the first order of business must have been to destroy this building. He saw burn marks and broken glass on the floor, evidence that flaming bottles had been thrown at it. There were the usual bullet holes and the roof had begun to collapse some time ago. Sabbath welcomed the refuge.

Walking inside the burned out husk, Sabbath carefully sat down on a splintered bench and unfolded the map of Blackheart. He dared not risk lighting a match, so he had to rely on the moonlight, the beams of light filtering down through the wood slats of the damaged roof. The city had a simple design, a square border of buildings with two gates, and a central square bisected by the main street. The church was located on the west side of the town and Steerwell's home was due east. The sheriff's office was to the south east corner and had a clear line of sight on Steerwell's home. He was dismayed to find that there was only one stable in town. Sabbath hoped to find another means of procuring a horse. It was then that his pointed nose began to twitch, smelling something distinctly foul. He recognized the stench instantly; it was the unmistakable odor of a rotting corpse. Sabbath quietly walked to the church's cellar door, the source of the odor, and opened it.

His eyes were greeted by a horrific sight. The bodies of many men,

....he made his way to the abandoned building...

women, and children were carelessly stacked and rotting away. He looked over the bullet riddled bodies of the townsfolk, the blood on their clothing had dried stiff long ago, and Sabbath felt a fury overtake his senses. He had planned to bring these outlaws to justice, but a hanging no longer felt proportionate to their murderous rampage. Sabbath vowed that each of these men would suffer for what they did, and that he would personally hunt down and punish every single outlaw of Blackheart. He surmised that everyon must have had a hand in the carnage, and there would be no exceptions.

Sabbath thought of Steerwell's law degree hanging on his fancy wall and it made him sick. How could a well educated man allow this to happen, or even more sickening, order it? Surely Steerwell had the wisdom and knowledge necessary to make this world a better place. Although Sabbath was not a saint, he felt in his heart that he had never killed anyone who could not defend themselves. The massacre of innocent people made his stomach turn.

Sneaking out of the church and back into the night, Major Sabbath looked to the next building. It was the schoolhouse, and Sabbath could see a candle faintly burning in one of the windows. Sabbath remembered the somber, beaten down look of the people he saw when he entered the town, and resolved to talk with them. They did not appear to be outlaws, and perhaps they could aid in his escape. His suspicions were further confirmed when he saw three armed guards lazily keeping watch outside.

The three were positioned all around the wooden building, guarding different sides. One was lazily carving away at a dilapidated wooden wall with his knife, one of sitting on the ground with his back resting against a rock, enjoying a cigar, and the third man had fallen asleep leaning against a fencepost. Obviously, Steerwell did not consider the people kept prisoner inside the schoolhouse a threat. Still, Sabbath did not want to risk raising an alarm, so he had to take out the men silently. He placed Diego's throwing knives in his hand as he crept closer.

His first target was the outlaw carving his initials in the schoolhouse. He seemed the most alert. Sabbath carefully angled himself and threw the knife with deadly accuracy, the blade piercing the outlaw's heart. Sabbath raced over and placed his hand over the dying man's mouth, stifling his final agonizing moans.

Sabbath aimed and hurled a knife at the sleeping man leaning against the post. It hit the outlaw square in the chest and he slumped over. Sabbath propped his dead body back up against the post and removed the blade. If a passerby were to see him, they would assume that he was asleep.

Sabbath then snuck around the rock and deftly cut the throat of the third man. With his grizzly task accomplished, Sabbath felt that he could enter the schoolhouse safely. Making sure that no one was looking; he crept around to the front of the building and quietly entered through the front door.

What greeted Major Sabbath was a dozen or so frightened citizens staring at him in terror. They appeared weak and frail, some malnourished. He saw several women of varying ages and some older, weak looking men. Sabbath silently concluded that Steerwell had already dealt with the ones he thought would offer resistance. The schoolhouse was primarily one large room with a chalkboard mounted to the back wall. The desks had been pushed to the sides to make room for the townspeople. There were two smaller rooms off to the side, and Sabbath guessed that one was perhaps an office and the other kept supplies.

"Who... who are you?" one of the women spoke up. She was middle aged and had a firm jaw and strong arms. Her eyes betrayed a weather-beaten sadness, yet one could feel a certain strength radiating from her. This woman appeared to be the leader of the group.

"I'm Major Sabbath, what's your name?" The people murmured at the mention of his name. The recognition of his name echoed through the room.

"Martha, Major." she replied "And if you don't mind me saying it, we could have used a man like you two months ago." Martha's Swedish accent was thick, and her tone was of a scolding nature.

Sabbath could not help but grin. "Steerwell and his men came into Blackheart two months ago?" Sabbath guessed. Martha nodded firmly.

"Yes they did. They took our men, children, and anybody else they didn't need and murdered them all! They stacked their..." Martha began angrily.

"I know, I saw it..." Sabbath interrupted. He did not wish to be unsympathetic, but he had to hurry. "Listen, Martha, I'm going to need you to help me fill in some gaps..."

"Whatever you need." Martha said proudly, but one of the older men stopped her, a look of fear was written on his wrinkled face.

"Don't Martha! If Steerwell finds out that you've helped him..."

"I'm tired of being his prisoner! If he wants to kill me, so be it, he'll have to get some one else to forge his letters!" Martha shot back at the man.

"What do you mean 'forge letters'?" asked Sabbath.

Martha sighed before continuing. "Steerwell has kept a few of us alive to keep the town running. He forces us to reply to any letters that come in to town and has us fill out any necessary forms the suppliers need. That way, nobody can say that they have received no correspondence from Blackheart. We thought of trying to write out some kind of a code, but the dirty bastard reads every word we write!"

"I take it that the lines are actually down. Utah Grizwald wasn't just pulling my leg?"

"Yes. Taken down the first day they showed up."

"So there is no way for me to get a message out asking for help?" Sabbath said in frustration.

"We've tried everything we could think of! The trouble is, even if some message were to get out, you don't know who will read it! Steerwell has blackmailed every law enforcement official around Blackheart, so whenever a marshal or bounty hunter goes missing..."

"Like the men on Blackheart's wanted posters?" Sabbath asked.

"Yes, Major! Whenever someone tries to investigate a disappearance, they're told by these lawmen that they've been promoted to Washington D.C. or someplace like that!" Martha said bitterly. "I don't know how he did it, but Steerwell has managed to figure out every angle to keep us trapped!"

Sabbath looked at the faces of these poor wretches, and they echoed the sadness of her tale. He did not wish to endanger these survivors, but he would need their help. A plan was beginning to formulate in his mind. It was a way to rid the town of the outlaws, but even if his scheme were to play out, there were simply too many of them for him to deal with.

Fate, however, seemed to favor Major Sabbath. A man could be heard staggering towards the schoolhouse's front door. Sabbath hid in the shadows while one of the younger women answered. A drunken outlaw bellowed:

"Hey, Hopkins, me and a whole buncha' the boys are gonna sleep it off! Git over to your damned hotel and give us service!" The outlaw wandered off.

Hopkins, a portly, meek man with a thick mustache and spectacles, nervously started to head outside. Sabbath spotted his opportunity and seized the man by the arm.

"Listen to me, Hopkins..." the Major began "I have a plan, but it would cost you your hotel."

"It hasn't been mine for months, Major Sabbath," Hopkins spoke quietly "I'll help you with whatever you need."

"Good, you head out first. I'll be along shortly, but I need you to..."

It was still dark, and many drunken voices could be heard coming from the saloon, so he had the advantage. He hoped that Steerwell and the other "officials" would still be occupied by Utah's sudden demise. There was no way that Sabbath could disguise himself, his wanted poster was hanging everywhere in town, so he would have to maintain his stealth and create a distraction. A gaggle of gallivanting outlaws howled and laughed like idiots as they stumbled down main street towards the town's hotel. It may have been respectable once, but now it was where the outlaws hung their hats. With a burning vengeance in his eyes, Sabbath determined that this would be their final resting place.

Lights inside revealed the silhouettes of various outlaws. Most Sabbath recognized, some he did not. They continued their drinking and merriment inside the hotel. Sabbath did not see any women in the hotel, only outlaws. The Major watched as Hopkins did as he said, hurrying away from the rear exit after the outlaws were served.

His conscious would be clear. Sabbath barred the front and back doors to the hotel by breaking pieces of lumber off a hitching post and slipping it through the handles, then the Major stepped back. The bounties no longer mattered to him, besides; some of the men were still worth a little something dead. Looking at the oil lamps hanging along the porch, Sabbath pulled out his rifle and blasted away at them, causing them to explode on impact! Within moments the crumbling hotel was starting to burn, and Sabbath ran to find a horse. Outlaws at the saloon drunkenly filed out onto the street staring dumbfounded at the fire as it increased in intensity. In all the commotion, Sabbath was ignored.

"Help 'em out!" yelled one of the outlaws as they rode up the street. As the group rode past Sabbath, he decided to seize his chance. The black horse he wanted was at the back of the pack, and in all the confusion, Sabbath made his move. As the rider drew closer to him, Sabbath took one of Diego's throwing knives and hurled it at the outlaw. The rider jerked his head back, revealing that Sabbath's knife protruded from his neck. The rider fell off his horse in a spectacular fashion, and went crashing into the banister of the general store, splintering the wood to pieces. Sabbath mounted the black horse and rode towards the nearest exit. He did not wish to leave Blackheart, but his scheme would work better if every outlaw thought that he had... Sabbath's target was Steerwell.

Major Sabbath barreled out of there, pushing the horse as fast as it could gallop. He was nearly there when he saw that his way was blocked by Val Smith (now patched up, however clumsily) and several other outlaws on horseback, all of whom carried shotguns aimed at him!

"Goin' somewhere, Major Sabbath?" Val asked condescendingly. "I'd figured it was you who killed Utah and started the fire, so me an' my boys thought you'd try and make a run for it, being the coward that you are!"

Sabbath desired nothing more than to blow Val's head off, but practicality ruled out. Realizing that Blackheart's main street was impassible due to the commotion caused by the fire, Sabbath jerked the reigns to the left. He would take the long way around town and head for the other exit. Anything to keep the outlaws in an uproar and draw Steerwell out of hiding. Fiercely kicking the horse, Sabbath raced along the street with the sound of thundering hooves gaining on him!

Shotguns blazed behind Major Sabbath! The bounty hunter ducked closer to his animal, hoping to avoid their blasts. Sabbath zig-zagged his horse along the street. A moving target is much more difficult to hit. The pellets from their shotguns had spread out, and Sabbath watched as the sides of buildings near him were plugged full of holes. Pellets that hit the ground caused large geysers of sand to fly up in Sabbath's face.

Turning around, Sabbath wildly fired back at the outlaws. He did not count on hitting them, but was hoping that the random shots would cause them to perhaps panic and lose focus. Sabbath flinched as one of the shotgun blasts blew apart a barber shop's sign that was near his head as he passed! Sabbath was surprised to see an apple cart discarded in the middle of the road up ahead. He did not have time to dodge it; his only hope was that the horse would be able to make the jump!

The powerful horse bounded over the cart. Sabbath went sailing through the air, gripping the horse tightly around its neck. The shock of the impact almost threw Sabbath off, and he quickly looked back to see how his pursuers fared. He saw that the outlaw's horses had not attempted the jump, which resulted in several of them being flung off. Val was cursing at them to get up while he struggled to get his own horse under control. Taking a chance, Sabbath raised his rifle and fired at Val. He had no idea if he had killed the outlaw or not, but he had more pressing matters to worry about.

Riding past the burning hotel, Sabbath noted with grim satisfaction that the post he had placed to prevent their escape was still holding strong. He quickly glanced to see that the flames had engulfed the second story rooms. A small group of outlaws were trying to throw buckets of water on the inferno. They might as well have been playing cards for all of the success they were having. The bounty hunter hoped that the townsfolk of Blackheart would be able to rest easier knowing that some of their murderers were now burning for their sins before heading to hell.

If he remembered the map correctly, Sabbath would keep riding straight through to the other exit. He could not see the gate as yet, but expected it to be guarded. Swinging his rifle forward, Sabbath was prepared to blast his way through. He was soon met by several muzzle flashes that ripped out of the darkness, and Sabbath was able to distinguish several men standing on the ground, shooting at him! The horse, frightened by the sudden gunfire, reared up. Sabbath steadied the horse and aimed in the general direction of the men and fired away. He hit two of them dead on.

As the horse regained its composure, Sabbath saw Steerwell wandering out into the chaos. He was demanding answers from some of the nearby outlaws, and Sabbath knew that this was his chance! He rode over to the Mayor and grabbed him, pulling the man onto his horse. Pulling back on the reins, Sabbath's horse came to a sudden stop, facing the outlaws. The outlaws did not have time to react before Major Sabbath pressed his gun into Steerwell's temple.

"Nobody move! If any of you try anything, I'll kill him and you'll never get your money!" Sabbath hollered. The outlaws were itching for action, but did as the Major ordered. Sabbath rode back to the schoolhouse with his prisoner.

When Major Sabbath arrived at the schoolhouse with Steerwell, he pushed the Mayor through the door. The townspeople grabbed a hold of him while Sabbath gathered the guns off the three dead guards outside. He passed them out among the survivors.

"Here, if any of the outlaws start coming this way, you give them a warning shot. Say that the next bullet is for Steerwell." Sabbath instructed. The people with guns stood by the open windows and aimed their weapons at the saloon across the street. The remaining outlaws were either inside or out on the saloon's front porch, eyeing the schoolhouse with worry.

Sabbath took one look at the townspeople, then at Steerwell, and knew that he had to separate them. He needed information from Steerwell and felt that it was only a matter of time before they tore him limb from limb. He firmly took the mayor by the collar and dragged him into the office. The townspeople began to protest, but Sabbath put his hand up in a calming gesture.

"You can have him when I'm done, but if you want to save your town then just bear with me and keep watch." The survivors begrudgingly relented as Sabbath closed the door.

The office was modestly constructed with a view of the church through the small window, but large enough to comfortably sit two people. A hand-me-down desk, two wooden chairs, and an old bookshelf were the only items of furniture in the room. Sabbath forced Steerwell into one of the chairs while the Major sat on the desk.

"I don't know how many bodies are in the cellar of that church, but if every last one of you was hanged it would not begin to settle that score."

"Oh, so you came across our dark little secret... I know that you must think me a monster, Major Sabbath. Believe it or not, in addition to being the Mayor of Blackheart, I was at one time..."

"A defense attorney. Yes, I saw the Harvard diploma. I was indeed surprised."

"Surprised? Most people would say impressed, Major Sabbath. Why would you say surprised?" Steerwell said, genuinely curious.

"I'm surprised a man of your intelligence would bother with these outlaws," Sabbath said. "You could have become a rich man legitimately... why all of this?"

Steerwell took a deep, long sigh. "You are right, Major Sabbath, I am far more intelligent than this lot... and frankly I'm glad you've managed to survive this long. I finally have someone with some semblance of intelligence to talk with."

"I'm glad we're best friends now." Sabbath said sardonically. "Now what the hell kind of mind justifies the massacre of an entire town?"

"It's a bit of a story... you see, after I became a defense attorney, I wanted a real challenge. I decided to head west and see if I could defend those who seemingly had no defense, represent the "outlaws" as you call them."

"I don't mind you defending them," Sabbath admitted "each piece of filth that you save from the noose becomes another bounty for me. An outlaw will always be an outlaw."

"The noose. Is that your idea of justice?" Steerwell said passionately "The men I was defending were doing wrong. They were exercising their rights as Americans to do what they want!"

"Their rights as Americans?" Sabbath repeated, confused by what Steerwell was talking about.

"What does the Constitution mandate? It states that all Americans have the right to life, liberty, and the pursuit of happiness! And these men, who are labeled as "outlaws" and "criminals" by men like you, are merely seizing their opportunity to create a better life for themselves! In pursuing this ideal, force is necessary. They found a city to their liking and changed it for the better. Like the Constitution states, they are living freely and happily. No laws, no..." Steerwell explained, as if Sabbath were a jury.

Not being able to listen anymore, Sabbath interrupted, "And how did you get to be their Mayor?"

"You see, I have successfully defended virtually every single one of these men. They owe me everything and they know it. I had to educate them about their Constitutional rights. I told them "Gentlemen, your paradise awaits you in Blackheart, and I would be proud to be your Mayor!" Regretfully, we had to displace the original populace..." Steerwell said, with a theatrical expression of distress on his face "however, the outlaws are quite contented here."

"I suppose you may bastardize the law as you choose, well... eventually all of you are going to have to answer to a higher law." Sabbath said.

"You mean God?" Steerwell asked in bemusement. "I stopped believing that superstition a long time ago. But tell me, Sabbath, are you not a murderer yourself? Have you not singlehandedly killed at least a dozen of my men?"

"I've killed a hell of a lot more than that in my time."

"I have no doubt, but if you are a murderer, the same as these men, how can you judge?"

Sabbath fixed Steerwell with a steely glare that froze his heart. The Mayor felt a chill run down his spine. Sabbath pulled out a knife, Diego's, and quickly placed it against Steerwell's throat.

"Because I don't murder women and children and justify it with fancy language. And furthermore, the only thing that keeps your men in line is that you are holding their money over their heads!" Sabbath said between clenched teeth. He wanted to plunge the knife into Steerwell's heart, but the Mayor's look of surprise was reward enough.

"What? But how did you..." he started weakly.

"Because I don't murder women and children…"

"And I'm willing to bet anything that you've hidden that map in plain sight, just to enjoy taunting them. I personally think that it's hidden in something you hold most dear... maybe behind that diploma you're so proud of?" Sabbath casually remarked. Steerwell's bulging eyes told Sabbath that he was right on the money.

At that moment, Major Sabbath saw movement outside the window. Looking cautiously out, he saw the slight figure of Elliot creeping out of the darkness. Somehow he had managed to sneak past the townspeople and circle around the back. Thinking quickly, Sabbath tossed Steerwell back into the main classroom and instructed the townspeople to keep him quiet.

Sabbath had a hunch about Elliot that he was willing to play. He hid in the shadows while the young thief crept in through the window, his gun drawn. Sabbath cleared his throat, causing Elliot to wheel around in surprise. Elliot did not shoot.

Sabbath glared at him, his dark, beady eyes cutting deep, down to Elliot's core.

"You're the one with the gun, and you're shaking like a leaf." Sabbath nodded towards Elliot's quivering hand. Elliot looked to it and tried to calm himself down, but his hand did not cooperate.

"Where's Steerwell? The boys say I'm a coward. I'm gonna prove 'em wrong and I ain't leavin' without him!" Elliot demanded, though his voice was wavering.

"You know, what Utah said about you is absolutely right... you're no killer."

"What? What do you mean?" Elliot said with defiance. "I am one of the most notorious bank robbers in the states! You saw the price on my head, Major Sabbath. The U.S. government thinks I'm one dangerous son-of-a-gun!" The way Elliot delivered his speech indicated that he was apparently used to saying it a great deal.

"The banks put the reward out on you because you are a damned nuisance. Furthermore, before I take a bounty I like to get to know who I'm going after, and in all of your robberies, not one single person was killed and few shots were heard." Sabbath started.

"What can I say? I strike fear into the hearts of..." Elliot began, forcing the bravado.

"Shut up!"

The bravado quickly faded as Sabbath continued. "One robbery with no killing is lucky, two robberies is a miracle... but near a half dozen robberies... I realized that I was dealing with a man who would not kill."

"You sayin' that I don't have the guts to kill a man?" Elliot said, clearly an accusation echoed throughout Blackheart. It was a sore subject for Elliot, but Sabbath pressed on.

"No, I'm saying that you have the wisdom not to kill needlessly."

Elliot paused and put his head down for a moment. He slowly raised his head and looked Sabbath straight in the eye. "What about you?" Elliot asked, genuinely interested in how Sabbath perceived himself.

The major sighed, thinking of his past. It was clear that the young man was beginning to listen, and telling Elliot the truth would help to gain an ally. "I kill men who deserve it. I haven't always been successful in that regard. But I have to ask you a question."

"What?"

"How long have you been in Blackheart?"

"Let me think... I heard about this town through the grapevine, you know... but I must have got here... I don't know... about two weeks ago? I was told it was an outlaw's paradise." Elliot said.

"I see, so you have no idea." Sabbath said looking downcast.

"No idea about what?"

"I need your help, Elliot. We're going to clean up this town."

"What? Why would I help you? I don't even know why I'm talking to you!"

Elliot pointed his gun at Sabbath once again. With lighting speed the bounty hunter snatched the weapon from his grasp, spun it around in his hand, and pointed it at the youth. Elliot instinctively put his hands up.

"Now you do exactly as I say and you'll come out of this in one piece. I know where Steerwell's map is and I think I know the combination of his safe. We need to get the map and the money for my plan to work."

"Why would I betray them? I've got some good friends in that saloon, and I'm not going to steal from a fellow outlaw!"

"How well do you know them?"

"Well enough."

Sabbath nodded. "There's something that you need to see."

Major Sabbath, with his rifle slung across his back and his pistols holstered, made his way with Elliot Castle across town under the cover of darkness. With the exception of the light from oil lamps in the saloon, the city seemed like a ghost town. The Hotel was nothing more than a pile of blackened wood and smoke. Sabbath heard rowdy voices coming from the saloon and estimated that possibly fifteen outlaws were packed inside, all of them voicing their opinions about Steerwell, Sabbath, and what was to become of them.

"Whatever you're planning to do, I suggest you do it right quick, Major Sabbath" Elliot whispered to him "it sounds like the boys are getting all worked up over there. It's only a matter of time before one of them goes off to try and rescue Mayor Steerwell."

"Don't worry, this shouldn't take long."

Sabbath led the way and a few minutes later the two were standing inside the burned out church. Elliot looked around the ruined structure with curiosity.

"I was told to stay away from here, like the whole building might collapse!"

"There's a good reason for that," Sabbath said as he made his way to the cellar, motioning for Elliot to follow him. "Have a look in here."

Elliot descended the stairs and immediately noticed a powerful, nauseating stench reach his nostrils. He stopped in his tracks, and was on the verge of retching, before Sabbath grabbed a hold of him and gave him a firm shake.

"Don't lose control now!" Sabbath snapped at the young man, annoyed that he was unwilling to continue forward.

"What is that smell?" Elliot asked, wishing he were anywhere else right now.

"It's time you learned something about the company you keep!"

With that Major Sabbath grabbed Elliot and lifted the cellar door. Forcing the young man to descend into the room, Sabbath watched as Elliot's hands flew to his face. He looked at the multitude of bodies stacked unceremoniously in piles on the floor and began to shake uncontrollably. Elliot turned away and faced the cold, hard glare of Sabbath.

"This is the foundation that your "outlaw's paradise" is built on." Pointing to the corpses, Sabbath growled, "Blackheart used to be their home before they met up with your friends. Utah, Val, Diego, Steerwell... they are responsible for this." Sabbath spoke bitterly.

"I had no idea about any of this..." Elliot said truthfully as tears began to form in his eyes.

"Any outlaw hangs his hat here is treading on their graves... and look at them... they weren't even given a decent burial or marker. Left to rot in a burned-out building. You keep company with these men and you are no better than they are."

"I'm not like this." Elliot said firmly. He felt a fire and determination well up inside him. Sabbath recognized that the young man suddenly had a desire for justice, and he put a hand on his shoulder.

"Then prove it by helping me."

"What do you need me to do?" Elliot asked, still shaking with revulsion.

"Elliot, you traitor! Sabbath, drop your guns!"

Sabbath and Elliot spun around to see Val aiming a pistol at them with an enraged look in his eye. Sabbath reluctantly complied as he placed his guns gently on the ground, the barrels facing Val. He motioned them to stand against the wall, and the two quickly obeyed. Gripping the gun handle tightly with his good hand, Val's moment with Sabbath had finally come. He looked angrily at Elliot.

"What the hell do you think you're doing, Elliot?"

"He... he took me as his hostage. I had to go along until I could make my escape! I was going to warn all of you..." Elliot lied. He hoped that Val would believe his story and separate him from Sabbath.

"I was going to see what was takin' you so damned long! I saw Sabbath leaving the building with you and decided to follow, figuring that you were his captive. I'd of believed you Elliot... except that you just renounced us boys in front of the bounty hunter! Suddenly we ain't good enough for you!" Val yelled.

Sabbath noted that Val was alone, and he could not hear anyone moving around upstairs. Hopefully Val decided to investigate alone. Val was yelling at the top of his lungs, but nobody came to see what the noise was about. Sabbath took that as a good sign: he could shoot without attracting attention. He knew that a move from him would result in Val blasting away. Val was known for his quick draw and itchy trigger finger, so Sabbath decided to let Elliot keep talking.

"It's not that I'm better... it's that..." Elliot looked at the bodies once more and straightened up, holding his head high, a righteous indignation filling him "Yes! You know what Val? I am better than you. I'm better than all of you! Because I would not have done all this!" he said pointing to the corpses.

"What? That?" Val said curiously, genuinely surprised that Elliot was upset by the sight.

"Yes Val, that! Steerwell fed me the same line about "the pursuit of happiness" in America, and how it was our right! And Blackheart was all about finding paradise. A home of our own! He never said it was built over dead bodies!"

Sabbath watched as Elliot was about to lunge at Val, and he knew that he had to move even faster! In the blink of an eye, Major Sabbath tucked into a forward shoulder roll, grabbed his pistol mid-roll from the cellar floor, and squeezed a shot as his body unfolded. The bullet struck Val in the shoulder, causing his shot to go wild. Elliot instinctively dove for cover behind a wooden pillar when he saw Sabbath make his move.

Val was wounded, but not dead. He began shooting as Sabbath dove behind a small grouping of barrels. The outlaw rapidly alternated his shots between Elliot and Sabbath. The bounty hunter knew that Val was going to run out of bullets real soon. Sabbath was able to grab his rifle without getting hit. Elliot stood like a statue pressed against the wood, doing his best to hide all of his body.

Val's gun clicked and he swore aloud. Sabbath popped up and aimed his rifle at Val. Val put his hands up and began to protest.

"Now... now listen Major Sabbath... killing me now wouldn't be fair! You're killing an unarmed man... and besides, I'm worth a lot more alive than dead last time I checked."

"It would be as fair as what you did to them..." Sabbath said grimly, nodding towards the bodies, but he lowered the weapon to his hip. "But I'll give you the chance to reload."

Elliot looked at Sabbath in disbelief and Val flashed a nervous smile. Although it was a struggle with his broken, jittery hand, he quickly loaded the bullets one by one. When Val dropped the sixth bullet into the chamber, a gunshot from Sabbath's rifle ended his life. The Major stood over the dead man and shook his head.

"I said that I'd give you a chance to reload... I didn't say I'd give you a chance to fire." Sabbath turned to Elliot and waved him over. "Pick up his weapon, he won't need it. Now here is what I need you to do."

Elliot sprinted towards the saloon in a panic, his hand holding onto his hat, lest it be blown off by his momentum. Tucked under one arm were large stacks of money in a saddlebag, and his fist held Steerwell's map. Several outlaws were loitering outside and spotted Elliot. They started to ask him questions but he raced past them, ignoring their inquiries as he swung the saloon doors open.

The saloon was a two story building and the rest of the outlaws were busy yelling at each other. Every seat at the bar was taken. The men held a discussion with the bartender, debating if Steerwell would divulge the location of his stash to the townspeople. A few of the tables were taken up by men having more private conversations, outlaws planning their own personal getaways should the situation with Steerwell turn against them. The once charming saloon with its beautiful carved wood paneling and beveled mirror which hung above the bar was now smeared with tobacco stains. Ashes littered the floor as smoke hung heavy in the air.

Elliot stepped into the middle of all the commotion. Putting his fingers to his lips, he whistled as loudly as he could and caught the attention of the saloon's patrons. Elliot did not have time to count, but he estimated that there were at least fifteen outlaws that he could see, and maybe more in the other rooms, but right now all eyes were on him. Sabbath had told him what to say, and on paper his plan was sound. However, now that he was in the thick of it, Elliot was beginning to have his doubts. After clearing his throat, he began to speak.

"Excuse me gentlemen..." he began.

"Where's Mayor Steerwell?" a man yelled from the bar.

"Yeah! I thought that you said you'd bring him back all by yourself! Where the hell is he!" another shouted from a nearby table.

"And where's Val?"

There was a general chorus echoing these questions at Elliot. He put his hand up and did his best to speak calmly over the men. Eventually they quieted down enough for Elliot to be heard.

"Now, I know that you're all concerned about the fate of Mayor Steerwell's stash..." Elliot did not get the chance to finish the sentence due to the unanimous (and expected) uproar that this statement caused. Some began to jump up on the tables, bellowing that they would lynch Mayor Steerwell if he failed to pay them. Elliot knew that if the outlaws were still united, the plan would fail. Elliot climbed up on a table and shot his pistol in the air to silence them. He held their attention once more and, having a feeling that this was the last chance he had, he needed to make the most of it.

"Now, the good news is that we no longer need Steerwell or his hollow promises! I managed to find his map, and here's the proof!" Elliot said as he opened the saddlebag and dumped the money out onto the table.

The outlaws looked at one another in disbelief. This was more money than most of the men had ever seen at one time. If they could get their hands on it, the outlaws would be rich beyond their wildest dreams.

"You know..." Elliot began "I don't know how much Steerwell stashed away, but I'm sure as hell glad Major Sabbath set fire to the hotel!" He noted the outlaw's expressions of disbelief and wonder, so he (according to Sabbath's instructions) explained. "I mean, however much money there is, at least we don't have to split it thirty ways! Now it's only, what? Fifteen or sixteen ways?"

Hidden across the street, Sabbath squinted to see the outlaws inside the saloon. Judging by the looks on their faces, his plan was working. In his experience as a bounty hunter, Major Sabbath had learned that the idea of "loyalty amongst thieves" was only an expression coined by some writer a long time ago. This expression is far removed from reality. His plan relied on the fact that outlaws act more like drowning rats on a sinking ship. They will bite, claw, scratch, and kill one another to survive. Even with his deadeye, Sabbath knew he would never be able to deal with all the outlaws and hope to make it out alive.

Major Sabbath watched as each of the outlaws looked at one another with hesitation, their hands slowly moving over their guns. Friendships were silently being tested, then torn apart as each outlaw planned on who he would shoot first.

"Fifteen ways..." one outlaw said eyeing the man sitting across the table from him, "why not fourteen? I haven't seen you lift a damn finger since you came to Blackheart!" He drew his pistol on the man.

"For that matter, why not thirteen?" another outlaw with a shotgun said as he pointed his weapon at a table of men. "I don't recall being a friend to most of yah in the first place!"

Elliot began to slowly, silently make his way towards the exit. Sabbath would breathe easier when the young man was outside, for he felt a sense of guilt sending Elliot into the proverbial viper's pit.

Elliot was almost at the door when Sabbath saw an outlaw place a hand on his back.

"Where do you think you're going?" the man demanded.

"Well... I was going to let you all decide how to handle the situation..."

"Well you have a vote! You're in this with us, kid!" the outlaw yelled as Elliot was shoved back into the center of what was soon to become an arena.

Sabbath cursed as he aimed. Elliot was in no immediate danger, and Sabbath resolved to keep the young man safe should the need arise. It was impossible for the outlaws to keep an eye on one another, so they would not notice if a shot from the outside set off this powder keg.

Major Sabbath's gunshot broke the silence! In an instant, an outlaw standing on a table grabbed his chest and fell, smashing a chair into a million wooden splinters. Time stood still and all bets were off! Bullets began flying through the air like a plague of locusts! Bottles shattered, the paneled walls were splattered with black burn marks and shards of glass from the bar mirror exploded, covering the room. Outlaws were shooting each other left and right. If any man had eyes on Elliot (who had the sense to drop to the floor and begin crawling to the saloon doors), Sabbath would shoot him dead.

Under Sabbath's protection, Elliot crawled out from underneath the saloon doors and raced towards the Major. Standing behind Sabbath, Elliot watched as the carnage abruptly stopped and the silence was unreal. The battle had lasted only a few minutes, but witnessing its fury and intensity would be enough to last a lifetime.

"Do you think they're all dead, Major?" asked Elliot.

Sabbath nodded and approved, however silently, at Elliot's phrasing of *they*. The young man had clearly distanced himself from his fellow outlaws. "Yes, Elliot. But I'll check for survivors."

Sabbath walked into the bar and began to survey the damage. The sight reminded him of a battle he was in, but he forced himself not to visit memories of the Civil War. He heard Elliot enter the saloon.

"Oh my god..." the young man said.

"It's just like I told you earlier, Elliot. There is no honor amongst thieves."

"Major, do you think what you did here... what we did here... do you think this is justice?" Elliot asked, obviously shaken by what he saw. Sabbath took him outside and they walked away from the saloon. The Major had witnessed many a fine young man lose their mind to the madness of war, and he hoped to spare Elliot this pain.

"Is it justice? I don't know. According to the law of our land, maybe not. According to the bible, I'm not sure..." Sabbath motioned towards the ruined church "the only ones that can really answer that question are down there. Hopefully their spirits will rest easier tonight... their murderers are finally in hell. The point is, Blackheart is safe for the townspeople once again."

Riding out of town on a newly purchased horse, Elliot looked back at Blackheart, his eyes filled with shame. The men that he once called compatriots were nothing but a bunch of murderers who had created a hell on earth. They were all gone now, and Elliot realized that he did not have a single friend in the world.

Elliot then saw that it was Sabbath following him. The bounty hunter was driving a two-horse, covered wagon. Inside the wagon lay a collection of the outlaw's bullet riddled bodies, as many as it could carry before the cart collapsed. There was a man sitting next to Sabbath, tied up and gagged (even though he was still unconscious). The Major met Elliot's surprised gaze.

"Each one of them had a price on their head. Even dead, this collection ought to earn a pretty penny. Worth more than you were alive, at any rate." Major Sabbath explained to Elliot with an attempted smile on his face. He nodded towards the man next to him "I knocked this one out when I escaped from the sheriff's office. He slept through the entire night... he's mine now."

"What about the rest of them?" Elliot enquired.

"I'll let the Texas Rangers know... let them sort out this whole mess. Besides, the townspeople are going to need help rebuilding... making this a real city again."

Sabbath looked back over his shoulder at Blackheart. "The West will be a good deal safer now that these men are dead."

Elliot nodded, but then grew curious. "Yeah, but what about you?"

"What about me?" Sabbath returned the question, not understanding the young man's meaning.

"Doesn't this make you sick? Don't you want to stop?" Elliot said.

Sabbath looked down momentarily before answering. "Son, there will always be evil men in the world... and men like me are meant to bring them to justice. What about you, though, what are you going to do?"

"I've been thinking about that... I decided I was going to change my name, head north... I'm not sure..." Elliot said uncomfortably. He swiftly changed the subject. "So, what do you think will happen to Blackheart now?"

"We left the townspeople Steerwell's stash, and they'll need it to fix up the town again."

Elliot nodded as the two took a somber look at the town. The Major turned to Elliot with a slight smile.

"You know, they'll probably need a sheriff. I talked to Martha about you, and the idea did not disgust her."

Elliot's eyes widened as he looked at Sabbath. He shook his head with a smile and slowly turned in the direction of Blackheart. The two parted ways and Sabbath rode off into the desert.

As the sun rose over Blackheart, the body of Louis P. Steerwell could be seen hanging in the town square, swaying gently in the breeze.

THE END

FILM TO TEXT

*I*t may sound strange to say, but the wild west is something that I have only recently become interested in. I did not grow up wanting to be a cowboy, or ride a horse, or anything of that nature. I have nothing against any of these things, it just held little interest for me.

However, things started to change a little while ago. At film school, my business partner and I were talking about films that we could make that would blow our classmates away (not that we were competitive or anything). One of the ideas tossed about was to do a western. Of course, we had seen a few, but could not claim to be experts in this area. So we decided to remedy that, and since then, I have become a fan of the genre, having watched many of John Ford's classics, the Dollars Trilogy, Django, etc... To date, our western has not been made (yet), but the knowledge and interest of the west has stayed with me.

A little while ago, I purchased a 20-pack of spaghetti western movies. Though some are of dubious quality, I enjoyed the ones that featured Lee Van Cleef (films such as Death Rides a Horse, The Grand Duel, and Beyond the Law). I had already seen him in the Dollars trilogy, and I like him as an actor. He says little, but his eyes speak volumes. He does not look like a conventional tough guy, yet you buy him as a force of destruction. I also enjoy the flavor of spaghetti westerns. They are more outlandish than the American westerns, but there is something hyper-real about them, their characters become almost mythic symbols. The violence is more exaggerated and plentiful.

When Ron first announced that Airship 27 would be putting out Major Sabbath, my first thought was "Boy that looks cool! I can't wait to read it". While I was writing for some of Airship's other characters, Sabbath kept popping up in my mind. I felt that after watching so many westerns, I *had* to do something with that knowledge. So I wrote to Ron and pitched my story.

I tried to capture everything I enjoy about those films in my story. I want it to feel, somehow, Italian. The characters have to be bigger than life, and the action has to be plentiful and spectacular. I joked with my uncle that I thought it was amazing that the west ever got settled, because (according to cinema history) there would be few people left alive. After I hung up the phone, that got me thinking... what if an entire town was against our hero?

My policy when writing this story was to try and write the ultimate Lee Van Cleef western (I'm not saying that I did, but I sure did try!). I love jailbreak movies and clever escape plans, so I wondered how one could escape from a city of enemies. I tried to walk through the town, putting myself in Sabbath's place, trying to figure out what he would do in the situation. I had it almost all figured out when the flu struck, and, if I may be so bold as to impart some advice to any writer... typing through a fever can give you interesting, but misguided results. Suffice it to say that after I recovered, plenty of rewriting was in order before I could send it to Ron.

Unsure of how many western stories I would write, I tried to get in as many different types of action scenes that I could. When making films, one always has to be budget conscious (thus one of the reasons our western has not been made yet), so when I was writing this story, it was fun to let loose! I decided to write in everything that we could not afford to shoot: horse chases, buildings burning, saloon gunfights, etc. It was freeing, but had the negative effect that I now wanted to go and film all of these scenes.

Maybe one day that film will be made, but until then I hope you enjoy my first attempt at a spaghetti western!

ERIK FRANKLIN - is a writer/actor/filmmaker based in Seattle. Recently graduating with honors from the Art Institute of Seattle in film production, he is the co-President of Franklin-Husser Entertainment LLC. He is working on two upcoming feature films for his company: A dinosaur action film "Revenge of the Lost" and the martial arts comedy "3 Morons Fighting Ninja". You can give the company page a "Like" at: https://www.facebook.com/pages/Franklin-Husser-Entertainment-LLC/290795021042906.

Drawn to pulp fiction through his love of history, literature, and Americana, he is grateful for Airship 27 Productions giving him the opportunity to write his first story. He looks forward to writing more adventures!

THE MISSION OF SHANGHAI JOE

BY FRANK SCHILDINER

*T*he man calling himself Jimmy Diamond was a ratfaced, shifty-eyed fellow was a quick grin that fooled many people. He was losing just enough at poker to get the big players at the Branded Bull Saloon to start betting big. That's when Major Sabbath confirmed the man's identity, recognizing the shift in the man's body language from wormless monied fool to rapaciously destructive gambler.

Jimmy Diamond smiled and pushed his still large pile of chips into the pot. His left eye twitched madly, telling the players he was bluffing. "I bet it all, gents! Every cent I have in the whole wide world!"

The other players tried to hide their grins as well while pushing their piles into the pot. They were risking everything, but this rich greenhorn needed to be fleeced and sent back East where he belonged. Major Sabbath laid down his cards and also pushed his money into the pot. He knew what the false Jimmy Diamond was about to do and this was his chance to reveal the man's true identity.

"Four deuces," Jimmy Diamond crowed, looking at the others. "Anyone can beat that? No? Then this pot is mine!"

Jimmy Diamond reached for the chips, his grin less lopsided now as he pulled the money towards his side of the table. Major Sabbath reached out and grabbed the man's arm, his grip in Diamond's wrist as strong as a vice. The major's other hand reached under his tie and pulled out a knife, which he used to slash open the man's silk shirt. Cards tumbled out of Jimmy Diamond's sleeve, spilling across the table before everyone's eyes.

"Cheat!" one of the gamblers screamed, reaching for his whiskey glass and hurling it at Jimmy Diamond's head. Like all present, he'd been disarmed before the game began and had no weapons.

"Okay, okay, you got me. But you didn't lose no money. Can't call me a thief unless I actually took the cash. That's the law." Jimmy Diamond stated, stepping back and raising his hands.

"But I can call you a murderer," Sabbath whispered, his hushed voice causing all present to fall silent. "Isn't that right, Johnny the Deuce?"

Jimmy Diamond's hands dropped, his face falling carefully neutral. "What did you call me?""

Major Sabbath stood up, the knife still in his hand as he looked around the room. Taking in every position in the room and mentally preparing for what was coming in a moment. This would go bad, fast. But he knew how to win; he always knew how to win these battles.

"Johnny the Deuce," Major Sabbath stated, his voice not hiding his disdain. "Gambling cheat, thief and, most importantly, murderer. I'm here to take you for the reward money. Alive or dead, your choice, of course."

"You're not Bart Maverick!" Johnny the Deuce snarled, hunching his shoulders and looking enraged.

"No, we just shop at the same tailor. The name's Sabbath, Major Sabbath. How do you want to play this one, Johnny?" Sabbath asked, lifting a hand in a languid gesture.

A man to right Johnny's suddenly pulled a Colt Peacemaker from a bag and tossed it to Johnny while he and a second man drew pistols from beneath their jackets. Major Sabbath threw the knife at the second man, the blade sinking deep into the gunman's eye. He shrieked and fell back, dead before he struck the floor.

From his sleeve Major Sabbath drew a tiny derringer, firing it twice at Johnny the Deuce's other friend. The man didn't have a chance to scream as the bullets hit him in the skull, a spray of blood flying behind him and into the crowd of onlookers.

"Bad move, Major!" Johnny the Deuce stated with a nervous giggle. He held the pistol in his hand and it shook slightly as he pointed it at the infamous bounty hunter. "You fired all your bullets at Bobby and tossed your pretty blade at Rico. Now I got the drop on you!"

"I guess you do, Johnny." Sabbath replied, a slight smile on his face. He pulled the trigger twice again and watched as Johnny the Deuce crashed to the ground, as dead as his friends.

"How'd you kill him?" the bartender asked the cash box for the game in his hands. He was a rolly-polly man with a full thick beard and short salt and pepper hair. Secretly owner of the saloon, he was always complaining that the "owner" wouldn't let him buy good whiskey and other items.

Sabbath smiled and turned the gun around, allowing the man to see there were four barrels. "He was a great card cheat, but not good at counting. Call the sheriff. Johnny and his friends are worth $4000 to me. Oh, and I will be taking the money I used to enter the game."

Two hours later, as he counted his reward money a second time, Major

Sabbath pulled out his pipe and began to light up. He was just beginning to puff away when one of the deputy's entered the jailhouse and approached him.

"Major Sabbath, sir? Telegram for you!" the deputy handed him a yellowing slip of paper. A skinny teen with a rash of acne across his chin, he was young enough to find the well-dressed bounty hunter to be an admirable figure.

"Thanks," Sabbath said and tossed the kid a fifty cent piece. He read the telegram and looked up, "When is the next train to El Paso?"

"You stupid little man," The Frenchwoman snarled as she slapped Stanley Spencer across his mouth. "You idiotic, tiny-minded, rapacious, lickspittle worm! Do you realize how your greedy foolishness has endangered our plans? Do you?!"

She was a tall woman, well-dressed with long silken blonde hair and perfect satiny skin. Her eyes were large and colored an odd, enticing shade of gray. Her lush figure caused men to stare and gasp. But right now this stunningly beautiful woman was the most terrifying creature Spencer ever encountered. With a word or gesture she could end his life, destroy his whole family and there was nothing he could do to resist her will.

Slapping him again she sat down behind his desk and stared at him with stormy eyes, "The All-Father is quite displeased with your actions. He knew you were greedy and base, but believed a simple task was within your realm of competence. All you had to do was hire very cheap workers and pay them just enough to survive. But instead you stole the All-Father's money and used bandits to kidnap Mexican peasants. All of whom you had murdered when your foolish schemes failed! Do I slander you, little man?"

Stanley Spencer, who was at least a foot taller than this French woman, only known as "The Countess", felt like a small boy standing before a particularly terrifying schoolmaster. Every time she mentioned their mutual master, the All-Father, he visibly shuddered with terror. The All-Father was a being of frightening power, the master of life and death on two continents. The rewards he offered for service were enormous, but the penalties for violating the terrible man's will were the stuff of legends.

"Miss...pardon me, Countess. I saved the All-Father much money. My work made us very profitable, you yourself told me I was the one making the most money in this region!" Spencer spluttered. He was a tall blocky man with long blond hair and a heavy blond beard. His eyes were tiny and dark and gave him a piggish visage. As always he was dressed in a white suit, his way of showing the world he was above all those who worked in the dirt. Of course now said suit was sweat-stained and looked closer to a beggar's rags than a wealthy man's symbol of his position.

The Countess nodded slowly before picking up an ink well and throwing it at Spencer's head. He ducked and heard the glass shatter against the wall, straightening in time to by struck by several pens and a notebook. "If I had known your reason for earning such money was because you were acting as the basest of jackanapes, I would have had you executed to save us all the troubles!"

"It wasn't my fault, Countess! All was going well until this Chinaman, Shanghai Joe the men call him, arrived and demonstrated impressive fighting skills. Instead of killing, as I offered to pay him, he began freeing my slaves and killing my men! I sent the best killers in the region after him and he murdered three and blinded another!" Spencer yelled, bowing his head in hopes that the lovely woman's rage.

"Continue," The Countess stated, leaning back in the chair and studying Spencer with cold eyes.

Spencer straightened slightly and breathed a small sigh of relief, "When that failed, I put out the word for a Chinese assassin; a master of whatever this Shanghai Joe could do. I found one, supposedly his equal, who filled me in on the truth. The man's true name was Chin Hao and he was member of a group called the Fire Lotus. When my Chinese killer failed, I had enough information to put on a wanted poster. There's now a $5000 reward on his head!"

"And in the meantime we have no workers and the Black Coats lose money every day." The Countess snapped, shaking her head. "I hope you have done more than spread a reward poster about the region."

Spencer nodded quickly, "I sent a telegram to the best bounty hunter in the business. He's called Major Sabbath."

The Countess nodded slowly, "Yes, Sabbath. I have heard of his reputation. We shall see if he lives up to his legend. But if he fails to do so, I have brought several of my own people. They will destroy this Shanghai Joe. Failure is not an option."

Stanley Spencer kept his mouth shut and tried to keep from quaking at the thought of this woman's killers in his home. He'd agreed to join the Black Coats for the promise of wealth, power and position. But there were people above him that were terrifying, true killers who lived for the sight of blood. Or callous men and women who's thought processes were plainly inhuman. Perhaps his choice was a sin, a greedy mistake, but Stanley Spencer knew there was no going back from the life he'd chosen. All he could do now was try and stay alive a little longer.

Costa Cruz was a content man. Having been tossed off the family farm at age thirteen for stealing from the church poor box, he took little time in joining a bandito gang. Now, almost twenty years later he'd risen to leadership of the gang and even made a successful deal with a rancher to supply slaves. Slave raiding was easier than fighting rich people, you found a farm or three and maybe a small town and attacked. The young girls would be shared, with Costa getting first pick and the rest would be handed over on the other side of the border. The money was good and if this kept up, he could buy a position with Diaz's government. Money and a willingness to enforce the rules with lethal force could lead to a Colonel's post or something equally powerful and prestigious.

But until he had enough gold, the raiding would continue. Fortunately the border had plenty of small towns that were unprotected and wouldn't be missed when Costa's band went on the rampage. The cave back near the Rio Grande was almost full and they could bring to that gringo Spencer a full load of slaves for labor or whatever he wanted. Costa didn't honestly care, he was just glad for the money and no longer being forced to feed their captives once a day.

"Nino!" Costa roared with a happy gap-toothed smile, seeing his best scout approaching. Costa was a giant of a man, well over six feet tall with a long, thick mustache and barely fitting clothing. He wore three pistols, two knives and a pair of long rifles across his back. Costa was lethal with guns, knives or his hands, rising to the top of his band because he was the smartest and easily the best killer of the bunch. His favorite activity was taking the toughest looking of the new prisoners and beating him to death in front of everyone. This sent a message to all their captives as to what could happen if they violated his rules.

But Costa's happiness was muted when he realized that Nino was alone. Costa always sent teams of four out to search areas out, usually under Nino's command. Nino was smart enough to seek out future targets and lead others, but was loyal and completely afraid of Costa. That made him perfect for their band, a follower with some brains, helpful and loyal like a dog but not about to get ideas about taking over one day. But seeing Nino missing the others in his team was worrying, were the Federales on their trail? The American Rangers? Doubtful, but Costa had to know.

"Hola!" Costa bellowed, hand on his pistol as Nino rode up and leapt off his horse. "What happened? Tell me fast!"

Nino, a hugely fat man with quick fists and the piggy eyes of a lifelong bully, was usually the jolliest man in the band. But now he was white faced and sweating with terror. "The man...the Joe...he killed them with his hands! Tore them to pieces!"

"One man with only his hands? Why didn't you shoot him?" Costa roared, pulling out his shiny Colt Peacemaker. He bought it a month ago in El Paso and polished the weapon daily. To Costa the revolver was a symbol of his status, the only one in the band with such a shiny item. It was his determination that one day he would also own a different shirt for every day of the week. That would be true wealth, especially if any of them were silk. Costa felt a silk shirt once, the ruin of one in fact. He'd killed a man and found his clothes were different from any he'd ever seen before in his life. It was then that learned that some men, wealthy ones, owned luxuries such as silk shirts and more than two pairs of pants. And indoor plumbing!

"I tried!" Nino wailed, holding up two bloody, bandaged hands. "He threw metal scorpions into my hand and let me go. All the others are dead. Santo, Oscar, Jose...he killed them, Costa. Killed them with his hands!"

"Metal scorpions?" Costa asked, taken aback by Nino's statements and behavior. He wondered if his follower spent too much time in the sun without a hat, or something else that drove men mad. Like the diablo weed the Indios used for their ceremonies. Some went loco and starved to death in the desert.

"Si! Little metal..." Nino gasped and fell over, nearly toppling into Costa. Sticking out of the back of his head were two pieces of metal in the shape of scorpions.

Costa drew his revolver and looked around. Nobody was nearby and the dust of Nino's trail was still slowly settling. The metal scorpions could have come from anywhere and Costa knew better than to try and shoot in every direction in hopes of hitting his attacker. That was a trick he'd used in the past, resulting in a lot of men dying with empty guns at the bandito leader's hands.

Keeping his horse nearby, Costa scanned the area twice more to be safe. Then he quickly mounted his horse and rode away. He kept his head low, hoping no lethal darts would follow. Waving on his men, all of whom were nearby watering their horses, they rode hard back to the caves they used as a base. Once surrounded by his band, he kept looking back over his shoulder, but the trail dust made any view impossible.

A short time later they rode up the small rise to their base and Costa leapt off his horse with the deftness of a much smaller man. "Amigos! Nino and his men were killed by some man with darts. Get your guns ready and shoot anyone who gets close!"

Moving through his men and giving them a pat on the back or two, he entered the cave. It was a deep one, regularly used by the locals in the past. Costa and his men killed the inhabitants, took their store of food and installed a wall of wooden bars in the rear of the cave. That way they had a place to store their victims before bringing them across the border to rich gringos like Stanley. "How many are still alive?" Costa asked Javier, the man guarding the gates. Javier was a small, thin man who was quick with a gun or a knife, but wasn't naturally cruel. The perfect choice for a jailer, he tried to keep all the men, women and children alive.

"All, Jefe," Javier replied, not rising for his stool. As always he was whittling a hunk of wood while keeping a careful eye on their prisoners. "Eight women, five men and five children. No sickness yet."

Costa was about to tell them they were going to bring them across the border for Stanley when they hit thirty or more, when a sound filled the cave. It was gunfire, rifles and pistols firing at a fast rate. Costa smiled and nodded, whoever their enemy was he would be dead soon enough. Slowly the gunfire tapered off and Costa sighed out loud, glad the latest menace to his authority was defeated with relative ease.

But then the screams began, some of agony, others of terror. Every few seconds there was a gurgled cough and another shriek would cut off. It was a terrible sound; the screams of torment, Hell come to Earth. Costa tightened his grip on his pistol and looked over to Javier. The smaller man had a derringer and a long knife in hand, his knuckles tight on the weapons with fear at the terrible sounds.

Nodding, they moved forward, the light of the lanterns in the cave suddenly causing their base to feel oppressive. Formerly a place Costa had found as good a place to sleep as any he knew, the cave suddenly felt like a tomb. Each step he and Javier took seemed to send the same hollow, dead echo causing them to breathe heavier with fear.

Suddenly a figured loomed up at the mouth of the cave, blocking the sunlight and raising an arm towards Costa and Javier. With a cry of terror, Costa fired his pistol, emptying all of his bullets in seconds. Next to him, Javier shot his derringer, but held onto his knife. The echo of their guns shook the walls of the cave and deafened them both for several seconds. But the figure in the front of the cave no longer blocked the light. His fallen form could be seen just outside the cave, unmoving.

"Ha! Not so dangerous now!" Costa shouted with a wide smile. Lowering his gun, he walked forward and gasped at the sight before his eyes. Suddenly the sounds and feeling he felt in the cave came to fruition. Costa was truly in Hell.

Costa's men lay strewn about the landscape, their bodies torn and destroyed. Limbs lay in heaps around twisted corpses. Men who fought and killed dozens of peasants and the occasional lone soldier or Indios were unrecognizable bodies that littered the area around the cave. The carnage was terrible and Costa stared in open mouthed horror, only realizing that he'd shot one of his own men, one who was beaten but still alive until shot by his leader.

"Run!" Javier screamed, turned and suddenly fell to the ground. Costa ran to his side and recoiled in horror. A metal spike in the shape of a scorpion protruded from his underling's skull. Javier's breathing was slowing and, with a harsh rasp, ceased altogether.

A sound of movement caused Costa to rise, but he stopped as the cold metal of a knife touched his throat. Freezing in place, he felt the blade press in against his neck. It wasn't a killing blow, just a silent way of forcing the giant bandit leader onto his knees.

"Drop your gun and your gun belt," stated a soft voice in English. The accent was odd, not like the gringos across the border, but understandable none-the-less.

Costa complied slowly, wondering why his attacker was talking to him after butchering his whole band. As the gun and belt hit the ground, the other yanked both of the bandit leader's rifles. Costa heard them being tossed off into the distance just as the knife moved off his neck.

"You may rise," the stranger said and stepped back several feet. Costa turned and saw a tall thinly built man in khaki pants and a loose dark shirt. His face was darker than the gringos in El Paso, but lighter than Costa and his men. His eyes were narrow and similar to the Indios, but he was clearly not one of those people. His black hair was pulled back in a ponytail that was thrown over one shoulder. There was a calm deadliness to the man, not in the least because of the blood that stained his hands

The carnage was terrible…

and arms.

"Who are you?" Costa whispered, confused by this terrible stranger. Why had he butchered their entire band? There seemed no reason for his actions, none at all!

"I am Chin Hao. They call me Shanghai Joe." he replied, sheathing an oddly shaped knife in his belt.

"Do we know each other? Did I kill someone in your family? Why are you doing this? You killed all my friends!" Costa howled. Looking about for his guns but realizing the closest one, his pistol, was useless. He fell for the same trick he was afraid of earlier, firing his gun out of fear and not reloading. Now Costa was, at the moment, helpless. But like a rat, he was always seeking a way to survive.

"No," Shanghai Joe replied, watching the bandit leader with an impassive face.

Costa's face broke into a smile, "Then is it the money? I have much! In gold! Back in the cave! You can have it! And, when I get a few more men, you can have a share of the slaves we're going to sell to some gringos from across the border!"

"No," Shanghai Joe said, a biting edge in his tone.

"Then what? What do you want?" Costa shouted, his hands balling into fists with frustration.

Shanghai Joe's face split into a mirthless grin, "I searched for you, Costa. You raid farms, kill anyone who fights. You and your men rape and steal and sell human beings as slaves. They were bad, but you were the worst. You liked to beat men, women and children to death. Showing you were greater."

"Yes, I did that. What is it to you? You're no Federale or Ranger!" Costa snarled, "You butchered my men for no reason!"

A touch of anger crossed Shanghai Joe's handsome face, vanishing as fast as it appeared, "I had good reason. Your treatment of mankind. Some would compare you to a pig. But this is incorrect. Pigs do not treat their own with such cruelty."

Costa smiled, seeing a chance to beat this fool. He was a do-gooder, the biggest fools alive! Do-gooders were easy to defeat, they were so easily outraged. All you had to do was torment them with some words and they would immediately make a mistake. "You're a do-gooder? Like a priest? I've killed priests like you. You all die badly. Screaming, like dogs."

Shanghai Joe felt a wave of disgust at the words of this beast of a man. But he breathed slowly, controlling himself as he'd been taught to do by Master Yang, leader of the Fire Lotus Tong. The Tong, an ancient organization, trained him in many areas the least of which was emotional control. As a child Yang tried to break his calm with dozens of emotional and physical attacks over the course of years. By the time Chin Hao mastered all of arts of the Fire Lotus Tong, emotional, verbal or physical assaults were easy to defeat.

"You like to fight with your hands, Costa?" Shanghai Joe asked his voice calm and even. He tossed aside two knives and a wide thick belt. "Good, we shall fight using only our hands. If you win, you will live to destroy more lives."

Costa chuckled, no longer afraid. He was used to killing people with his hands, he was far better at that then he was at rifles or revolvers. And he really enjoyed fighting. The feeling of a man's jaw shatter beneath his fist or a rib caving under his knee...it was better than sex. Even his own men knew that Costa had a need for fighting and would sometimes indulge him and give up before they were injured too badly. Nino and the others, seeing when Costa was getting bloodthirsty, would take him into a cantina and wait as their leader picked a fight with someone. Usually this ended in murder, but better some stupid peon then one of their band.

With a roar, Costa charged toward Shanghai Joe, his huge hands swinging at the smaller man's head. These punches were capable of killing a man with ease, shatter a skull or neck instantly. Usually he liked to prolong a battle like this one. But after seeing all of his men slaughtered, Costa wasn't taking any chances.

But the man called Shanghai Joe wasn't there, he had moved to the left just out of reach. Costa stumbled, but stopped himself from falling. Turning, he charged again, arms outstretched to grab this man and knock him to the ground the way a bull would an enemy in his pasture.

But this time Costa was shocked as Shanghai Joe leaped in the air straight over the giant's head and landed with almost no sound. Then he was on the move again, charging the shocked bandito and striking Costa's huge arms with a series of quick painful shots along his arms. Shanghai Joe then back flipped three times and landed in an odd pose, watching his enemy.

Costa stared at the welts on his arm and began to laugh. He'd received bee stings that were more painful than those little pokes. He was about to clap his hands together in happiness when he discovered something frightening. His arms were not working. Costa could feel them, could feel the sweat beading down his body, but they would not move. His hands could flex and move, but would not move from his sides!

"What? What did you do to me?" He screamed, trying in vain to lift his arms. They were like meat hanging at his side, useless.

Shanghai Joe's face didn't change, but he did appear content at the results of his actions. "Snake style. Assault of the fangs and the tail. Now let me show you the scorpion."

Costa opened his mouth to respond, but Shanghai Joe was on the move again. He rolled forward and leaped in the air. His foot struck Costa in the face, knocking the giant bandito backwards. But Shanghai Joe's feet barely touched the ground before they were lashing out, striking Costa in both legs and his chest. He dropped to his knees, his legs and body feeling as if they were on fire. And just like his arms, Costa realized his legs were unable to move!

"The sting of the scorpion's tail. Quite painful. If I left you here, you would probably die of hunger or thirst. Or possibly the coyotes would eat you alive. But it matters not. I have never done that to another human being. Even one as loathsome as yourself. Instead I shall dispatch you through the use of the centipede. You will die in pain, but it will be quick." Shanghai Joe explained and struck an odd fighting pose.

A moment later he moved forward, his body a blur of motion that was almost impossible to see with the naked eye. But there was an odd, inhuman grace to his actions as he stopped before the fallen bandito leader. Shanghai Joe's hands lashed out, striking Costa's body with the speed of a lightning bolt and the force of thunder. Each time he hit the body of the huge criminal, the man's bones shattered. In mere seconds Costa's torso was a destroyed mass bones and blood. He collapsed without a sound, slipping to the ground, a pool of blood slowly forming around his body.

Shanghai Joe looked down at the body without a trace of regret. These men ravaged the land and destroyed the lives of innocent men, women and children. Death at his hands was simply justice. The authorities of this region appeared unable to respond, so he stepped in and was acting for the downtrodden. It was making him a criminal to some, but Chin Hao didn't come to this region of the world to be popular.

Suddenly there was a clapping sound from a distance away. Shanghai Joe spun in place, knowing his darts were nowhere nearby and he might be vulnerable to a bullet. How had someone sneaked up on him? His awareness of his area was almost absolute, that was also part of his training. Even when he was asleep, he was aware of his surroundings.

Major Sabbath leaned against a rock, his arms crossed across his chest. He was smiling as he watched Chin Hao aka Shanghai Joe work. The young man's skills were nothing short of amazing, which was why he stationed himself well outside of throwing range. Because this was not the simple job he'd been sent after dealing with Johnny the Deuce. This man was fighting the bandits of the region, the ones who were acting as slavers for the wealthy. This caused Major Sabbath to pause and not shoot the man down, to merely step back and find out the truth about this story. Because one of his main rules as a bounty hunter was to never become a criminal. In fact if a criminal hired you, it was acceptable to pocket the money and betray the crook.

"Now son, let me apprise you of the situation. You're fast, but a bullet's faster. And I'm far enough away to get you with three or more shots." Major Sabbath stated, tapping the pistol strapped in the front of his belt. It was a large silver revolver with a twelve inch barrel, able to fire at distances far beyond that of a normal pistol.

"You are a bounty hunter?" Shanghai Joe asked, not advancing, but looking for a means of cover or escape. Nothing was available, but oddly enough this man wasn't moving to attack. He had the look of a professional killer, a dangerous man this one, used to bringing death to his fellow man.

"I am. Major Sabbath is my name and I was offered five thousand dollars to bring you in alive or dead." Major Sabbath explained, smiling and showing his perfectly white teeth within a sardonic smile.

Shanghai Joe studied the man called Major Sabbath for a moment, "You planned your position, a careful distance from me but within range of your weapon. What is your plan now?"

"Your actions, they interest me. I can see you're a killer; that much is obvious." Sabbath stated, nodding at the corpses that lay strewn about the countryside. "But you seem to have a mission in mind. All those you've murdered were bandits and killers, the scum of the Earth. I'd like to know why before I take any action."

Shanghai Joe stared at the older man, recognizing this was no common bounty hunter. The few he met in his life were only slightly more legal than the bandits and killers they hunted. This Major Sabbath was a clever, thoughtful type, as well as a dangerous gunman. That was a deadly combination, one that would make him a terrible enemy should a clash occur.

"You wish to know why I exterminate such scum?" Shanghai Joe asked and began to walk towards the cave. "Follow and you will have your answer."

Major Sabbath kept his long pistol in hand, but relaxed and at his side as he followed the infamous Shanghai Joe up the slope and to the cave. The cave emitted a stench that was nearly a physical force, a scent of fear and neglect, of terror and death. Yet the blood-soaked Chinese warrior stepped into the depths with a lack of fear that was impressive, even to a trained killer like Major Sabbath.

The cave itself was clearly a combination of a natural formation and man's clever use of tools to destroy his environment. New and ancient supporting timbers were visible in the sparse light and signs of recent habitation. It appeared the bandits used the cave for storage more than a home, with casks of dried meat and ammo for guns and rifles visible as they stepped deeper in the depths. But it was in the rear that the source of the horrific smells emerged. People, more specifically men, women and children stood and squatted at the rear of the cave, their eyes the lost look of those who suffered tragedies beyond human reason. They were held behind a well-built structure of metal and wood, a makeshift, if highly effective jail. The small space available could probably hold six to eight men, yet twenty or more stood, their dead eyes staring at the two men, their faces expressionless.

Major Sabbath knew at once what these bandits were doing and why the man known as Shanghai Joe was attacking them regularly. They were slavers, marauders who attacked settlements throughout Mexico and stealing all the living bodies for a short life of servitude. Though he served in the Confederate forces in the war back home, Sabbath always despised slavery. The very act was a blight on the world, an inhuman practice he fought while living in his home state. But he disliked government more and took the side of his home state in the war. In the end the Union won, but the one positive from the terrible loss of life was the destruction of the institution of slavery.

But it appeared to be in full practice here, in Mexico where those of Native decent, known as Indios, were treated as second class citizens. Sabbath had full sympathy for Shanghai Joe's cause, if the young man was performing his act for the right reasons. If he was merely fighting the bandits to take the Indios for his own profit, Major Sabbath would execute Shanghai Joe and free the imprisoned men, women and children on his own.

"I see," Major Sabbath stated, watching Shanghai Joe without any visible expression, "When you free them, what's your plan, young man?"

Shanghai Joe didn't turn around; he merely stepped up to the bars and began to pull with all his might. The metal and wood shook, but stayed in place, a well-made prison. "Plan? I will take them to a mission town maintained by my...my friend. She will help them find new lives. I will check the bodies, take all the guns and sell the weapons. That helps support the town, keep the people safe. Then I'll go back out and find the next group Stanley Spencer is sending out."

Holstering his pistol, Major Sabbath reached into his belt and pulled out a ring of keys of various shapes as well as pieces of metal. He stepped next to Shanghai Joe and stated, "Allow me, son. You're strong, but sometimes it takes more than muscle to accomplish a task."

Shanghai Joe stepped aside and watched with a wary eye as the older bounty hunter fiddled with several keys and bits of metal. He was just beginning to get impatient, when there was the metal snap and the door swung open. Major Sabbath waved the men, women and children out, instructing them to get food and water and get out of the foul cave.

It was some time before horses, carts and burros could be rounded up and a slow train of men, women and children were lead off down the trail. The children were too shocked by the horrors they experienced at the hands of their captors to cry or even laugh as they rode in the wagons. They chewed their dried beef with metronomic slowness, their dead eyes staring at the white man and the Chinese man who killed the bandits and recoiled even at the touch of their own mothers. The men and women were grateful, though wary and frightened. Many were quietly praying, hoping they were not trading one nightmare for another. Two days later, seeing the walled mission, some grew hopeful, if still cautious, about their future.

The mission was at least one hundred years old, a tower structure of light colored stone and high walls. It looked closer to the den of a particularly prosperous robber, despite the huge crucifix that towered over the highest spire. There were men, most with the dark skinned look of Indios, on guard on the walls. They appeared suspicious but happy to see Shanghai Joe and more rescued men, women and children. The gates were large and made of thick, dark wood and they opened as the party approached, shutting behind them as the last rider, Major Sabbath, entered the grounds.

Major Sabbath spurred his horse further on, passing the people and stopping near Shanghai Joe. He was speaking to a young man in priestly robes, a tall handsome figure with dark hair and eyes and the soft skin of a born aristocrat.

"...to the capital. There the bishop and my grandmother will speak to President Diaz or General Jertado. They both respect her and will us." The priest was explaining to a crestfallen Shanghai Joe.

Shanghai Joe nodded unhappily and then waved at Major Sabbath,

"This is Major Sabbath. He helped saved the lives. He's a killing man."

The priest performed the sign of the cross and nodded Major Sabbath direction in a neutral manner, "I have heard of the Major, he is well known in Mexico as a bounty hunter. But sir, you have my thanks. You are a man of honor. Sadly there are more bands of men who will take the place of the group you both destroyed."

Major Sabbath dismounted his horse and tied the animal to a nearby post facing a trough. Tipping his hat back slightly on his head, he nodded slowly, "Your problem is, you're treating the symptom and ignoring the disease."

"I'm sorry?" The priest asked, looking puzzled. He took a small step closer to Shanghai Joe, knowing his friend was capable of dealing with gunmen and madmen. Was the legendary Major Sabbath planning treachery? It seemed unlikely, given his history, but a life spent spilling the blood of your fellow man did change a even those with the best intentions.

"Please explain, sir." Shanghai Joe stated, sensing the older bounty hunter had a notion.

"You mentioned Stanley Spencer two days back. He was the one who hired me, a rancher." Major Sabbath said, pulling out a small cigar and lighting it with a monogrammed lighter.

"Yes," Shanghai Joe and the priest both stated at the same time.

Major Sabbath blew out a long stream of smoke into the air and watched as the people they rescued were taken to places to eat and rest, "A rancher needing slaves? Doesn't make any sense. Cattle hands are skilled workers, not slaves. And Stanley doesn't have any farms on either side of the border. Which leads me to ask, why does he need all these slaves? And why children too?"

Shanghai Joe and the priest exchanged a look of surprise, realizing they were missing an essential element that was right before their eyes. A rancher like Spencer didn't need slaves; he had a great many men, all of whom were also armed killers, working on his ranch. What would he do with so many others?

"I don't believe we ever considered that," The priest explained and offered his hand, "I am Father Herando Lerdo-Diaz, priest of this mission. I was brought in to help our friend here and his lady love, Maria. I understand your metaphor now, sir. You are saying we were so concerned with saving lives, we did not realize Stanley had a larger plan in mind."

Major Sabbath shook the priest's hand and gave them both a wolfish smile, "Nice to meet you, Father. And you are correct. Slaves, they're no use at all on a ranch. And children, they're not much help on a farm. Which leaves?"

"Mining!" Shanghai Joe yelled, his eyes widening. "Back home some terrible men send children down small tunnels, to mine."

Major Sabbath frowned, "Not just back in your home. We need to find out where they're mining and what. And put a stop to it. Or these slave runs will keep happening, but they'll start carrying weapons that will take out armies. You're good son, one of the best I've ever seen with your hands. But a Gatling gun will cut you apart before you take two steps."

Shanghai Joe ignored the jibe and stepped forward, "You will help?"

Major Sabbath smile grew wider and there was a coldness in his whole demeanor that caused both men to pause. This was the professional bounty hunter and war hero that was so feared by men throughout the territories and Mexico. A pure, cold-blooded gunman with a clear sense of honor. But a dangerous killer none-the-less, one that few men would wish as an enemy, "I'm in." he replied and turned away, "We leave in the morning, young man."

Stanley Spencer was a frightened, nervous man. Normally he was big, blustery and full of Texas pride, a lord among men. He was wealthy, prosperous and was good-looking enough to have mothers regularly throw their heiress daughters his way. As a widower with a son making his own wealth in Mexico, he was a prime catch, a man to be envied.

But this was all lost since the woman, the representative of his master, came to El Paso. She was staying in his home, sleeping in his bed and forcing the lord of this house to sleep in a guest room. She appropriated his library and living room and sent for him like a common peon. And when she spoke, her words were harsh, cruel and filled with mockery and contempt. Her manner seemed to indicate that that Stanley Spencer, the cattle baron of El Paso Texas and points north, west and east, was a creature not worthy of her attention. This would have sent him into a killing rage, but one thing held him back, terror. This woman and their mutual master, a man known as the All-Father, were capable of violent retribution so savage, Comancheroes would flee in terror at their handiwork. Years before, when Spencer was an underling of Jacob Tyler the leader of this area for the Black Coats, Tyler made the mistake of stealing from the organization and attempting to hide the truth. The All-

"Nice to meet you Father."

Father's minions captured a barricaded Tyler, his wife, mother and three children and staked them out in the desert. There the whole family was slowly consumed by a colony of fire ants, a lingering and horrific death for all. But the message was clear, the All-Father and his organization were not to be trifled with, ever.

Knocking on the door to his library, he heard movement within, but knew better than to walk inside. Doing so days ago earned him a riding crop slash across his cheek by the lovely, yet frightening woman within. Several minutes passed before her softly accented voice stated in a clear tone, "Enter."

Stanley Spencer straightened, knowing he needed to be strong, despite the bad news he was about to impart. You didn't show fear to predators like this terrible woman. To do so was like the scent of blood to a mountain lion, they would tear you apart for the sheer pleasure of the kill. Therefore outwardly Spencer was standing tall and firm, his white suit spotless, his thick blond beard tidy and well-cared for, the model of a prosperous confident man. But inwardly he was as frightened as a child in a thunderstorm, quaking with terror.

"Miss, may I speak to you?" Spencer stated, humbling himself as he knew he must at all times to this woman.

The woman known as the Countess looked up slowly from the piece of paper she was examining and raised one perfectly sculpted eyebrow. Her rose colored lips turned up slightly with derisive amusement and she replied, "You already are, silly man. What do you wish to say?"

Spencer shuffled slightly, but maintained his dignity and met her piercing gaze as he shut the heavy oak door, "I have news. Apparently the bounty hunter I hired, Major Sabbath, is assisting Chin Hao in resisting our slavers. I confirmed this information before I brought it to you now."

Surprisingly the Countess nodded with some degree of respect, "You did correctly and I do not fault your choice of agent. Major Sabbath was well-known, a master bounty hunter. We will merely add him to the list of those who must die. None may thwart the All-Father's will."

She stood and stepped past him, throwing open the door before he could react and heading out of the house. She circled around his home, never looking back but confident that Stanley Spencer was following in her wake. Several of Spencer's men trailed behind, sensing something important was about to occur and ready to support their leader.

They stopped before the large series of caravan wagons that brought her to Texas, a small train of small homes on wheels. The attendants, upon seeing their mistress, all stood at attention, a mass of men and women behaving like soldiers despite being thieves, murderers or worse. But fear, pure and simple fear, made them obedient and polite in their service to the Countess, and through her, the All-Father.

"Bring them to me," the Countess ordered to nobody in particular. The throng of criminals that made up her entourage appeared to melt back, a hushed body as three figures emerged from the wagons.

The first was a tall man, a head higher than Stanley but with a spare hard body. He possessed the lean muscles one often saw in lifelong farmers, men who toiled by hand day and night for years. But it was his face and eyes that caught your eye. The face was the sharp lined disapproving glare of a hellfire preacher standing before a sinner of the worst order. And his eyes were hard, black and unyielding, the face and gaze of a fanatic. This was a terrible man, a killer who viewed the world as fools awaiting a much needed execution.

"Reverend Jacob Stiller, the Righteous Killer." The Countess stated, giving the man an approving nod. "Fastest gunman in the world."

"The Lord," Reverend Stiller whispered, his voice a harsh grating sound, "adds swift wings to his loyal servants. As the good book said, 'I will beat down his foes before his face, and plague them that hate him.' Amen!"

The Countess smiled as a giant of a man stepped into view. Though giant was a misnomer, the man enormous in every way. Standing taller than even the Reverend, his head was huge and as hirsute as a buffalo. His body was bloated, with a paunch larger than a small child and rolls of blubber that covered him, making him resemble a shaved bear more than a human. Yet he moved with a light step and wore a huge bloodstained leather apron with dozens of knives and cleavers strapped and visible.

"Butcher Babon, the Cajun Slaughterer. He has been shot fourteen…" The Countess said, but was interrupted by Babon.

"Excuse me, cher. But I been shot sixteen times." Babon said his voice light and musical.

The Countess nodded and favored Babon with a small smile, "My apologies, sixteen times. The deadliest man with a blade alive. And nearly impossible to harm."

The final figure was about the same height as the Countess, with short red hair and large green eyes. She was attractive, not beautiful, but attractive. She was dressed in men's clothing and appeared to study Spencer with a marked lack of interest.

"Lisette du Monde," The Countess introduced, "The most feared killer in France."

One of Spencer's men, a portly but powerful bully named Clem, began to guffaw, "That little thing, deadly? What's she do, screw a man to death?"

Lisette du Monde looked the Countess direction, still appearing disinterested. The Countess smiled fully and gave her servant a small nodded and stepped aside, turning fully as Lisette strode past. She licked her lips in anticipation.

Lisette stepped up to Clem, staring up at the taller man. Her head cocked to the side for a moment and then her foot lashed out, striking Clem in the groin. He doubled over in pain, but the smaller woman was on him, her hand reaching out and wrenching something hard. She kicked Clem in the side of the head and sent him sprawling to the ground, where he began to shriek in pain. Turning, Lisette walked to Spencer and dropped an object at his feet from her blood soaked fingers. The object hit the ground with a wet slap and she met Stanley Spencer's eyes.

"Your men need to learn manners in front of a lady." Lisette stated in heavily accent English.

Stanley Spencer stared at the object on the ground, fighting back revulsion as he waved his men to take Clem to the local doctor. But he couldn't take his eyes from the object at his feet…Clem's tongue, torn out by this tiny woman's hands. Stanley Spencer felt another wave of fear fill his whole body, knowing failure would mean this woman, or the other three evil murderers, would be sent to destroy him and his family. The All-Father's servants were more terrible than he ever imagined.

Major Sabbath thought up a plan in short order and gathered together enough supplies and times for them to rest. The plan itself was simple enough, find a group of bandits working for Spencer and follow them to wherever they brought the captives. This way they could destroy Stanley Spencer's plans at the source, rather than constantly searching for bandit gangs working for the evil Texan.

The hardest part of the plan would be to keep Shanghai Joe from attacking the slavers. Major Sabbath knew the young man was a fierce warrior, one that believed in retribution towards evil men. Holding him back from attacking the bandits was essential for Major Sabbath's plans, otherwise there was little chance they could find Spencer's mine. The deserts of Texas and Mexico were vast, dangerous places. These lands were one that felled even the strongest men, a force of nature few could resist.

Four days of searching without results lead both to wonder if Spencer's plans changed. The small villages appeared untouched, the people happy and content with their lot in life. Both were close to returning to Joe's adopted home when a familiar scent Major Sabbath's nose. It was a slight trace of a smell, a sickly sweet whiff of cent that vanished as fast as it arrived. He dropped off his horse and took several steps away, waving Shanghai Joe to silence. After five minutes of gently smelling the air, Major Sabbath discovered the direction of the smell, one he remembered every time he suffered a nightmare.

"I think I found them," Major Sabbath explained, climbing on his horse and checking his pistol. "Just west, several dead and burned bodies. The smell is...unmistakable."

"You experienced such in your war? Or killing men for money?" Shanghai Joe asked his voice slightly edgy. He was unhappy they hadn't found Spencer's men and was getting ready to demand that they take the battle to the wealthy monster himself.

Major Sabbath studied the younger man without expression, "War. The War Between the States. Many of the battles were bloodbaths. At times something, cannons, gunshot or the like, would cause an explosion. You never forget the screams of a man dying being burned to death. And the smell in unmistakable. A nurse I knew referred to it as, 'Hell's breath'. I didn't disagree with her sentiment."

Shanghai Joe didn't reply, but immediately felt some shame at his attitude towards the older bounty hunter. Though his profession wasn't honorable, Major Sabbath was a decent man with a clear set of morals. He lived a life of blood and death but managed to maintain his soul. That was an amazing feat unto itself, one that deserved respect.

After a few minutes, Shanghai Joe cleared his throat and replied, "My apologies, sir."

Major Sabbath waved his hand, understanding the younger man's frustration and not taking offense by his words, "We're several miles from the dead bodies. Do you mind if I ask you a question?"

Shanghai Joe shook his head, "Ask away, Major."

The Major smiled, his white teeth glinting in the strong sunlight, "This is a little personal. If you don't wish to answer, I'll get it."

Shanghai Joe smiled and shook his head again, "My life is, as an English writer once said, an open book. Ask away."

Major Sabbath nodded and took a quick pull from his canteen, "I watched you in action against the bandits. You used skills I've never seen, not even from other Chinese men I've met in California. Some used their hands and feet in impressive ways, but not like you. What's your secret, son?"

Shanghai Joe nodded, suspecting this would be the Major's question. The bounty hunter was an incredibly observant man, one who would notice that his skills were far from common in a battle. The story wasn't a secret, though parts of it were only known to his brotherhood in China. But Shanghai Joe didn't feel the need to protect his temple. Major Sabbath wouldn't repeat the information and the story wouldn't serve to help him in any way in the future.

"It is a long tale, but interesting." Shanghai Joe began, imitating the Major and taking a drink. "Many years ago, hundreds of years in fact, a clan known as the Poison Claw Clan was formed. The creators of the clan were masters of an unusual style of fighting, called the five arts. Each were styles of combat, unique and deadly."

"Hundreds of years ago?" Major Sabbath asked, surprised by the statement.

Shanghai Joe nodded, "China is an ancient land, sir. As I was saying, the Poison Claw five arts were very deadly. The leaders of the clan decided to try and take power, killing many people in the process. They lost, the pretender to the throne they backed was executed and the majority of the clan were killed by slow torture. The remaining members went into hiding, training in secret."

"But this changed," Major Sabbath asked, interested despite himself.

"Yes," Shanghai Joe acknowledged with a nod, "A master of the clan trained five pupils, each specializing in one art form. He then pitted them against each other with the secret fortunes of the clan as the prize. A good man, the master of the Lizard style, named Meng won. He took the hidden gold and recreated the clan as a temple, a secret one. The main purpose was to create men who would fight for the good of mankind."

"What is a Lizard style?" Major Sabbath asked, frowning. Was the younger man telling him tales?

Shanghai Joe chuckled for a moment and smiled again, "Forgive me. I forget that I'm telling this to someone who wasn't raised in our traditions. As I said, the original clan had five art forms. Each represented a style of fighting. They were named after poisonous animals. The first is the centipede, a fast striking form that hits with devastating power. The second is the snake, a style using incredible agility and nerve strikes. The third is the scorpion, who strikes with terrible kicks and claw like strikes.

The fourth is the lizard, also agile and fast and using incredible acrobatics. And the final, the fifth, is the toad. The toad is a defensive style, powerfully strong and hard to injure."

Major Sabbath raised an eyebrow, realizing the young man wasn't jesting in any way. Was it possible that people from China lived in secret temples and devoted themselves to training in secret and highly dangerous fighting styles? An army of men like this would be a deadly power. If they were also trained in modern warfare styles, they'd be the most dangerous force on Earth.

"Which did you learn? You said there were five styles. You moved fast, so centipede?" Major Sabbath asked.

Shanghai Joe shook his head, "No. I master all five arts. That's why I'm on my own. A master of all styles is expected to go out in the world and do good. Then when the time is right, you return and teach others the skills of the clan. This part of the world was known to be lawless, so I came here to be a cowboy and save lives."

"Quite a story, young man. And you do appear to be following your clan's traditions. Freeing people from slavery is the right way to act." Major Sabbath stated and nodded ahead. "I believe we have arrived. Prepare yourself. This will be a sight that is hard on the eyes."

A moment later, they reached the top of a small rise and a scene of horror greeted their eyes. The remains of a small town lay before them; the buildings burnt and destroyed frames. Shattered clay pots and broken wooden buckets could be seen as they approached the detritus of the lives of the former inhabitants. But the true horror became more visible within moments.

A cloud of flies hung above a small pile of corpses, a buzzing swarm of insects whose sheer volume could be heard at a great distance. The sound was horrific, a ripping, tearing noise that caused both warriors to wince slightly. And then the scent struck them full force. It was a sickly smell, a corrupt stench that caused both men to cover their noses and mouths to prevent involuntary retching. The corpses were torn and destroyed, barely recognizable as human. There were four, all seemingly men and their bodies and skulls were burnt, melted waxen figures that were picked apart after death. The scene was terrible, even for a pair of men who witnessed death, many times caused by their own hands, in the past.

"There's nothing left here. These poor men must have been killed weeks ago. Their bodies are almost gone. We missed the killers!" Shanghai Joe snarled bitterly and waving away the flies.

Major Sabbath shook his head slowly, "No, these are recent. No more than a few days. We can find their trail and catch up quickly. Walking men, women and children will not be fast."

"But the bodies..?" Shanghai Joe began, hopping off his horse and pulling out a shovel. At the very least he could cover the corpses and give the poor men some dignity in death.

"The desert, young man." Major Sabbath explained, pulling out his own shovel. "Coyotes, buzzards, rats, mice, insects. The desert takes care of anything that dies, feeds on it and absorbs the remains. This is recent. We'll find them soon enough, son."

Two hours later, they were back on the trail, the bodies covered and the trail found by Major Sabbath's hunting skills. The direction was south, deeper into the desert, a desolate area avoided by all since there was no life in that desolate zone. A hot desert wind blew on both men's faces, but the scent of the rotting corpses still lingered in their noses for many hours.

They discovered the bandits less than a day later, leading a train of men, women and children. The trail was easy to follow, the bandits weren't bothering to cover their tracks and their captives were too frightened to even contemplate such actions. The path towards the mountains was clear and the bandits weren't stopping often, merely providing water to anyone who needed it to keep them alive. Their actions weren't done out of kindness, they needed as many alive as possible to fulfill their contract with Spencer.

The leader of the raiders was a man of medium height and a thick beard and mustache. He wore the remains of a Federales uniform with a Captain's insignia visible on the shoulders. His followers were also dressed in the remnants of military uniforms, a most were older and looked as if they came from the United States. They were well-armed, carrying new and clean looking pistols and rifles and their horses appeared to be strong and healthy.

Looking down on the bandits from a rise, Major Sabbath closed his telescope carefully and chuckled, "That's where he's been hiding. Well, well, well."

Shanghai Joe swore quietly in Chinese, his face a mask of fury, "You recognize that murderer?"

"I do, son." Major Sabbath replied, sliding back and heading for his horse. "Felipe Diaz, murderer. He is wanted in Texas, two thousand dollar reward. He vanished a few months back after robbing a military base. It seems he went south, into the mountains where nobody lived. Stole the uniform from a man he killed in Mexico City, had his followers wear similar ones. Probably meant to make a deal with the next junta."

"There are only eight. Let's kill them all and save the people! I can't stand by and watch them suffer!" Shanghai Joe stated, climbing on his horse.

Major Sabbath grabbed Shanghai Joe's arm, his face as fierce as the younger man's but far colder. The younger man's arm was like grasping a python, as strong as steel yet very much alive and dangerous. "Hold yourself, son! I don't like watching those people suffering. But we need to find out why Stanley Spencer is kidnapping people. Once we find that out and destroy the source, the theft of people will end!"

Shanghai Joe shook off Major Sabbath's arm and snarled, "And those murderers will get away!"

Major Sabbath shook his head and smiled, showing his teeth. He looked more like a growling wolf than a man at that moment and even the fierce and dangerous Shanghai Joe was forced to pause, "Not a chance in this life, young man. Now that I know where Diaz and his men are hiding, I'll track them down. And deliver their bodies to the authorities in Texas."

Shanghai Joe thought for a full moment before he nodded his head, "You are right. Forgive me, it's very hard to watch them drag these poor people away from their homes."

"It never gets easier, son. But I've been in this business for a long time. You learn to make hard choices." Major Sabbath explained, "I never liked slavery, even when it was a part of daily life when I was young. The only good result from the war was that, no more slaves in the States."

Shanghai Joe sighed unhappily, but knew the older bounty hunter was correct. Though he didn't respect the man's profession, hunting humans for money was a terrible way to live. But the Major was a man of honor, one who continued to prove his ethics regularly in his every action. "You've lived a unique life, Major."

Major Sabbath chuckled and adjusted his hat unnecessarily, "To say the least son, to say the least. But I promise you, we'll make Diaz and his men pay right after we're finished with Stanley Spencer."

They continued to trail Diaz and his captives for two days, two very difficult days. Diaz and his men, though keeping the men, women and children alive, were cruel, dangerous and often violent. They each carried whips, which they used any time they saw a hint of resistance or attempts to flee. The people from the small village were constantly reminded that their death was only being prevented by following the rules. It wasn't long before the captives were dull eyed and listless, following Diaz and his men out of fear of beatings or worse.

Shanghai Joe had to fight his desire to charge in and attack every time Diaz or his men acted. But he managed to hold himself back, hold his desire to battle in check with the constant knowledge that they needed to wait until finding where the captives were being transported. Still, the struggle was difficult and every night he went into the desert and trained himself into exhaustion. The pain of his muscles followed by a long bout of meditation enabled the young warrior to maintain himself as they followed the captives.

But it was on the second day that Diaz stopped and waited, forcing the captives to stand in a huddled mass. They waited in the hot sun for one hour, before one of the men pointed out a dust train coming from the west. The dust cloud grew larger, and seven men slowly emerged in the distance. They were all better dress than Diaz and his men, with long rifles strapped to their saddles and pistols in quick draw fashion on their belts. After a brief shouted conversation, one of the men tossed Diaz and large bag and the latter looked inside and replied while waving to his men. Within a moment, Diaz and his band were gone and the new men were forcing the captive men, women and children onto the trail.

The trip into the mountains wasn't a long one, but it was difficult for Major Sabbath and Shanghai Joe. They needed to stay well back to avoid being seen, yet close enough that they could see which trails the captives were being lead. The leaders of this band were calmer than Diaz's brutes, giving some food in addition to water to the men, women and children. But their pistols and rifles as well as their polite disinterest made them a far more frightening group to the kidnapped townspeople. Diaz and his men were brutes, nasty bullies with guns and whips. These were professionals, composed and quiet, but far more deadly. The captives knew, without being told, that the first sign of resistance or flight would result in a bullet in the back of their skull. And then the men would go about their business, leading the people to their slow death by overwork or disaster.

The trip into the mountains took the better part of the day, though the distance was probably no further than a few short miles. The twists and turns in the hills and valleys that made up this land were deceptive and a

"I promise you, we'll make Diaz pay…"

weapon against prying eyes. For many years native tribes like the Apache and the Yaqui used this land as a means of trapping enemies and escaping from greater forces. If you were unfamiliar with your route, you could get lost and eventually die of thirst or starvation. Major Sabbath marked his trail, carefully placing pictograph cuts into the walls. This left them an escape route and a direction for leading the captives from the hidden mines. But this was slow work, worse because he had to accomplish the actions with a careful hush. Sound carried easily over these mountains, though the movement of the townspeople did appear to mask his operations.

"They'll probably have the people in a box canyon," Major Sabbath said as they wound down a wide trail. "That's a small canyon with only one trail in and out. It's the easy way to make sure nobody can get in or out. Also makes guarding people easier."

"I can climb in or out without being seen." Shanghai Joe replied, "We can free the people and lead them away."

Major Sabbath shook his head, "No, that's second in the plan. First we deal with the mine and the men running it. Those people and any others won't be safe unless we destroy the whole operation. Spencer and his friends will just send Diaz, or someone like him, out looking for more farmers to kidnap."

Shanghai Joe frowned, but nodded gravely. If they destroyed all of Spencer's operations, the people of these lands had a better chance of being safe and leading full lives. If the mine was left operational, the deaths and slavery would continue unabated. "The odds are not in our favor, eight men."

Major Sabbath chuckled and smiled again his cold grin, "Probably closer to twenty, son. But with the proper planning, we will be able to overcome the numbers. Mines are dangerous places, after all."

It wasn't long after those prophetic words before they watched as the people were forced down a small trail by two of the men, while the rest rode on over a small rise. There was a medium sized lean-to at the top of the trail and a pair of riflemen sat in the shade and watched. Climbing up above the trail, Major Sabbath and Shanghai Joe watched as the captives were placed in a small box canyon, just as predicted. After the men women and children disappeared into the small valley, the gunmen that accompanied them moved on, following the trail of their team.

"We can circle around on foot," Shanghai Joe said and waved for the Major to follow him. The younger man was a gifted climber and could sense the best route to follow. He was moving at a slow pace for the Major's benefit, but it was clear he could move through these mountains with the skill and deftness of a mountain goat.

It took over an hour, but they arrived at a rise overlooking a wide valley. A huge tunnel was cut out of the rock face of the mountain and a stream of men, women and children could be seen walking out with loads of dirt in their arms. The people were bent backed, exhausted and some appeared barely able to stand. A huge man could be seen in the mouth of the tunnel, a black snake whip in each of his enormous hands. Standing head and shoulders above all of the slaves, he possessed the powerful muscular body and enormous fists of a lifelong brawler. The giant man was laughing loudly and occasionally cracking the whip above the heads of the men, women and children as they walked in and out of the mines in a long, endless line.

"That's the overseer. They're usually bullies who like to fight. When the time is right, you'll humiliate him." Major Sabbath stated, pulling out his telescope and beginning to scan the mining area. It wasn't hard to discern the operation; the setup was the same around the world. There was a bunkhouse for the guards and a small building they probably used to eat and keep entertained during the hours the mine wasn't working. A small shack for the overseer and the mining engineers and a well-built brick building some distance for the mine and other buildings. The horses and a group of wagons were visible in the distance, far enough away to be safe but close enough for easy access. A small stream bubbled along near the horses and the animals could be seen drinking from the clear water. A very standard setup for mining in a desolate location.

"Humiliate him? I want to yank his heart out of his chest," Shanghai Joe snapped, seeing the man laugh as one of the slaves cowered beneath his whips.

Major Sabbath shook his head, "You'll just scare these people worse. They need to see him beaten down, worse than them and left to slowly die in the wilderness. It will give them some of their spirit back. But we need to do a little work tonight. That brick building, that's the answer. They'll keep the explosives inside. Here's what we'll do…"

After a night of hard, careful work and a fair amount of rest, Major Sabbath and Shanghai Joe returned to the mine. They intended to finish this today, free the people and destroy Stanley Spencer's plans for good. But fate had far more in store for them than their original plans. The mine site was surprisingly quiet as they approached that morning, the sounds of the large overseers roaring laughter the only noise that floated to their ears.

Climbing to a high point to observe, Major Sabbath and Shanghai Joe were greeted by a horrific spectacle. Five men and five women were standing, tied to posts with the large overseer striding back and forth, leather whips coiled in each hand. He paused every so often to slash one of the bound victims, howling with laughter at the moans of pain. The guards were visible, ten men standing with their rifles at the ready in strategic shooting points in the canyon.

"They know we are here!" Shanghai Joe hissed, seeing the overseer slap a weeping girl who looked like a girl just becoming a woman.

Major Sabbath nodded, "I expected that much. Plus there will be more surprises to come. Spencer is no fool. But this is all part of the plan, son."

Shanghai Joe looked as if he was going to argue, but all he managed to spit out was, "We can't leave those people to die!"

"Nor will we, young man. But we need to draw out the real enemy. This is just the opening act. The circus starts once are presence is known. Watch." Major Sabbath explained and pulled out a rifle stock. He attached it to his long barreled pistol. He then added a piece of metal that extended the barrel, transforming the pistol into a rifle. He carefully sighted and let out a long slow breath. He then fired the rifle, just as the overseer was about to bring his whip down on the young woman. The whip flew from his hands and a second later another shot tore the second whip away. The huge overseer shook his hands in pain, but retreated back behind the captive men and women.

"Now we'll see the real players here," Major Sabbath stated, calmly reloading the two chambers. "I suspected we might be found out. And Spencer has probably hired outside talent."

And Major Sabbath proved to be right once again. Three figures emerged, each standing close to the captives, but very visible from every rise surrounding the canyon. The first figure was tall, lean and hard. He was dressed in black and moved with the smooth stalking stride of a mountain lion. The second was a giant of man; towering well over the overseer and weighing probably double of that huge man. He was so hairy he appeared inhuman and he was dressed in a leather apron large enough to cover several men. The final was a slight figure, an athletic looking woman with bright red hair. They were cautious in their movements, each scanning the heights of the canyon with watchful eyes.

"Reverend Stiller and Butcher Babon. Very dangerous, very expensive to hire. Spencer has impressive connections. Stiller may be the fastest gun alive and Babon is a knife master who claims to be too tough to die. No idea about the woman." Major Sabbath explained. "If she's treated as equal by them, keep an eye on her."

Before Shanghai Joe could respond, the harsh, grating snarl of Reverend Stiller rose from the canyon floor. The gunfighter sounded as if he was whispering, but his voice was clearly audible, even at the great distance between him and his audience, Come out, Major. Come out sinner, it is time for you to feel the hand of Lord as he chastises you for your sins. As the good book says, 'Who shall be punished with everlasting destruction from the presence of the Lord, and from the glory of his power!' God is reaching out with his mighty fist to crush a murdering sinner such as you and your heathen servant!"

"Servant?" Shanghai Joe asked, looking at Major Sabbath with a quizzical expression. The Major seemed disinterested and was taking apart the additions to his long barreled pistol.

"He means you. The man has a limited view of the world, don't take it personally." Major Sabbath explained and then slid a little closer and called out, "Good afternoon, Reverend! Hiding behind the skirts of a woman? Not exactly the brave warrior of the Lord I've heard about in Tombstone, Mexicali and the Pecos."

"Merely avoiding a foul trick by your heathen servant. I know you to be a man of your word. Give your word that you will commit no foul tricks and will meet myself and these two saved souls. In response, I will send away the sinners tied to these posts." Reverend Stiller replied, his harsh voice almost sounding amused.

"You have my word. We'll come down once the people are gone." Major Sabbath replied and took a long drink of water. "Drink up, young man. Thirsty work ahead."

Shanghai Joe took a long drink from his canteen and watched as the rifle carrying guards freed the prisoners and two ushered them back to box canyon. He and Major Sabbath stood up once the captives were out of sight and slowly made their way down to the mine. The mouth of the mine proved to have eight men with rifles, each standing and watching the older bounty hunter and the young Chinese warrior as they stepped about twenty paces away from Stiller, Babon and the female killer who rarely seemed to speak.

"This is the little man who has been giving cher Spencer so many troubles. Cannot be!" Butcher Babon stated with a hearty laugh, pointing at Shanghai Joe.

Reverend Stiller stared at Shanghai Joe and replied, "Never underestimate the cleverness of the heathen. Their souls are as damned as their eyes are misshapen."

Major Sabbath sighed, pulled out his cigar case and placed a long thin cigar in his mouth, "I can see this won't be done pleasantly. I guess you want to test your draw against me, Reverend. Shall we?"

A slight twitch to the ends of Reverend Stiller's mouth was as close to a smile as the man was able to provide. "As I hoped for, sinner. As the good book says, 'we live unto the Lord; and whether we die, we die unto the Lord.' You shall die and, if repentful, will see the Lord and not a lake of eternal fire."

Major Sabbath pulled out his lighter and lit the cigar, his other hand hovering over the large barreled pistol. "If men like you are there, Stiller, I'll take the flames."

Reverend Stiller's face became a mask of fury, rage emerging from his whole body like a force of nature, "Sinner!" he snarled and his hand reached for his pistol.

There was a quick sharp explosion of sound and a body fell to the ground, unmoving. It was Reverend Stiller, his face down in the dust, blood leaking from beneath his body. Everyone stared in shock, seeing that Major Sabbath's right hand was still hovering above his large pistol. Instead a small trail of smoke emerged from his left fist. Dropping the lighter into his right hand and replacing it in his coat, a small palm pistol lay in his left hand, the barrel still emitting a tiny trail of smoke.

"Never fight another man's fight," Major Sabbath stated, blowing a long plume of smoke from his lips. He then drew his pistol, spun in place and fired just above the entrance of the mine. The loud crack of the bullet was followed by a massive explosion from the top of the mine, causing the structure to collapse in on itself. There was a quick shriek from the men inside, before they were cut off by the snapping tinders and falling rocks.

Major Sabbath then spun again, firing at the bunkhouse, explosive storage building and overseers hut. Each exploded with a roar of noise, a thundering hammering sound followed by debris and men being tossed every direction. Scanning through the smoke, he fired twice more, killing guards as they tried to rise and return to the fight.

That was the plan all along, to use the explosives from Spencer's mine to kill the majority of the guards and destroy the mine in the process. Had the explosives been out-of-reach, the Major had an idea using alcohol and fire to accomplish the same goal. It far safer than attempting to take out the men all at once or piecemeal. Also the Major suspected that Spencer would have more dangerous men to help protect his interests now that he was working with Shanghai Joe.

Shanghai Joe caught up to the Major a moment later, "It worked. Now leave these two to me. Save the people."

Major Sabbath nodded and smiled, "Good luck, son," before walking out of the canyon and towards the captives.

Butcher Babon emerged from the smoke, brushing a piece of wood from his back, "That was mighty clever, no? But not that clever, cher. You got me to deal with still. Butcher Babon is taking your head."

Despite his size, Butcher Babon moved fast, a cleaver in each hand, he stepped towards Shanghai Joe and swung fast with both weapons. Shanghai Joe danced back and assumed a pose, a fighting stance with his two hands extended and his left foot in front. He ran forward but suddenly changed directions, stepping to Babon's left side and began striking the man with palm heel and knife hand blows, each designed to shatter the ribs of the victim.

But Butcher Babon didn't fall back or scream in pain like every other person Shanghai Joe attacked in the past. Instead he roared with laughter and swung his cleaver in a back handed attack, slicing the smaller man across the chest. Shanghai Joe leapt back and out of reach, his eyes wide in surprise, but his face otherwise calm.

"Ho ho, you think to break Butcher Babon? Butcher Babon don't break, cher. He break any who get close." Butcher Babon laughed, swinging his cleaver theatrically.

Shanghai Joe wasn't impressed by the puffery and boasting of the giant man, everyone, even a giant like the Butcher possessed a breaking point. And there were many ways to tear a man down, especially when they relied on size and weapons as a means of defeating their enemies. Suddenly Shanghai Joe's stance changed, his movements becoming more fluid, his hands moving in a more sinuous fashion. His right hand suddenly was shaped like a claw while his left had two fingers extended.

"That's very pretty, you look like a dancer." Babon jeered and stepped forward, swinging his cleavers high and low.

But Shanghai Joe was ready for such an attack. Bending his body to the left, he dove between the blades and landed next to the Butcher's exposed flank. His hands then began to strike, quick piercing blows aiming for the giant man's nerve endings. Strike a man in the right way, in an exact location and he would be weakened or even killed. The Snake style mastered these attacks, each blow meant to pierce the nerves like the venom of a poisonous serpent.

Butcher Babon roared in pain and swung his heavy arm at Shanghai Joe, knocking the smaller man off his feet. He rolled quickly out of the way as the giant man swung his cleavers in fast, dangerous downward slices. Butcher Babon was injured slightly, but not nearly as much as a normal man. The giant's layers of blubber appeared to act as armor, protecting the exposed nerves from attack.

"This taking too long and Butcher be getting hungry. No more playing little man." The Butcher snarled and charged forward. Though huge in size, he, like the bison he resembled, moved with astonishing speed. The knives in his giant fists slashed through the air with a whistling sound as he bore down on his enemy. The sight was terrifying, an inhumanly powerful force bearing down on the slight figure of Shanghai Joe. Any man would attempt to flee in terror, but not Shanghai Joe, he never ran form a fight.

Shanghai Joe screamed and ran forward, towards the Butcher. Within a heartbeat they were upon each other and the smaller man leapt into the air, over the giant's blades. He spun in the air and his rear leg slashed out, the heel striking the side of Butcher Babon's exposed throat. A loud snapping sound, like that of the bough of a tree being shatter by a strong wind filled the air and the Butcher dropped his knives and began to grab his throat. Low pitiable sounds emerged from his huge mouth and a moment later he dropped to his knees, his face turning purple.

"A jumping, spinning hook kick to the throat," Lisette du Monde said, her heavily accented English not hiding her amusement. "A dangerous maneuver to attempt upon one so large and fast."

Shanghai Joe watched as Butcher Babon's face began to turn black. The giant man fell to the ground, still twitching but not making any more sounds. He looked at the smaller woman, her red hair shining in the sunlight. "Dangerous, yes. But the best means to end this battle without any further injury. You are next?" he asked, feeling body weakening slightly from the cut.

"Oui," Lisette replied, smiling and bowing slightly. Too many men, especially trained killers like this one, assumed she wasn't dangerous. This made defeating them all the more enjoyable. But occasionally one recognized that she was no mere slip of a girl and demonstrated honor. This she paid tribute to by treating the other with equal respect. "Allow me to introduce myself. I am Lisette du Monde. Please, drink if you wish. I would not wish you to be anything but at your best. You are Fire Lotus Tong, the Five Deadly Venoms forms?"

Shanghai Joe nodded, "And you?"

Lisette du Monde nodded and began to move, her hands and feet weaving fast and hard to follow patterns in the air. Her movements were faster than Butcher Babon's, probably equal to that of Shanghai Joe when he was using the Centipede style of fighting.

Shanghai Joe watched for several minutes and asked, "Pradal serey style? From ancient Angkor and parts of Cambodia?"

Lisette bowed, "Well done, Chin Hao. I may call you by your real name, no? Good! My mother learned the art from her grandfather, a master of the style. I have never seen the Poison Claw styles in the past. You mastered more than one? All five? The kick, that must be the Scorpion. The others were Centipede because of many fast attacks like the many legs. And the last, the Snake, the nerve strikes and agility. Impressive."

"All five," Shanghai Joe acknowledged, "Shall we?"

"Oui!" Lisette replied and kicked Shanghai Joe in the chest. He was knocked back several feet, but transformed the fall into a series of leaps and flips, landing on his feet several paces away.

They stared into each other's eyes for several seconds, unmoving and unblinking. This was the real battle; they would know who would be the victor in this fight. They were both masters of their art, expert warriors capable of killing with a blow. A true master of martial arts didn't need to fight a long drawn out battle, one look would tell it all. This was the highest form of the art, a metaphysical battle that took place with one look.

"Walk away," Shanghai Joe whispered, "You cannot win. We both know this much."

"Sadly, non. I would rather die on my feet than hang my head like a dog. Farewell, Chin Hao." Lisette du Monde whispered back. And then she screamed a primal roar more like that of a leopard about to strike its prey than that of a human. She slid forward, her hands and feet cutting the air like knives.

Shanghai Joe merely exhaled and blocked the French woman's impressive attacks. She was fast, strong and skilled, probably one of the best on Earth. In a few years she would be his equal, but not today, not here in the middle of the Mexican mountains, where the dead outnumbered the living. Not wishing to prolong the battle, Shanghai Joe swept Lisette to the ground and swung a hard axe kick down upon the back of her head. A sickening crunch filled the air and the young warrior closed his eyes with disgust. She should have walked away, lived to fight another day. But her pride was her downfall, he knew that when they met eyes. Lisette du Monde was too proud of her skills, her ability to defeat men far larger and stronger. It weakened her and left her vulnerable. A martial artist needed to be humble at all times, no matter how skilled or powerful in battle. There was always someone better in the world.

"You didn't have any choice, son." Major Sabbath stated, lighting another small cigar. Behind him were a growing mass of people, many so emaciated they resembled skeletons more than human beings. The stronger were helping the weaker and children, all sad eyed and frightened, clung to each other and adults.

Shanghai Joe bowed to the corpse of Lisette du Monde, "I know. But that doesn't make it easier."

Major Sabbath nodded, "Good. Never enjoy killing. Especially when the person didn't give you a choice but to take their life."

He was about to say more, when the overseer stumbled into view. He was torn, battered and bloody, having been hit by many splinters caused by the exploding shed. He stared, open-mouthed and shocked at the devastation before his eyes.

Major Sabbath smiled a wolfish grin, reached down and picked up a large piece of timber. He handed it to the strongest looking man nearby and said in clear, loud Spanish, "Hit him with it."

The man took the wood, his eyes wide with fear. Shanghai Joe stepped over to the overseer and slapped the man across the face, a loud sound that rung through the valley. The overseer clutched his face, but didn't respond. He saw what the smaller man could do in a fight.

But that was all that was needed. The captives, following the man holding the wooden shard, charged forward, even the weakest picking up a bit of wood or a rock. They fell on their tormenter, who shrieked as he was pummeled on all sides by the furious people he tortured and murdered for money and pleasure. Within moments he was dead, a torn ruin on the canyon floor.

"The other guards?" Shanghai Joe asked, suspecting the answer.

"I shot them down," Major Sabbath replied, inhaling deeply on his cigar. "Now, we'd best scrounge up some food and gather some barrels for water. Between the horses and wagons, we should be able to lead these people back to your mission. Oh and make sure we throw plenty of those sacks in too. Wouldn't want to leave a few million in gold behind."

"Gold?" Shanghai Joe asked, surprised.

Major Sabbath chuckled, "You think Spencer was out here digging for tin? Only gold would make a man willing to murder so many people!"

Stanley Spencer sat alone in his library, knowing the end was near. The Countess left, disgusted by the failure of Spencer's operation, not to mention the death of her best killers. She didn't bother to threaten him; her cold look was enough to know the All-Father would demand his slow and agonizing death as recompense. Spencer looked at the pistol in his hand, unable to use it to bring about a quick end to his suffering. He placed the silver gun back on the desk and sighed, hoping the All-Father would at least spare his son.

"You should have taken the bullet, the quick death." a whispery voice said in his ear as the cold steel of a knife blade was pressed against Stanley Spencer's neck. "My end for you will be far longer and more terrible. You should not have failed the Black Coats and the All-Father, little man…"

THE END

NEVER THOUGHT...

I never thought I'd write a western. I've written many tales of adventure over the years, but a Western, like a Sherlock Holmes story, always appeared out-of-reach. It's not that I disliked cowboy tales, either books or films, quite the opposite! I love them, growing up viewing everything from old Tom Mix and Roy Rogers films to the least know Euro-westerns. But a concept never seemed to click in my head, give me the needed inspiration for the story.

Then enter my good buddy, Rick Lai. Rick's an amazing guy, a man possessing an encyclopedic memory who I've been friends with for over a decade. Rick was creating his Major Sabbath universe, when he contact me with a suggestion, write a tale with the good Major and Shanghai Joe. Suddenly I was like John Belushi in THE BLUES BROTHERS, singing, "I have seen the light!" (though sadly no James Brown to make the scene complete).

For those of you who don't know me, here's a simple fact; I live for martial arts. I'm an instructor at Amorosi's Mixed Martial Arts and when I'm not training, I'm usually watching or reading about fighting forms from around the world. Martial arts saved me, changed me in so many ways and the reason any writing of mine is out there in the world is thanks to the training I received at my dojo.

Now Rick knows me well and he hit on a film, which turned out to be public domain, that I haven't seen in years. MY NAME IS SHANGHAI JOE and the rotten sequel, RETURN OF SHANGHAI JOE were a pair of Euro-westerns with a Chinese martial artist coming to the west and fighting for good. They're silly films, good fun and both, surprisingly, have legendary screen actor Klaus Kinski in them playing two different parts. The difference between Shanghai Joe and the man they obviously were copying, Kwai Chang Caine (played by the also legendary David Carradine) in KUNG FU was simple. Where Caine, a holy man, would turn the other cheek until he had no choice but to fight, Shanghai Joe would attack on the first insult. The character was a dangerous customer, sadly the film isn't great and the sequel stinks. But that fired my imagination, Major Sabbath and Shanghai Joe versus the servants of the famous French gang, the Black Coats!

Now a humorous aside on this tale of the story. The last time I viewed these films, I was a 22 year old who only watched martial arts. As a 49 year old martial artist, I viewed it again and nearly passed out laughing. During a scene in which Shanghai Joe was telling about his training, the tale had a flashback to his temple. There the hero was demonstrating his skill. But my trained eye noticed that his style, which was said to be Kung Fu, was in fact an Okinawan style known as Shotokan. This style, which was a part of the style I practice under my mentor and spiritual older brother, Shihan James Amorosi, is a famous system based in Okinawa and Japan, not China. The idea of a Chinese martial artist practicing a modern style in a Chinese temple in the 1800's had me laughing good and hard. But hey, we take our fun where we can get it, right?

Still, the world of Major Sabbath was a fun place to visit. I certainly am grateful Rick Lai, Ron Fortier and Rob Davis let me visit. And I'm grateful my wife, and top support, Gail Schildiner, put up with my viewing Euro-westerns over and over for the time I was writing this tale. At one point I think even our cats were sighing with annoyance as I sat down for another poorly dubbed but fun western from Italy. It's been a fun ride, hope to visit this world once again!

FRANK SCHILDINER - has been a pulp fan since a friend gave him a gift of Philip Jose Farmer's TARZAN ALIVE. Since that time he has published articles on Hellboy, the Frankenstein films, Dark Shadows and television's Lovecraftian links. He is a regular contributor to the fictional series TALES OF THE SHADOWMEN and his writing has been published in SECRET AGENT X Volumes 3 and 4; RAVENWOOD, STEPSON OF MYSTERY; THE BLACK BAT MYSTERY by Airship27. For Pro Se Productions his writing has been published in THE NEW ADVENTURES OF THUNDER JIM and THE NEW ADVENTURES OF RICHARD KNIGHT. His work also appears in THE AVENGER: THE JUSTICE FILES by Moonstone. Frank works as a martial arts instructor at Amorosi's Mixed Martial Arts. He resides in New Jersey with his wife Gail who is his top supporter.

ORIGINS OF MAJOR SABBATH

BY RICK LAI

INTRODUCTION

While the United States was flooded with Westerns on television during the 1960's, very few people in Italy owned a television. Italians went to the movie theatre to see largely American Westerns in the early 1960's. Inevitably Italian studios began to crank out their own Westerns, but these were pale imitations of the American product. The early Italian Westerns were staunch morality plays with incorruptible heroes versus despicable villains. It wasn't until Sergio Leone made A Fistful of Dollars (1964) that a distinct style was created for what came to be known as the Spaghetti Western, although some fans prefer the term Euro-Western.

Two American television shows heavily influenced the Euro-Western. *Have Gun, Will Travel* (1957-1963) featured Paladin (Richard Boone), a gunfighter for hire. *Wanted: Dead or Alive* (1958-61) recounted the adventures of Josh Randall (Steve McQueen), a bounty hunter. Prior to these two TV series, professional gunfighters and bounty hunters were portrayed as unscrupulous men who made life difficult for heroic sheriffs and marshals. Both Paladin and Randall had firm codes of honor which trumped their desire for money. Many an episode of *Wanted: Dead or Alive* had Randall killing a vicious criminal, but turning over the bounty money secretly to the dead outlaw's relatives.

The Euro-Western took the Paladin and Randall characters and created equivalent anti-heroes motivated by greed. The first such example of this anti-hero was the so-called Man with No Name played by Clint Eastwood in the "Dollars" trilogy of Sergio Leone, A Fistful of Dollars, For A Few Dollars More (1965) and The Good, the Bad and the Ugly (1966). Eastwood's character, who functions as a bounty hunter in two of the movies, is primarily influenced by a desire for money, but he always commits at least one unselfish act in each film. He helps a woman escape enslavement by a bandit leader (A Fistful of Dollars), remains loyal to a partner he took on reluctantly (For A Few Dollars More), and ends needless slaughter in the Civil War by blowing up a bridge (The Good, the Bad and the Ugly). However, the so-called Man With No Name performs blatant criminal acts. For example, in *The Good, the Bad and the Ugly*, the bounty hunter engages in an elaborate scam where he constantly turns in a vicious criminal for the reward and them helps him secretly escape execution.

For A Few Dollars More featured the only canonical appearance of Colonel Douglas Mortimer (played by Lee Van Cleef). Wearing a black hat and an Inverness Cape, this bounty hunter dressed like Hatfield, the ill-fated gambler played by John Carradine in John Ford's classic Western, *Stagecoach* (1939). Dressed in black clothes and using a derringer, Mortimer was influenced by Paladin. While making a living as a bounty hunter, Mortimer was mainly motivated by vengeance in *A Few Dollars More*. He was pursuing his sister's murderer, a bandit who recently broke out of a Mexican jail.

A character very similar visually to Mortimer was Sartana (who appeared in five films officially). Sartana wears clothes very similar to Mortimer and uses a derringer-like weapon.

Sartana was played by Gianni Garko in all films except the third where the role was briefly taken over by George Hilton. The Sartana films are 1) *If You Meet Sartana Pray for Your Death* (1968), 2) *I Am Sartana Your Angel of Death* (1969), 3) *I Am Sartana, Trade Your Guns for a Coffin* (1970), 4) *Have a Good Funeral, My Friend... Sartana Will Pay* (1970), and 5) *Light the Fuse . . . Sartana is Coming* (1970). Sartana was both a bounty hunter and a con artist. The typical Sartana ending has him not only collecting the bounty on the bad guys, but successfully absconding with the money they stole. The Sartana films are in the public domain. In fact, there were many unofficial Sartana sequels in the 1970's. None of them were any good. However, there were two films, *They Called Him Cemetery* (1971, also called *A Bullet for a Stranger*) and *The Price of Death* (1971) in which Gianni Garko played characters who were essentially Sartana in everything but name, Garko's surrogate Sartanas were called the Ace of Hearts in *They Called Him Cemetery* and Mr. Silver in *The Price of Death*. To complicate matters, Garko also played two different outlaw characters named Sartana Liston in *1,000 Dollars on the Black* (1966) and Sartana in *Sartana Killed Them All* (1971). Sartana was also called the Preacher in the canonical film series (particularly in *Light the Fuse . . . Sartana is Coming*). Stephen Boyd played a Sartana-like character called the Preacher in *Hannie Caulder* (1971) with Raquel Welch.

The Mr. Silver character in *The Price of Death* is further complicated by an earlier film, *Killer Calibre 32* (1967). Both films were made by Lorenzo Gicca Palli (also known as Enzo Gicca). *Killer Calibre 32* featured a very similar Mr. Silver played by Peter Lee Lawrence. Apparently Gicca wrote *The Price of Death* as a sequel, but couldn't get Lawrence to repeat his role. Therefore, Gicca cast Garko and rewrote the Mr. Silver character to be more like Sartana.

One year after the first Sartana film was made, the creators of that series decided to fashion a similar hero, Sabata. Lee Van Cleef was hired to play their role. Although the character was similar to Sartana, major decisions were made to make him very close to Colonel Mortimer in the first movie in the series, *Sabata* (1969). Besides dressing almost exactly the same (the black hat is a slightly different shape), Sabata has an arsenal that parallels the weapons utilized by the bounty hunter from *A Few Dollars More*. Like Mortimer, Sabata has a long-range rifle which enables him to easily pick off enemies whose bullets can't reach him. Mortimer employed a derringer in the gunfight with the hunchback (played by Klaus Kinski). Sabata has a four-barreled derringer with three extra barrels hidden in a secret compartment inside the handle.

The movie even suggests that Sabata may really be Mortimer in the closing scene. A character asks Sabata "Who the hell are you?" His enigmatic reply is "Didn't I ever mention it?"

Sabata mimicked Mortimer by being a bounty hunter. In the tradition of Sartana, Sabata was a bit of a trickster but with a significant difference.

Whereas Sartana often secretly confiscates stolen property for his own profit, Sabata will return it to the rightful owners. This isn't an unselfish act on Sabata's part because he always manages to collect a reward for retrieving the stolen goods.

While Sabata claims to stay within the law, he often withholds vital information from local law-enforcement officials, This characteristic has its precedent in Colonel Douglas Mortimer's blatant neglect to tell the authorities of El Paso that the Indio gang is planning to rob the bank. This action is prompted by the desire to collect all the bounties on the gang with the help of the Man with No Name. If Josh Randall had been in a similar situation in *Wanted: Dead or Alive*, he would have immediately warned the Sheriff of El Paso.

In 1970, the owners of the Sartana and Sabata franchises made a Western movie starring Yul Brynner as a new character named Indio Black. Indio, the Spanish word for "Indian," had been the name of the brutal villain in *For a Few Dollars More.* When the Indio Black movie was being dubbed into English, a decision to change the protagonist's name to Sabata in order to cash in on the success of the earlier Lee Van Cleef film. The movie was released in its English version as *Adios, Sabata*

There is an Internet legend that *Adios, Sabata* was originally intended to be a genuine Sabata film with Van Cleef. Supposedly Van Cleef was unavailable because he was filming *The Magnificent Seven Ride* (1972). In that film, Van Cleef played Chris Adams, a role which Brynner originated in *The Magnificent Seven* (1960) and *The Return of the Magnificent Seven* (1966).The gap of two years between the releases of *Adios, Sabata* and *The Magnificent Seven Ride* causes one to doubt this Internet story.

Van Cleef returned to the role in *Return of Sabata* (1971). While the first film emphasized the character's similarities to Mortimer, the second film began to introduce differences. Sabata was a Major rather than a Colonel in the Confederate Army. There were strong hints that Sabata was the illegitimate son of a prostitute. In the both *For a Few Dollars More* and *Sabata*, Van Cleef made no effort to disguise the fact that he was partially bald.   In *Return of Sabata*, the actor wore a wig.

In 2005, my first short story, "The Last Vendetta," was published in *Tales of the Shadowmen #1*. This somewhat convoluted story was a homage to Euro-Westerns. Inside the story was a brief summary of the career of a bounty hunter called Gunsight Eyes, who was a composite of Colonel Mortimer and Sabata. During the Civil War, a bandit called the Indian (alias for Indio in *A Few Dollars More*) murdered the bounty hunter's sister and her husband. When the war ended, Gunsight Eyes sought to track the killer down. Unfortunately the bounty hunter confused the Indian with the Black Indian (alias for Yul Brynner's Indio Black/Sabata). Gunsight Eyes killed the Black Indian in Mexico before realizing his error. After slaying his sister's true killer, Gunsight Eyes became embroiled in a blood feud in Utah (this was borrowed from flashback scene in a highly regarded Euro-Western called *The Great Silence* (1968)). During the events in Utah, Gunsight Eyes was tricked into nearly killing an innocent man. Remembering the similar tragedy in Mexico, Gunsight Eyes decides to take the Black Indian's surname in order to always remember to avoid the mistake of hunting an innocent man.

The central premise of the bounty hunter's origin came from two sources. First, another of Lee Van Cleef's Euro-westerns, *The Big Gundown* (1966), had him playing a bounty hunter manipulated into pursuing an innocent man. The second inspiration was "Genesis," a 1962 episode of *Have Gun, Will Travel*. That episode revealed that Paladin had adopted the attire and methodology of Smoke (also played by Richard Boone), a gunfighter whom he had been tricked into killing in a duel.

THE BIG GUNDOWN

LEE VAN CLEEF - TOMAS MILIAN
WALTER BARNES - MARIA GRANADA - FERNANDO SANCHO
Dirigida por SERGIO SOLLIMA - Música de ENNIO MORRICONE
TECHNICOLOR - TECHNISCOPE

The same story also created a sort of "Spaghetti Western Universe" by incorporating other characters from movies in the same genre. For example, Franco Nero made a famous Western, *Django* (1966), in which the central character was a gunfighter who dragged a coffin containing a machine gun. Since Nero has a heavy Italian accent, his lines were dubbed by an American actor in the English version. In later Westerns, Nero wanted to dub his own lines, Therefore, the screenplays made him a European immigrant (usually Polish or Swedish). In "The Last Vendetta," I created a variation on Django called Djanko, a Croatian immigrant.

I long intended to write an expanded narrative detailing the origin story of the Mortimer/Sabata character. I broached the idea to Ron Fortier of Airship 27. He liked the concept, but wanted me to jettison the Gunsight Eyes name. He accepted my alternative of Major Sabbath. In writing stories about the Major, it can be implied that he's also known as Colonel Mortimer and Sabata, but those names should never appear. Characters from Leone's the Dollars Trilogy and the Sabata films can appear, but they must have different banes than those used in the movies.

There are several recurring anomalies in Euro-Westerns for which I have provided explanations.. One example is the usage of anachronistic weapons. Starting with *A Fistful of Dollars*, many films had machine guns in the 1870's. Machine guns weren't invented until 1884, although the Gatling Gun was invented during the Civil War. *The Good, the Bad and The Ugly* had dynamite being used to blow up a bridge in 1862. Dynamite wasn't invented until 1867. I rationalized these inaccuracies by having characters from some of the movies invent fictional forerunners of these weapons.

One traditional setting for a Western was Mexico during Emperor Maximilian's reign in the 1860's. Maximilian was supported by French troops, In American Westerns such as *Vera Cruz* (1954) and *Major Dundee* (1965) set in Maximilian's time, villains were French soldiers.

When Euro-Westerns such as *Adios, Sabata* were made in the same time period, the filmmakers didn't want to antagonize French audiences. Since Maximilian was Austrian, the fiction was created that his government was supported by Austrian troops. I explained this inaccuracy by having an elite squad of Austrian mercenaries.

THE MAIN PROTAGONIST: MAJOR D. M. SABBATH

Basis: For A Few Dollars More (1965)
Sabata (1969)
https://www.youtube.com/watch?v=Hye7KJOhudY
Adios, Sabata (1970)
https://www.youtube.com/watch?v=udNde1qpczs
Return of Sabata (1971)
https://www.youtube.com/watch?v=wdacywm3iiM

The man known as Major D. M. Sabbath was born in 1825 (based on the reference that Colonel Douglas Mortimer was almost fifty in *For a Few Dollars More*). His father was a South Carolina plantation owner named Mortimer (that surname should never be used in the stories). His mother was a prostitute. The previous statement is based on three scenes in *Return of Sabata*: First, the Major made an amused look upon being told (by Bronco) that he would distrust even his own mother. Second, the Major tells Lieutenant Clyde (known as Lieutenant Tervis in our stories) that if both their mothers walked the street, the Major's had a better clientele. Third, when it is revealed that the Major has fathered an illegitimate son, Bronco remarked that he feels sorry for the boy who won't be raised by a strong father like the Major. Clyde then whispered something in Bronco's ear. Bronco looked shocked, and wondered if there were any virtuous women in the world.

The prostitute christened her child Douglas (this name should never be used). The plantation owner married later in life. His daughter, Rosemary Mortimer, was born in 1840. When the plantation owner's wife failed to produce a male heir, he recognized Douglas as his son in 1845. During The Mexican War (1846-48), Douglas served gallantly in the American Army and rose to the rank of Colonel. The young man legally adopted the name of Douglas Mortimer (this name should never be used). Young Rosemary never challenged this decision. She totally embraced Douglas as her brother. During The Mexican War (1846-48), Douglas served gallantly in the American Army and rose to the rank of Colonel. When their father died in 1855, Douglas became Rosemary's legal guardian. The Colonel left the military to run the family estate.

In 1860, Rosemary married Robert "Bob" Galloway, a wealthy Texan. Douglas gave Rosemary away at her wedding. As a wedding gift, Douglas had two watches made containing a picture of Rosemary. Each played a musical lullaby. Douglas also had at had a third watch made for himself.

When the Civil War began, Douglas joined the Confederate Army. He was given the rank of Major and assigned to Colonel Jonas Leland in the Hellbender Regiment. A hellbender is a salamander, and an image of that lizard adorned the regimental flag, The Hellbender Regiment fought in Tennessee.

In 1862,the Major was wounded at the battle of Stones River in Tennessee. The top joint of the middle finger was shot off. He recovered at a military hospital run by Mrs. Elizabeth Leland. During his 20 days of convalescence, the Major discovered a drunken Colonel Leland beating his wife. The Major warned Leland that he would kill him if he ever beat her again.

In 1864, Lieutenant Clyde Tervis joined the Hellbender Regiment. This is Clyde from *Return of Sabata,* and his first name should never be mentioned in our stories. At the Battle of Nashville in 1864, Tervis saved the Major's life. Tervis was awarded a medal for heroism.

When the war ended in 1865, the Hellbender Regiment was disbanded. Colonel Leland took the defeat of the Confederacy very hard. He became exceedingly cruel to his wife, and this resulted in her committing suicide. Holding Colonel Leland responsible for his wife's death, the Major sought to challenge Leland to a duel.

However, Leland had fled Tennessee with his three sons, Nat, Jeff and Ben. Only Ben was Elizabeth's son. Nat and Jeff were the offspring from an earlier marriage. Jonas Leland had embarked on a criminal scheme to steal over a million dollars to fund a revived Confederacy. This scheme resulted in the death of the whole Leland family in New Mexico during 1865. This event is depicted in the film *The Hellbenders* (1967). In that film, the Colonel (played by Joseph Cotton) was only referred to by his first name (the surname Leland comes from a character portrayed by the same actor in *Citizen Kane*).

Before leaving Tennessee, Colonel Leland and his two older sons spread a false rumor that the Major had "chewed" off his own finger in 1862 in order to romance Elizabeth in the hospital. Furthermore, it was claimed that she had committed suicide because the Colonel had refused to resume their affair. Although blatantly false, the story was widely believed by many people including Lieutenant Tervis.

At the close of the Civil War, the Major met Pickled Joe (this is Josiah Pickles from *Return of Sabbath*). Pickled Joe was a member of the Hellbender Regiment. A former engraver, he forged documents for the

Hellbender Regiment to perform secret missions behind enemy lines. Colonel Leland used Pickled Joe to forge a Union Army military permit to bury Captain Ambrose Allen of the Confederate Army in New Mexico. Actually the coffin contained a million dollars that the Colonel had stolen from the Union Army. In a series of bizarre circumstances (told in *The Hellbenders*), the stolen millionaire ended up being buried in a military cemetery in New Mexico. The money was in a coffin under a headstone bearing Captain Allen's name in Fort Brent. There are no records of it ever being dug up.

The Major's family plantation (located near Columbia, South Carolina) was ravaged by Sherman's soldiers in 1865. With his estate in ruins and his reputation damaged by the Leland scandal, the Major viewed his prospects in the eastern United States as dim. He decided to join his beloved sister Rosemary in Texas. There he found only tragedy and horror.

During the war, Robert and Rosemary Galloway had been murdered by a Mexican bandit, the Crazy Indian (this is the character called Indio in *For a Few Dollars More*). Robert's brother, Lee "Red" Galloway (the character called Banjo in *Sabata*), was residing in a Union POW camp of Batterville as a consequence of having participated in the ill-fated 1862 New Mexico campaign of Confederate General Henry H. Sipley. He had been totally unaware of the murder of his brother and sister-in-law until his return home after being released from the POW camp. It was Red Galloway who informed the Major of the brutal murders by the Crazy Indian.

Equally impoverished by the war, Red Galloway convinced the Major to partner with him as bounty hunters in order to track down the killer of their relatives. They had two leads. The Crazy Indian had stolen the two musical watches from the Galloways. the bounty haunters also had a description of the killer, a bearded man with a full head of hair.

In 1867, the Major and Galloway mistakenly believed that they had located the killer. They heard rumors of a mysterious mercenary, Christian Adam Sabbath Sr. alias the Black Indian (this is a disguised version of Sabata/Indigo Black from *Adios, Sabata*). The bounty hunters suspected that the Crazy Indian and the Black Indian were the same man. Traveling to Mexico, the two partners changed their minds when they spied the Black Indian from afar. He was a clean-shaven man who was totally bald.

While their quest to find the Crazy Indian remained fruitless, the two bounty hunters had a profitable partnership until 1872. Briefly separated from the Major while pursuing outlaws in New Mexico during late 1871,

Galloway had joined a poker game at the Sunlight Saloon in Signo Amarillo, New Mexico. There he met Valentin L'Ollonaise alias Jimmy Ballantrae (this is Ballantine from *Adios, Sabata*). L'Ollonaise was not only an old enemy of Christian Sabbath, but also a sometime business associate of the Crazy Indian. L'Ollonaise convinced Galloway that Christian Sabbath had used makeup to disguise himself as the Crazy Indian.

The 1872 events of "Thy Name is Sabbath" then unfolded. In Mexico, the Major slew Christian Sabbath. When the Mexican authorities arrest the real Crazy Indian, the Major had a bitter falling out with Galloway. The partnership was dissolved in Mexico.

In the course of "Thy Name is Sabbath," the Major befriended munitions dealer Arthur Gordon, met Sheriff Priam Ramsey, got revenge on Valentin L'Ollonaise , formed a temporary alliance with Jake Sartana, and earned the animosity of the Gentlemen of the Night.

In 1874, the events of *For a Few Dollars More* unfolded. The Crazy Indian (Indio) broke out of prison. Allied with the Drifter with Many Names (the Man with No Name), the Major (Colonel Douglas Mortimer) finally tracked down and killed his sister's murderer. The placement of the movie's events in 1874 stems from Colonel Mortimer consulting the newspaper archives from 1873 in order to identify the Man with No Name (who is actually called Manco in the film).

In 1875, the major trained a man called Specs as a bounty hunter (this is a disguised version of Thomas Luther Price from *Hannie Caulder*). In the course of this training, the Major created the following Rules of the Bounty Hunter Code.

1) Once you embark become a bounty hunter, you'll never be the same man. Think twice before choosing the livelihood of a killer of men.

2) Before you draw, watch a man's hands.

3) Remember you're a target as well. Learn to position your body sideways.

4) One bullet may not be enough to kill a man You might have to shoot him twice.

5) Never pull the trigger of a gun in jest, even if you think it's unloaded.

6) When faced with many enemies, kill the swiftest first.

7) Most men in our profession are untrustworthy. Be careful if you ever choose a partner.

8) Never tell a competitor about a bounty.

9) Stay always within the law. Never pocket any stolen goods for yourself.

10) If a man pays you to commit a crime, you're within you rights to pocket the money and betray him.

The 1876 sequences from "Thy Name is Sabbath" then transpired. In Snow Hill County, Utah, the Major was nearly tricked into killing Arthur Gordon's son, John, by a corrupt Justice of the Peace. In the subsequent events of the story, the Major failed to prevent the murder of John and his wife as well as the maiming of their son. A devastated Major adopted the name of Sabbath in order to never repeat the mistake of pursuing an innocent man.

In 1877, the Major apparently had an affair with his sworn enemy, Delilah L'Ollonaise, in Redstone, New Mexico. Delilah gave birth to a son whom she claimed to be the Major's. Her six brothers swore vengeance on the Major for deserting their sister. The brothers claimed that the Major deserted Delilah at a church. Adopting the surname of Sabbath, Delilah's son appeared in *I am Sartana, Trade your Pistols for a Coffin.*

At this Redstone, the Major gained the allegiance of two acrobats, Angelos (Alley Cat in *Sabata* and Angel in *Return of Sabata*) and Bion Varno (Bionda from *Return of Sabata*). The Varno brothers had originally been entertainers at Delilah's casino in Redstone. The acrobats became the Colonel's spies. Hearing that Red Galloway (Banjo) was in Daugherty, Texas, the Major dispatched Angelos there to observe the gunslinger. There Angelos assumed the identity of a mute Indian Learning that the McIntock family was controlling Hobsonville, the Major sent Bion there.

In 1879, the Major discovered that his former wartime comrade, Pickled Joe, was traveling with a circus. Believing that the engraver was engaged in a counterfeiting scheme, the Major decided to infiltrate the circus. In order to do so, he needed to establish a theatrical act. Gordon Munitions developed for him phony bullets that were filled with red paint that looked like blood. The Major debuted in a theatre in El Paso. His act consisted of members of the audience engaging in a fake shootout with him. The theatre owner didn't want the Major to use the name Sabbath because church-goers might consider the name sacrilegious. Thus, the Major took the stage name Sabata, an alias that Christian Sabbath had used in Mexico.

The Major's performance was observed by Red Galloway in the audience. The Major noticed Galloway as well, and trailed him after the performance to Daugherty, Texas, There the two became untrustworthy allies in the events described in *Sabata*. Besides getting a reward for foiling a gold robbery, the Major swindled a corrupt banker. The banker paid Galloway to kill the Major. The Major then faked his death in a gunfight with Galloway. At the conclusion of this affair, Galloway tried to cheat the Major by running off with all the money. The Major foiled this attempt, and punished Galloway by only giving him a small share of the money. Angelos Varno assisted the Major in this enterprise, but pretended not to know the bounty hunter in order to fool Galloway, Once this exploit concluded, Angelos was sent to Hobsonville to rejoin his brother Bion.

Still using the Sabata name, the Major then joined the same circus to which Pickled Joe belonged. After touring for two months, the Major arrived in Hobsonville, New Mexico, where the events of *Return of Sabata* unfolded. Teaming up with Lieutenant Tervis (Clyde), the Major retrieved the money embezzled by a corrupt politician. When Tervis tried to betray the Major, the tip of his trigger finger was shot off by the Major.

In the course of this Hobsonville exploit, the Major killed Delilah's six brothers from Redstone. Hobsonville was very close to Redstone, whose large casino was owned by Delilah. *Return of Sabata* doesn't identify the state where Redstone and Hobsonville were located, but there is a town called Redstone in New Mexico.

Both *Sabata* and *Return of Sabata* are placed in 1879 for two reasons. First, both mention the Civil War as not being that long ago. Second, phonographs are present in both films. Edison invented the phonograph in 1877, and we have to allow time (2 years) for this invention to become prevalent.

After the Hobsonville incident, the Sabata alias was dropped by the Major and the surname of Sabbath was resumed. The name Sabata should never be used by the Major in our stories, but reference can be made that he once used a odd Spanish alias in stories set after 1879.

During his stint with the circus, the Major vainly wore a wig to cover up his partial baldness. Realizing that the wig made him look foolish, he quickly abandoned it.

The Major uses the following weapons:

1) A two-barreled Remington derringer (used in 1874 during the events of *For A Few Dollars More*). Remington derringers first became available in 1866,

2) A four-barreled derringer with three hidden barrels in the handle whose bottom opened on a hinge (from *Sabata* and *Return of Sabata*). In "Thy Name is Sabbath," we learn that Gordon Munitions made this weapon twice for him. The first derringer was purchased by the Major in 1872, and was damaged in the same year. The Major purchased a replacement for the weapon in 1874 (after the events of *For A Few Dollars More*).

3) A modified Winchester 1866 Yellow Boy (from *Sabata*). Altered by Gordon Munitions, it has a separate long barrel which can be attached to give the weapon a range of up to 600 feet. A leather bracelet has slots that stores bullets for the rifle. The Major purchased this weapon in 1872.

4) A revolver with a twelve inch long barrel (seen in *For A Few Dollars More*). Created by Gordon Munitions in 1872. Stuart N. Lake's inaccurate *Wyatt Earp: Frontier Marshal* (1931) wrongfully claimed that this weapon was called the Buntline Special. Lake asserted that dime novelist had this weapon made in 1876 by Colt, and then presented it to Earp, Bat Masterson, Bill Tlghman, Charlie Bassett and Neal Brown. Since neither Tilghman nor Brown were lawmen in 1876, this assertion has been dismissed as a fabrication. In our fictional Major Sabbath universe, this weapon was "really" made in 1872 by Gordon Munitions for the bounty hunter. The revolver has detachable rifle stock.

5) A palm gun (used in *Return of Sabata*). Circular with a small barrel, it carries up to ten bullets in a revolving magazine. The gun is fired by squeezing. In reality, this weapon was known as the Protector and created in France during 1882 by Jacques Turbiaux. However, the film anachronistically appeared in Euro-Westerns set earlier. A palm gun can be seen in the Civil War gun shop where Turco Ramirez stole a gun during *The Good, the Bad and the Ugly*. A protector gun also appears in *Johnny Yuma* (1966), a Euro-western set in 1881. Therefore, I had Leroy Bailey, later the chief gunsmith of Gordon Munitions, develop a forerunner of the Protector just before the Civil War.

The Major has owned three different palm guns at different points in times during the 1870's. In 1876, he confiscated one of these weapons from Delilah L'Ollonaise during "Thy Name is Sabbath." The Major discarded the weapon after it jammed. In 1877, he purchased another palm gun for 12 dollars (this is briefly cited in *Return of Sabata* as happening two years earlier). In Hobsonville, the Major purchased the same weapon for a more expensive price

6) A dart fired from a cigar (used in *Return of Sabata*).

7) A throwing knife hidden under a necktie (used in *Return of Sabata*). "Thy Name is Sabbath" reveals that the Major got this idea from Anton Niklas Petersen.

In addition to the weaponry cited above, the Major had additional paraphernalia, His clothes were made by Gino Di Marco of San Francisco (identified as Paladin's tailor in "The High Graders" episode of *Have Gun, Will Travel*). Gino's clients also included Hatfield, the doomed gambler from John Ford's *Stagecoach* (1939), and Jake Sartana.

As shown in *Return of Sabata*, the Major had used magnets to manipulate roulette wheels in dishonest gambling halls. These magnets have been hidden at various in his cigar case, his cigar and the heel of his shoe.

Prior to 1874, the Major smoked a pipe. In that year, the Drifter with Many Names introduced him to a small thin brand of cigar. These cigars were made by the J. V. Harden Tobacco Company (from a reference to John Vincent Harden, a tobacco millionaire, in Arthur Conan Doyle's "The Adventure of the Solitary Cyclist").

The Major kept the cigars in a gold case. When he assumed the alias of Sabbath, the Major had a black "S" stamped on the case.

The Major owned a black signet ring (purloined from Deliah L'Ollonaise in the 1876 sequence of "Thy Name is Sabbath"). Sartana wore a similar ring in two films: *If You Meet Sartana Pray for Your Death* (set 1878) and *Have a Good Funeral, My Friend... Sartana Will Pay* (set in 1899). Either Sartana had an imitation ring made, or the same ring swapped hands multiple times in poker games between the Major and Sartana.

In my story, "The Last Vendetta," the Major's weapons were sold in the First Assassins Auction in New Orleans during 1900. This was an auction organized by the Black Coat crime syndicate. Was the Major alive in 1900? He would have been about 75 years old if he still lived.

Were the weapons stolen from him? These are questions that probably should remain unanswered.

SUPPORTING CHARACTERS:

BAILEY, LEROY ("LEE")   - Based on the Bailey character played by Christopher Lee in *Hannie Caulder*. Bailey was a gunsmith living in New Orleans. Before the Civil War, he devised an early palm gun that was sold in gun stores up until 1882 when it supplanted by the Protector.

When Louisiana seceded from the Union, Bailey made weapons for the Confederacy. When Union forces occupied New Orleans in 1863, Bailey fled to Mexico. There he married a local woman and fathered several children.

In 1865, Bailey became Arthur Gordon's silent partner in Gordon Munitions. Bailey would design weapons in Mexico while Gordon would mass produce them in El Paso, Texas.

Certain individual pieces were made for select clients who were allowed to visit Bailey in Mexico. Those client include Christian Adam Sabbath (who met Bailey in 1865), Major Sabbath (who learned about Bailey in 1872), Jake Sartana/Mr. Silver (II) (who learned about Bailey in the same year), Specs (whom the Major introduced to Bailey), Ignacz Djanko (who met Bailey in 1876) and Ana Sartana (who met the gunsmith in 1882).

Bailey was a tall, lean man, He had a dark beard and a ingratiating smile.

BALLANTRAE, JIMMY - Disguised version of Ballantine from *Adios, Sabata.* A swindler with many aliases, his real name was Valentin L'Ollonaise. He belonged to the American branch of the Gentlemen of the Night, a crime syndicate based in London.

Under the alias of Ballantine in 1867, L'Ollonaise infiltrated the Mexican household of Heinrich Von Skimmel, an Austrian mercenary guarding gold for Emperor Maximilian. Forming an alliance with Christian Adam Sabbath, L'Ollonaise promised to steal the gold for the Juaristas. In reality, L'Ollonaise intended to double-cross his allies and keep all the gold for himself. Christian made sure that L'Ollonaise arrived empty-handed in the United States. L'Ollonaise became determined to get revenge on Christian.

Von Skimmel was knifed to death by Christian. The Austrian mercenary's relatives and associates blamed his demise on L'Ollonaise's betrayal. They became determined to locate the swindler and slay him.

Altering his name to Jimmy Ballantrae, L'Ollonaise was hiding out at the Jean Lafitte Saloon in Bougival Junction, Texas. In 1868, one of Von Skimmel's former subordinates, Otto Stejar, located L'Ollonaise. The events of "Thy Name is Sabbath" then unfolded.

After shooting Stejar in the back, Jimmy Ballantrae became wanted for murder in Texas, Under his real name, L'Ollonaise took ownership of the Sunlight Saloon in Signo Amarillo, New Mexico.

In 1871, L'Ollonaise tricked Lee Galloway into believing that Christian was the murderous bandit known as the Crazy Indian. This trickery led to a series of events that resulted in the death of both Christian and Valentin in 1872. The swindler was hanged by Heinrich Von Skimmel's cousin, Gustav Von Schulenberg.

Valentin L'Ollonaise was a handsome man with blond hair. He was a talented painter of portraits. Claiming falsely to have a bad memory, L'Ollonaise always wrote down everything in a journal that he always carried. The book actually contained a hollow compartment where a revolver or other weapon could be hidden.

Valentin's cousin was the treacherous Delilah L'Ollonaise.

BATTERVILLE - Union POW camp in *The Good, the Bad and the Ugly*.
    During the Civil War, both Lee "Red" Galloway and El Rojo were imprisoned in Batterville.

BEN, BUDDY - friend of Jake Sartana in *I am Sartana, Your Angel of Death*. In 1878, Buddy Ben had escaped released from prison after being sentenced to a term for bank robbery. He was attested due to information provided by two accomplices whose sentences were reduced in exchange for their betrayal. Once his treacherous associates were released, Buddy Ben gunned them down. The bank robber then helped Jake proved his innocence of the Northwestern Bank Robbery.
    Buddy dressed like a hobo. Right-handed, he wore his holster on the left side of his belt and drew sideways. Buddy always looked like he needed a shave,

BENNET'S RAIDERS - Gang of outlaws in the movie *Face to Face* (1967).
    The movie takes place sometime during the Grant's Administration (1869-76), but makes an historical error. One of the characters was the real-life Charlie Durango of the Pinkerton Detective Agency. In actuality, Durango wasn't a Pinkerton until the 1880's.

BLACK COATS - International crime confederation that loosely united such disparate gangs as the Camorra of Naples and the Gentlemen of the Night in London. The Black Coats were depicted in crime novels by Paul Féval: *The Parisian Jungle, Heart of Steel, The Sword-Swallower, 'Salem Street, The Invisible Weapon, The Companions of the Treasure* and *The Cadet Gang*. The leader of the Black Coats during the 1870's and 1880's was the mysterious All-Father, a Corsican recluse who many believed to be the immortal Colonel Bozzo-Corona. The Camorra was fiercely loyal to the All-Father, but the Gentlemen of the Night was openly defiant of his authority.

BOUGIVAL JUNCTION - Texas town from the movie *Frenchie King* (1971).
    Founded by French settlers in 1858, the town was celebrating its 30 year anniversary in *Frenchie King*. This fact suggests the movie was set in 1888, but a land deed was dated "May 31st, 1894" in the same film. The inhabitants prefer to speak French rather than English.

In "Thy Name is Sabbath," Jimmy Ballantrae lived there in 1868.

BOYETTE, DUKE - the character called Duke from *A Bullet for a Stranger*. Born in 1840, Duke was the illegitimate son of a Missouri prostitute and a visiting European nobleman. The nobleman left behind a collapsible drinking cup. Duke later had the letter D imprinted on the metal cup. Although this fact is unknown to Duke, the metal cup is a keepsake owned by members of the Von Schulenberg family of Austria.

During the Civil War, Duke fought on the Confederate side. After the war ended, he continued to wear his military uniform. Duke was a hired killer whom Jake Sartana befriended during his outlaw days in the late 1860's. From 1872 onwards, Jake and Duke often found themselves on opposite sides of conflicts. However, their liking for each other caused them to avoid killing each other. One such stand-off transpired in Texas during 1885 (see the events of *A Bullet for a Stranger*).

Duke's half-sister was Madame Boyette. He had brown hair and a mustache.

BOYETTE, MADAME (DORA) - conflation of an offstage character from *Return of Sabata* and the Madame character from *Hannie Caulder*.

Born in a St. Louis brothel during 1842, Madame Dora Boyette was Duke's maternal half-sister. When she reached adulthood, she became owner of the brothel. Her most popular prostitute was Red Margot (Maggie from *Return of Sabata*). At some point before 1879, Major Sabbath visited the brothel. In 1879, Red Margot left Madame's employ in St. Louis and moved to Hobsonville, New Mexico (see *Return of Sabata*). In 1880, Margot moved to a Texas town. She tried to run the local brothel on her own, but this proved beyond her capabilities. Therefore, she summoned Madame Boyette who gladly agreed to take charge. In 1882, both Madame and Margot encountered Ana Sartana on a staircase in a saloon (see *Hannie Caulder*).

Madame Boyette was buxom woman with blonde hair.

BROCKSTON-MORTON RAILWAYS - conflation of the corrupt railway companies in *The Big Gundown* and *Once Upon the Time in the West*. Mr. Brockston of *The Big Gundown* employed Baron Von Schulenberg (Gustav Von Schulenberg in "Thy Name is Sabbath") to do his dirty work. Mr. Morton of *Once Upon the Time in the West* gave the same duties to Frank (William LeFrank Gordon in "Thy Name is Sabbath") to perform the same function. Brockston and the Baron died in 1877. Morton and Frank died in 1883.

BURNETT, GIDDY - based on Gideon Burnett in *The Great Silence*. In 1872, Giddy was one of Priam Ramsey's two deputies in Signo Amarillo, New Mexico. After serving in the Calvary, he returned to law enforcement. In 1898, Burnett was appointed Sheriff of Snow Hill County. Unfortunately he was slain by a bounty hunter (see *The Great Silence*). Burnett was born in 1851.

CORREDOR, EL - disguised version of Manuel "Cuchillo" Sanchez.
    Basis: *The Big Gundown* (1966)
    http://ishare.rediff.com/video/entertainment/the-big-gundown-o-dia-da-desforra-1966-lee-van-cleef-low-/8171974
    Run, Man, Run (1968)

Manuel Sanchez, a petty thief, was the illegitimate son of a corrupt Mexican police captain. He became known as El Corredor ("the Runner") because he was constantly being pursued. He was an expert knife-thrower. He kept at least six knives hidden on his person (two were in the soles of his shoes, two up his sleeves, one on his back, and one in his long black hair). His two known exploits both occurred in 1877. In *The Big Gundown*, he was framed for the rape and murder of a young girl in Texas. In *Run, Man, Run*, he was embroiled in a search for gold needed to fund a revolution against Porfirio Diaz.
    El Corredor seems to have been a bigamist. He was married to a woman named Rosita in *The Big Gundown*, but engaged to another woman named Dolores in *Run, Man, Run*.

CHADWELL, MAJOR - Based on Captain Chadwell from *Charge!* (a. k. a. *Those Dirty Dogs*). In 1863, Chadwell performed admirably as a cavalry officer at the Battle of Gettysburg. In 1873, Chadwell investigated the Rio Grande Massacre performed by the outlaws of San Miguel, Although he couldn't prove it, he believed that the bandits had performed the atrocity with a rapid-fire weapon manufactured by Gordon Munitions. In 1875, Chadwell, along with Lt. Younger and Sgt. Boomerang Smith destroyed the private army of General Lopez in Texas (see *Charge!*). As a result of this exploit, Chadwell was promoted to Major.
    Chadwell had brown hair and a mustache.

CHIN HAO - See SHANGHAI JOE.

CRAZY INDIAN, THE - Disguised version of Indio from *A Few Dollars More.*

The Crazy Indian caused the death of Major Sabbath's beloved sister during the Civil War. During 1872-74, he was in a Mexican prison for a period of 18 months. After escaping prison, he was killed by the Major.

CROWN, HIRAM - criminal gunsmith from *I am Sartana, Your Angel of Death.*

For corrupt sheriff Manassas Jim, Crown designed a four-barreled derringer-like weapon that Jake Sartana confiscated for his own use in 1872. Six years later, Crown was fatally shot by Philip "Hot Dead" Holden.

Crown was a white-haired man who operated out of a shop in Poker Falls, Wyoming.

CUTTHROAT, JUDGE - disguised version of Pollicut from *The Great Silence.*

As Justice of the Peace in Snow Hill County, Utah, the man nicknamed Judge Cutthroat engineered an 1876 campaign to persecute Mormons and steal their land (see "Thy Name is Sabbath"). This campaign resulted in the deaths of John Gordon and his wife as well as the maiming of their son Louis. Taking advantage of an amnesty by the territorial governor, Cutthroat was able to escape punishment for his crimes

When Utah became a state in 1896, Judge Cutthroat resumed his campaign against Mormons. In 1897, Louis Gordon shot off the Judge's right thumb to prevent him from handling a gun. One year later, Louis fatally shot Cutthroat (see *The Great Silence*).

DAUGHERTY - Fictional town in Texas from *Sabata.*

The Major visited this town in 1879, The town also appeared in Quentin Tarantino's *Django Unchained* (2012), a movie set in the 1850's. There is a real-life Daugherty, Texas, but it wasn't founded until the 1900's.

DEGUEYO - bounty hunter from *I am Sartana, Your Angel of Death.*

A self-styled "gentleman of the South," Degueyo lived in a luxuriant southern plantation. Originally he and Jake Sartana were friends. In an unrecorded adventure, Jake helped Degueyo kill a man named Lassiter. Degueyo was so grateful for Jake's assistance that he offered to give Jake a valuable pocket watch as a gift. Jake declined the offer. When Jake was unfairly accused of bank robbery in 1878, Degueyo tried to collect the 10,000 dollar bounty on hid former friend's head. Jake was forced to fatally shoot Degueyo.

DELPHINE, MADAME - Disguised version of Delphine Yant from Louis L'Amour's The Proving Trail.

Delphine was the supreme leader of the American chapter of the Gentlemen of the Night. She reported directly to Jim Nemo (alias Professor James Moriarty) in London.

In 1884, she attempted to rob a young man of his inheritance (see The Proving Trail).

DELTA VALLEY - fictional California community where an American adopted the name of Paladin in the "Genesis" episode of Have Gun, Will Travel.

In the conclusion of "Thy Name is Sabbath," the Major visited Delta Valley.

DIABLO, EL - alternate name for the Devil from Djanko Strikes Again.

Aristig Olowsky Sandorf was the younger brother of Count Mathias Sandorf (see Jules Verne's Mathias Sandorf). He was an Hungarian officer in the Austrian Navy. In 1864, he resigned his naval commission to become one of Gustav Von Schulenberg's mercenaries fighting for Emperor Maximilian. When Maximilian was overthrown, Aristig remained in Mexico to terrorize the countryside as the river pirate called El Diablo ("the Devil"). he raided villages to recruit slaves for an abandoned silver mine that he discovered.

Aristig was married to Ivonne Von Schulenberg, Gustav's sister. In 1868, Ivonne died giving birth to a daughter, Marga. Aristig's daughter would leave Mexico to pursue a career as an assassin in Europe (see my "Sisters of the Shadows" series).

El Diablo was a fanatical butterfly collector. His great ambition was to find the legendary Black Butterfly.

In 1898, the events of Djanko Strikes Again occurred. After slaying Lee Galloway in a raid on a Mexican village, El Diablo kidnapped Ignacz Djanko's daughter. Rescuing his offspring, Djanko permitted El Diablo to be ripped to pieces by the slaves in the silver mine.

DJANKO, IGNACZ - Disguised version of the original Django.
   Basis - *Django* (1966)
   https://www.youtube.com/
watch?v=6VNSWhhTy8k&list=PLE313F5D7697236E3
   Viva Django (1968)
   https://www.youtube.com/watch?v=P8jblBxhQqU
   Djanko Strikes Again (1987)
   https://www.youtube.com/watch?v=UbzQxgE1ROM
   Prologue to *Djanko Strikes Again* (Italian with English subtitles)
   https://www.youtube.com/watch?v=roRaHaThCGk

The original *Django* with Franco Nero spawned a lot of unofficial sequels with other actors. Only *Djanko Strikes Again* starring Nero again is an official sequel. All the other sequels are ignored as non-canonical with the exception of *Viva Django*, that film is included because 1) actor Terence Hill looks a lot like Franco Nero, 2) dressed the same as Nero in the earlier film, 3) used a machine gun, and 4) *Django Strikes Again* borrows the ploy of hiding the machine gun in a graveyard from *Viva Django*.

The original *Django* concluded with a gunfight in a graveyard. There was a gravestone bearing the caption «Mercedes Zaro, 1833-1889.» This 1889 is problematic for many reasons. First, Django is an ex-Union soldier battling ex-Confederates in the film. 1889 is a little late for that. Second, Mercedes is generally believed to be the ex-lover whom Django was avenging in the film. It would make more sense if she died in 1869 at the age of 36. Some articles on the film (such as the Wikipedia entry) even cite the graveyard dates inaccurately as «1833-69.» My argument (first advanced in «The Last Vendetta») is that a drunken gravedigger inscribed1869 inaccurately as 1889.

The 1889 date would explain Django's usage of a machine gun. Sir Hiram Maxim in vented the machine gun in 1884. However, anachronistic machine guns crop up in other Euro-Westerns set in the 1870's (e. g. *A Fistful of Dollars* and *Light the Fuse . . . Sartana is Coming*). therefore the explanation is that an inventor (the Phantom of the Opera) created the machine gun in the 1870's. This weapon was later modified by Leroy Bailey of Gordon Munitions.

I place the events of *Django* in 1878, In the movie, a gang of ex-Confederate outlaws had taken over a Texas town. This is most likely to have happened once Federal troops were pulled out of Texas with the end of Reconstruction in 1877. Also Django was using an 1873 Colt Peacemaker revolver in the film. There were also Mexican rebels in the film who could only be opposed to President Diaz, who seized power in 1876,

Viva Django has some intriguing chronological issues as well. The movie began with a gold shipment robbery that results in the death of Django's wife. Django was severely wounded in the same ambush. We then see Django finishing a grave with the marker «Django 1887.» We are then told in another scene that five years had passed since the robbery. I always assumed that Django buried his wife in 1887, and the majority of the film transpired in 1892. However, the conclusion revealed that Django's machine gun was buried under the 1887 marker and that his wife was buried under a marker labeled Lucy Cassedy. Therefore, the robbery could have occurred in 1882, and the burial scene could have happened five years later (1887).

Django Strikes Again opened with Django as a monk named Brother Ignatius in a monastery. The «youtube» link to the film that I included here is missing a prologue scenes in which two aged cowboys reminiscent about the old West before being slain by El Diablo's pirates (there is a separate «youtube» link for the prologue). A reference to Butch Cassidy in that scene compels me to place the film in 1898. The same missing scene also contained speculation that Django was an Indian name.

There are plans for Franco Nero to reprise his iconic role in *Django Lives!* This movie will reportedly have Django working as a Hollywood consultant in World War I. He will be pitted against gangsters and white supremacists.

The idea to make Django a Croatian stems from the fact that Franco Nero in later Westerns played Poles, Swedes and Russians in order to be able to dub his own dialogue in the English soundtracks. Nero also had himself cast as an American Indian in *Keoma* (1976) to justify his foreign accent. The Italian version of *Django Strikes Again* hints that Django was part-American Indian. As an elaborate in-joke, *Jonathan of the Bears* (1984) had Nero playing a Polish immigrant raised by American Indians.

Ignacz Djanko was born in Croatia, then part of the Austrian empire, in 1843. In 1851, Djanko and his family fled Europe when one of their relatives participated in a horrific assassination (for details of this atrocity, see «The Heir of Pistolet» in my *Shadows of the Opera: Retribution in Blood*). Settling in the United States, Djanko gained an intense hatred of slavery. In 1861, he joined the Union Army to fight in the Civil War. Rising to the rank of Sergeant, he served under General Sherman. During this period, he befriended Sgt. Boomerang Smith. During his exploits, people has a tendency to mispronounce Djanko's name and call him «Django.»

When the Civil War ended in 1865, Smith and Djanko were sent on a secret mission to Mexico to sabotage a French factory manufacturing chemical explosive for the Maximilian regime. Accompanying them as a guide was Christian Adam Sabbath Sr. in the course of this exploit, Djanko was captured and imprisoned by the Maximilian regime. In jail, he met Hugo Rodriguez, a Juarista rebel. Djanko and Rodgriguez escaped from prison together. In the course of the jail break, Djanko saved Rodriguez's life.

Djanko fell passionately in love with Mercedes Zaro of Texas. In 1869, she was slain by the Red Scarf Gang, a group of outlaws who were all ex-Confederates. Swearing vengeance, Djanko spent the next several years searching for his beloved's killers. In 1876, Djanko made a bargain with Arthur Gordon of Gordon Munitions. If Djanko served him faithfully for two years, Gordon would give him a Bailey gun, an early form of machine gun developed by Gordon's partner.

Together with Jake Sartana, Djanko traveled to Mexico to receive such a weapon from Gordon's partner. They returned successfully with the machine gun to El Paso, Texas. Jake then departed for private reasons of his own. Together with Major Sabbath, Djanko and Gordon transported the machine gun to Utah (see «Thy Name is Sabbath»). There the weapon was sold to the enigmatic Count Kowalski.

In March 1877, President Rutherford B. Hayes removed Federal troops from Texas. The Red Scarf Gang seized control of the town where Mercedes Zaro was buried.

In late November 1876, Porfirio Diaz ousted President Lerdo of Mexico in a military rebellion. In 1877, a revolt against Diaz's rule broke out led by an ex-Juarista, General Santillana (see the movie *Run, Man, Run*). Santillana's rebellion was crushed, but his subordinate, Hugo Rodriquez, led a ragtag band of survivors into Texas. Arthur Gordon saw an excellent business opportunity. In 1878, he moved nine of Bailey's machine guns to a shack along the Pecos River. A tenth gun was given to Djanko. The Croatian-American gunfighter would contact Rodriguez and offer to sell him the ten machine guns. In order to demonstrate the weapon's potency, the gunslinger would use it to kill all the Red Scarf Gang. This would satisfy Djanko's need for vengeance.

The events of the film *Django* then unfolded. The Red Scarf Gang was wiped out, but Rodriguez never purchased the machine guns. His rebel forces were slaughtered by the Mexican Army.

Djanko related this exploit to Count Kowalski, who was in reality Count Salvatore Corbucci, a criminal member of both the Camorra and the Black Coats. Returning to Italy in 1879, Corbucci wrote a popular novel, *The Undertaker's Big Gun*, about Djanko's extermination of the red Scarf Gang. This novel was published outside Italy under the pseudonym of Stanley Corbett.

By 1882, Djanko was living in New Mexico married to a woman named Lucy Cassedy. The events of *Viva Django* then unfolded. While guarding a gold shipment, Djanko saw his wife murdered by outlaws. Shot three times, Djanko was left for dead by the bandits. However, he survived. Five years later (1887), Djanko slew Lucy's killers.

There is a lot of mystery about the five year gap in *Viva Django*. Where was he? The answer seems to be in Mexico because he fathered a daughter, Marisol, in 1884. Her mother was a wealthy Mexican woman living in the town of San Vicente.

During the 1887 sequence in *Viva Django*, Djanko took the job of a hangman in New Mexico. He saved the lives of many wrongfully convicted men by developing a harness that could be hidden under the condemned's clothes. As a hangman, Djanko would tie the noose to the harness, and then put a hood over the condemned's hood to hide the fact that no rope was around the neck. A sham hanging then occurred.

In 1896, Djanko grew disgusted with all the violence and killing in his life. He hoped to make amends by becoming a monk. He entered a monastery in San Vicente. There he became known as Brother Ignatius. In 1898, just as he was preparing to take his final vows, Marisol, Djanko's 14-year old daughter, was abducted by El Diablo («the Devil»), the notorious river who had originally been a Hungarian mercenary employed by Emperor Maximilian. The events of *Django Strikes Again* transpired. Abandoning his plans to be a monk, Djanko rescued his daughter and destroyed El Diablo.

Supposedly Djanko later worked as a movie consultant in Hollywood circa 1916, but this is not yet confirmed.

In the 1870's and 1880's Djanko generally wore his union hat and Inverness cape. In the 1890's, he wore a poncho. When not using his machine, he would house it in a coffin. Sometimes the coffin would be buried in a graveyard under a maker either bearing the name «Django» or «Djanko.»

DRIFTER WITH MANY NAMES, THE - disguised version of the Man with No Name from Sergio Leone's Dollar Trilogy. Although the character was marketed as the Man with No Name, he actually had a name in each film. He was called Joe in *A Fistful of Dollars*, Manco (Spanish for «left-handed») in *For A Few Dollars More*, and Blondie in *The Good, the Bad and the Ugly*. In our fictional universe, these names translate as Joe Limbo (based on the fact that *A Fistful of Dollars* borrowed its plot from the Japanese film *Yojimbo*), Lefty and Rubio (Spanish for «blonde»). there also is a connection suggested with Clint Eastwood's *High Plains Drifter*.

The Drifter's real name was Joseph Duncan. His brother was James Duncan, a Marshal murdered in the mining town of Lago. He began his career as a bounty hunter during the Civil War. The events of *The Good, the Bad and the Ugly* happened in 1862 (based on the references to the Confederate campaign in New Mexico), *A Fistful of Dollars* in 1873 (based on a tombstone), and *For A Few Dollars More* in 1874 (based on Colonel Mortimer finding a 1873 newspaper in a library).

The Drifter helped Major Sabbath avenge his sister's death in 1874. The right-handed Drifter was called Lefty then because he wore a gauntlet over his left hand. The Drifter usually wears a poncho that he acquired in 1862.

Some time after the events of *For A Few Dollars More*, the Drifter went to Lago to avenge his brother's murder (*High Plains Drifter*). Although the final English version of the film implied the Drifter was a disguised ghost of the dead Marshal, the original script made him the Marshal's brother. The Italian, German and French dubbings of the film also made the Drifter the brother.

The Drifter smoked cigars made by the J. V. Harden Tobacco Company.

GALLOWAY, LEE («*RED*») - conflation of Banjo from *Sabata*, Lee Galloway from the misleading entitled *Sartana in the Valley of Death* (1970; Sartana isn't in the movie at all) and the unnamed gunslinger from the prologue sequence of *Djanko Srikes Again* (1987). All three character were played by William Berger.

Sartana in the Valley of Death can be viewed here (the soundtrack is English with Russian subtitles):
https://www.youtube.com/watch?v=ViGb1z9lI_c#t=220

Prologue to *Djanko Strikes Again* (Italian with English subtitles)
https://www.youtube.com/watch?v=roRaHaThCGk

Sartana in the Valley of Death is in public domain. I used the nickname of Red for Lee Galloway In «Thy Name is Sabbath» simply because I also had characters named Leroy and Leland in the same story.

Born in Texas, Lee Galloway was nicknamed Red because of his red hair. In 1860, his brother Bob married Rosemary Mortimer, the sister of Douglas Mortimer (the future Major Sabbath).

When the Civil War broke out, Lee served in the ill-fated 1862 New Mexico campaign of Confederate General Henry H. Sipley. Captured by the Union forces, he spent the last three years of the war in the Batterville POW camp. Released from the camp in 1865, he discovered that his brother and sister-in-law had been by the Crazy Indian (the character called Indio in *For a Few Dollars More*). Joining forces with Douglas Mortimer, Lee became a bounty hunter in order to track down the killer. In 1867, the Major and Galloway mistakenly believed that they had located the killer. in the person of Christian Adam Sabbath Sr. alias the Black Indian (Sabata/Indigo Black from *Adios, Sabata*). Believing that the Crazy Indian and the Black Indian were the same man, the two partners journeyed to Mexico. There they discovered that the bald, clean-shaven Sabbath didn't resemble the Crazy Indian at all.

Although unable to locate the Crazy Indian, the two bounty hunters had a profitable partnership until 1872. Briefly separated from Mortimer while pursuing outlaws in New Mexico during late 1871, Lee had joined a poker game at the Sunlight Saloon in Signo Amarillo, New Mexico. There he met Valentin L'Ollonaise alias Jimmy Ballantrae (Ballantine from *Adios, Sabata*). L'Ollonaise was not only an old enemy of Christian Sabbath, but also a sometime business associate of the Crazy Indian. L'Ollonaise convinced Lee that Christian Sabbath had used makeup to disguise himself as the Crazy Indian.

The 1872 events of «Thy Name is Sabbath» then unfolded. In Mexico, the Mortimer slew Christian Sabbath. When the Mexican authorities arrest the real Crazy Indian, Mortimer had a bitter falling out with Lee. The partnership was dissolved in Mexico. When he split from Mortimer, Lee had begun to carry a concealed Winchester inside a Banjo.

In 1878, Lee was in Denver, Colorado. He fled the territory for Mexico due to a dispute with the five Clayton brothers.

In 1876, Mortimer had taken the name of Major Sabbath. In 1879, the Major altered his Sabbath to appear in a theatrical act involving phony bullets in El Paso. The Major debuted in a theatre in El Paso. The Major's performance was observed by Lee in the audience. The Major noticed Lee, and trailed him after the performance to Daugherty, Texas, There the two became untrustworthy allies in the events described in *Sabata*. Besides getting a reward for foiling a gold robbery, the Major swindled a corrupt banker. The banker paid Lee to kill the Major. The Major then faked his death in a gunfight with Lee. At the conclusion of this affair, Lee tried to cheat the Major by running off with all the money. The Major foiled this attempt, and punished Lee by only giving him a small share of the money.

By 1884, Lee was a wanted outlaw with a 10,000 dollar bounty on his head. The events of the confusingly titled *Sartana in the Valley of Death* then unfolded. In California, the Craig brothers had successfully stolen a U. S. government gold shipment that also contained a document with a vital diplomatic secret. Lee made a deal with the U. S. Army. In exchange for the gold and free passage to Mexico, he would recover the document. Successful in his mission, Lee fled to Mexico.

He lived in seclusion in Mexico for 14 years. In 1898, the events of the prologue from *Django Strikes Again* unfolded. Lee was killed by river pirates under the command of the notorious El Diablo. In this sequence, Lee mistakenly said all the great gunfighters of the West including Wyatt Earp and Butch Cassidy were dead and buried. Both Cassidy and Earp died later.

GENTLEMAN OF THE NIGHT, THE - crime syndicate based in London. It first appeared in *The Mysteries of London* (1844) by Paul Féval. In the 1830's, the Gentlemen of the Night was led by Fergus O'Breane. He was a combination of Captain Nemo, the Count of Monte Cristo, Professor Moriarty and Auric Goldfinger. An ardent Irish nationalist, he was determined to destroy the British Empire. After building a fortune as a pirate who only attacked British ships, he established the false identity of the Brazilian aristocrat, the Marquis de Rio Santo. Arriving in London as the Marquis, he gained ascendency over the criminal gang called the Gentlemen of the Night, He dispatched agents around the world to sow the seeds of the Opium War, the French-Canadian revolt in Quebec, and the Oregon dispute between Britain and America. When his criminal activities were finally exposed, O'Breane was plotting to rob the Bank of England.

O'Breane's title was His Honor, and his top lieutenants were called Lords of the Night. By 1872, the title of His Honor was abandoned. There was only one Lord of the Night, and he was the supreme authority in the Gentleman of the Night. From 1872 to 1891, the Lord of the Night was man whose alias was Jim Nemo. His real name was Professor James Moriarty (from Sir Arthur Conan Doyle's Sherlock Holmes stories). The idea that Moriarty would have agents in the United States is not far-fetched. Doyle's *The Valley of Fear* linked Moriarty to an American gang, the Scowrers.

Paul Féval's *The Invisible Weapon* made the Gentlemen of the Night a branch of the European crime cartel called the Black Coats. Louis L'Amour's *The Proving Trail* (1978) created an unnamed criminal organization led by the Yant family. This gang was essentially an American version of the Black Coats. The Black Coats robbed the heirs of wealthy legacies and were opposed by a detective called Pistolet (French for «pistol»). The Yant family robbed the heirs of wealthy legacies and were opposed by a gunslinger called Pistol. L'Amour even had agents of the Yant family dress in black coats. *The Proving Trail* was set in 1884.

L'Amour mentioned that the Yant family also used the aliases of Carbanus and L'Ollonaise. Therefore, I have the American branch of the Gentlemen of the Night run by the L'Ollonaise family.

Members of the gang identify each other through this ritual:
«*Gentlemen of the Night,*»
«*Family's Son,*» .
"*Will there be daylight.*»
"*It will be daylight from midnight to noon if it's the will of the Lord of the Night.*"

GORDON, ARTHUR - this character originated as an offstage sinister American in Emile Gaboriau's *Baron Trigault's Vengeance* (1870). I transformed him into an amoral arms dealer in «The Last Vendetta» and other stories in my «Shadows of the Opera» series.

A cousin of Edgar Allan Poe's Pym family (from «The Narrative of Arthur Gordon Pym»), Arthur Gordon was born in Nantucket during 1817. At the age of 16, he became a sailor. He jumped ship in Vera Cruz, Mexico. In the Texas Revolution of 1836, Arthur led a band of guerilla marauders. From 1837 to 1843, he commanded a ship in the illegal slave trade.

Arthur married Francine Xavier, an actress who used the stage name of Xaviera LeFrank, in Austin, Texas. Raised as a Baptist. Arthur had three sons by Francine: William (born 1838), John (b. 1840) and Barton (b. 1842).

Arthur became a Mormon in 1843. Since his religion initially sanctioned polygamy, he decided to take a second wife. During a trip to France in 1843 Arthur seduced Hermine du Chalusse, a Parisian heiress.

Hermine's brother, Raymond, challenged Arthur to a duel. after Raymond was severely wounded, Arthur and Hermine fled to the United States where they were married in Richmond, Virginia. Hermine gave birth to a son named Wilkie. Although Hermine was aware of Arthur's other wife, the fact remained secret because of the anti-polygamy laws in the United States. For six years, Arthur maintained two families, one in Virginia and the other in Texas. In 1850, Hermine left her husband. Taking Wilkie with her, she returned to Europe. For more on Hermine and Wilkie, see Emile Gaboriau's *The Count's Millions* and *Baron Trigault's Vengeance*.

Following Hermine's flight, Arthur and his other family all moved to Utah. His children by Francine were all raised in the Mormon faith. In 1855, Arthur took another wife. She bore him a son, James Arthur Gordon (the protagonist of Robert E. Howard's «The Dead Remember»), in 1856. In 1860, one of Arthur Gordon's closest friends, Mitchell Stangerson, was revealed to be the leader of a criminal gang in Utah. While Arthur was never publicly accused of complicity in Stangerson's crimes, he began to be ostracized by the Mormon community.

During the Civil War, Arthur supported the Confederacy. He commanded a ship that regularly ran the Union blockade. When Brigham Young decided to support the Union, Arthur severed all his ties to the Mormon faith. With the exception of John, the rest of the Gordon family followed Arthur's example. despite the religious rift between them, Arthur and John remained on good terms.

When the Civil War ended, Arthur founded Gordon Munitions in El Paso, Texas. Leroy Bailey became his «silent' partner and chief weapons designer. Arthur also established a subsidiary in Paris. He regularly spent part of the year in Europe. Arthur was able to negotiate a contract with the Spanish government to supply weapons to the troops in Cuba, In Paris, he pursued a romantic love affair with a blonde female criminal who used the alias of Countess Cagliostro. This liaison led to the birth of a illegitimate daughter, Josephine Balsamo, who would grow up to be the archenemy of Arséne Lupin, the master thief whose exploits were written by Maurice Leblanc.

In 1870, the man known as the Phantom of the Opera approached Arthur. The Phantom had then established the false identity of Enrique Claudin, a disfigured veteran of the French military campaign in Mexico. Always wearing a mask, the Phantom hired Gordon to make an organ that was really a massive arsenal including two canons and a early form of a machine gun. This organ had been constructed from blueprints designed by the Phantom. Impressed by the specifications , Gordon secretly made two organs. The other was sent to the United States. In the chaos of the Franco-Prussian War (1870-71) and the Paris Commune (1871), the Phantom jettisoned his Claudin identity. Arthur hired the Chupin Detective Agency to find Claudin, but that organization only unearthed that the masked client had been utilizing a false identity.

Leroy Bailey left his abode in Mexico to study the organ in the El Paso headquarters of Gordon Munitions. He concluded that the machine inside could be the basis for a more portable weapon. In 1872, Arthur sold the organ to Jake Sartana (see «Thy Name is Sabbath»). in the same year, the munitions dealer also sold a four-barreled derringer and several rifles to Major Sabbath.

By 1873, Bailey succeeded in making a portable machine gun. This weapon would become known as a Bailey gun. Arthur tried to sell the Bailey gun to the U. S. War Department, but his request to give a practical demonstration were rebuffed due to his Confederate past. Arthur then tried unsuccessfully to peddle the Bailey Gun to the Lerdo Administration in Mexico. Lerdo was actually buying arms from the American government in a series of secret transfers of gold for guns along the Rio Grande.

Arthur's next hope was to sell the Bailey Gun to General Porfirio Diaz, who was plotting to overthrow Lerdo. A man professing to represent Diaz did purchase a Bailey gun from Arthur in 1873, but the buyer was actually a member of the notorious Rojo gang from the Mexican town of San Miguel. The Mexican outlaws used the Bailey gun to massacre American and Mexican troops conducting one of the clandestine guns for gold transfer along the Rio Grande (this incident was depicted in *A Fistful of Dollars*).

An investigation into the massacre was conducted by Captain Chadwell of the U. S. Army. Based on Arthur's previous letter to the War Department, Chadwell believed that a Bailey gun had been used in the massacre, Fearful that he would be indicted as a accomplice in the massacre, Arthur told Chadwell falsely that the Bailey gun had been abandoned by Gordon Munitions due to overheating. Chadwell believed Arthur was lying, but couldn't prove it.

As told in «Thy Name is Sabbath,» Arthur sold a Bailey gun to Count Kowalski (alias Count Corbucci) in Utah. During the course of the negotiations, John Gordon and his wife were murdered by Judge Cutthroat's henchmen in Snow Hill County, Utah. Arthur took custody of his grandson Louis Gordon, whose vocal cords had been severed by the murderers of his parents. Arthur trained the young boy to handle a gun.

In 1878, Arthur moved ten Bailey guns to a shack located along the Pecos River. One of these weapons was given to gunslinger Ignacz Djanko, who had been working for Arthur for the last two years. Djanko was supposed to persuade Mexican revolutionary Hugo Rodriguez to buy all ten machine guns, but the plan ended disastrously (see the movie *Django*).

In 1887 at the age of 70, Arthur retired from the munitions trade. In 1898, Louis Gordon was killed in Utah by a bounty hunter (see the film *The Great Silence*). In 1900 at the age of 83, Arthur tried to slay the bounty hunter in New Orleans, but ended up being murdered himself (see «The Last Vendetta»).

Arthur was a fan of *The Undertaker's Big Gun* and other novels written by Stanley Corbett. Just before his death in 1900, Arthur learned that Corbett was Count Corbucci of the Camorra. However, he never discovered that Corbett/Corbucci was the Count Kowalski who purchased a Bailey gun in 1876.

GORDON, BARTON - Alternate name for Black Bart from *El Rojo* (1966).
   https://www.youtube.com/watch?v=cVW3cqMNXkQ

Born in 1842, Barton Gordon is the third son of Arthur Gordon and his first wife, Francine Xavier. In unknown circumstances, the lower portion of his face including his nose was disfigured during the Civil War. When the war concluded, Barton became the gunslinger called Black Bart. A brown clay mask with a nose covered the lower portion of his face. He wore a black ensemble consisting of hat, shirt, pants, shirt, vest. gloves and boots

In 1868, the events of *El Rojo* unfolded in New Mexico. Barton was hired by a mine owner, Ortega, to protect him from the vengeful El Rojo. Barton betrayed Ortega and let El Rojo killed him. At the conclusion of the film, Barton forced El Rojo to become his partner.

The movie has a confused chronology which is discussed in the entry for *Rojo, El.*

GORDON, JAMES ARTHUR - Based on James Arthur Gordon, the protagonist of Robert E. Howard's «The Dead Remember.»

Born in 1856, James was the son of Arthur Gordon and his third wife. In 1877, James was living with his older brother, William LeFrank Gordon, in Antioch, Texas. After killing a white man and his black mistress, James participated in a cattle drive to Kansas. In Dodge City, the ghost of the black woman caused James's death.

GORDON, JOHN - based on Silence's father (briefly called «Gordon») in the flashback sequence of the film *The Great Silence*.

John Gordon was the second son of Arthur Gordon and his first wife, Francine Xavier. Born in 1840, John was raised originally as a Baptist. In 1850, he converted to the Mormon faith when the family moved to Utah. Although Arthur and other members of the Gordon family left the Church of Latter-Day Saints when Brigham Young supported the Union in the Civil War, John remained faithful to the Mormon religion. Staying in Utah, he married a Mormon woman (his only bride). The couple had a son, Louis, born in 1866. Despite the religious rift between them, John remained on good terms with his father. Arthur frequently visited his son's home in Snow Hill County.

In 1876, the corrupt justice of the peace known as Judge Cutthroat used the anti-polygamy laws as a pretext to dispossess Mormon settlers in Snow Hill County. John Gordon organized opposition to Cutthroat's persecution The judge falsely labeled John with the nickname of Marrying Jack even though he only had one wife. Placing a bounty on John's head. the judge tried to unsuccessfully manipulate bounty hunters to kill the homesteader (see «Thy Name is Sabbath»). When the bounty hunters failed, the Judge hired men to impersonate the newly appointed Sheriff of Snow Hill County and his deputy. The bogus lawmen fatally shot John and his wife. Their son Louis survived, but he was rendered speechless by the severing of his vocal cords.

GORDON, LOUIS («LOUIE») - Disguised version of Silence from *The Great Silence*.

Born in Snow Hill County, Utah, during 1866, Louis was the son of John Gordon and the grandson of Arthur Gordon. In 1876, the ten-year old Louis saw his parents slain by Judge Cutthroat and two other men. Louis's throat was cut with a knife by a man pretending to be the Sheriff of Snow Hill County. The jugular vein had not been severed, but Louis would have bled to death if he hadn't been found by a group led by his grandfather (See «Thy Name is Sabbath.» Among Arthur's allies was Anton Niklas Petersen (an alias of the notorious Dr. Antonio Nikola), who saved Louis's life. However the severing of his vocal cords made Louis a mute for the rest of his life.

Arthur taught his grandson how to handle a gun. In 1897, Louis returned to Snow Hill County. Avenging his parents' death, he killed Judge Cutthroat's two accomplices and shot off Cutthroat's thumb to prevent him from handling a gun. For the next year, Louis became the paid protector of Mormon settlers persecuted by ruthless bounty hunters. The Mormons called Louis «Silence» (a name we shouldn't use in our stories) and «the Mute Shootist» (a name I invented in «The Last Vendetta»). Louis used a C96 Mauser in 1897-98 (the gun was invented in 1896) .

In 1898, the events of *The Great Silence* transpired. After fatally shooting Judge Cutthroat, Louis was gunned down by a bounty hunter.

GORDON, WILLIAM LEFRANK GORDON (a. k. a. FRANK) - conflation of Frank from *Once Upon a Time in the West* (1968) and William L. Gordon from Robert E. Howard's «The Dead Remember.»

Link to film: https://www.youtube.com/watch?v=MQhZB86WJJU

Born in 1838, William LeFrank «Frank» Gordon was the oldest son of Arthur Gordon, Until he was twelve, he lived in Texas, In 1850, he moved to Utah. William's activities from 1860-71 are totally unknown other than that he lived in El Paso for some point during this period. By 1872, he was working as a subordinate to Baron Gustav Von Schulenberg in the private security force of Brockston-Morton. William then operated largely out of the Gustav's Texas ranch, When Gustav died in Mexico during 1876, William moved his younger half-brother, James Arthur Gordon, to Antioch, Texas. In the same year, William a married. His son, Francis Xavier Gordon (see Robert E. Howard's El Borak tales), was born in 1877.

In 1877, the events of Robert E. Howard's «The Dead Remember» unfolded. After arriving on a cattle drive from Texas, James died in weird circumstances in Dodge City. Shortly before his death, James wrote William a letter.

By 1883, William was the chief enforcer for Brockston-Morton Railways. He was fatally shot by the brother of a man whom he had lynched (see *Once Upon a Time in the West*).

William LeFrank Gordon was always called Bill by his parents and brothers. When he reached adulthood, he took the nickname of Frank.

HEYWOOD, MARTY - Honest gambler from the film *Wanted* (1967).

https://www.youtube.com/watch?v=dL2bl38yMGs

In 1872, Heywood played poker at the Sunlight Saloon in Signo Amarillo, New Mexico (see «Thy Name is Sabbath»). In 1881, Heywood cleared Sheriff Gary Ryan of a trumped up murder charge in Greenfield, New Mexico (see *Wanted*).

Heywood has dark hair and a mustache.

HOBSONVILLE - fictional town from *Return of Sabata*.

Hobsonville was controlled by the McIntock family in 1879. The town was located near another community called Redstone. I have placed both communities in New Mexico because there is an actual Redstone there. However, I couldn't discover if the real-life Redstone existed in 1879.

HOLDEN, PHILIP «HOT «DEAD» - Bounty Hunter from *I am Sartana, Your Angel of Death*. Although only called «Hot Dead» in the English version of the film, several websites give his surname as Holden. The first name of Philip is my own invention.

In 1872, Holden was a gambler who participated in a card game at the Sunlight Saloon in Signo Amarillo, New Mexico (see «Thy Name is Sabbath»). Hearing of the apprehension of Jimmy Ballantrae, Holden decided to become bounty hunter. As a gambler, Holden was an abject failure. He consistently lost. Any bounties he collected were frequently lost at poker.

In 1873, Holden lost 5,000 dollars to Jake Sartana. In 1878, Jake was falsely accused of bank robbery (see *I am Sartana, Your Angel of Death*). Holden settled the debt by declining to collect the bounty on Jake's head.

Holden had a wife and son living in Fillmore, Utah. His son, Scott Holden, grew up to be the bounty hunter who slew Louis Gordon in Snow Hill County during 1898 (see *The Great Silence*). Scott used the alias of Loco in the film.

Holden generally doesn't load the first chamber in his gun because of his impulsive nature.

HOLY BOOK - Disguised version of Koran from *Charge!* (a. k. a. *Those Dirty Dogs*).

Link to the movie:

https://www.youtube.com/watch?v=HPjf3XVa4nQ#t=22

Holy Book's real name was Jackson Kirby. Before the Civil War, Kirby read about two real-life Americans, Josiah Harlan and Alexander Gardner, who explored Afghanistan. Seeking to follow their footsteps, Kirby visited Afghanistan during 1861-67. While in that remote area, he converted to Islam. In an 1863 adventure (which I intend to write for *Tales of the Shadowmen*), Kirby met the Phantom of the Opera in a lost city of Erlik cultists in Afghanistan (Gaston Leroux's novel had the Phantom traveling all over Asia before occupying the Paris Opera House). The Phantom was being held prisoner by the cultists. Kirby helped the Phantom escape his captors. In gratitude, the Phantom gave Kirby two weapons that he had invented: 1) an early version of a submachine gun disguised as a parasol and 2) a long rifle that fired explosive bullets.

Returning to the United States in 1868, Kirby proceeded to study the Indian tribes of Texas. In 1871, Kirby became an army scout at Fort Concho, Texas. During the events of *Charge!* in 1875, he fought alongside Captain Chadwell, Lieutenant Younger and Sgt. Boomerang Smith against the outlaw army of General Lopez.

During his time as an army scout, Kirby earned the nickname of Holy Book because he always quoted the Koran.

In 1877, Kirby resigned as an army scout to be a bounty hunter alongside Boomerang Smith.

ISAIAH - Disguised version of Prophet from *For a Few Dollars More.*

Isaiah was an elderly resident of El Paso, Texas. He was reputed to know everyone who passed through that community. Living near the train station, he was always kept awake by noisy Brockston-Morton trains.

In 1872, he met Douglas Mortimer (the future Major Sabbath) in El Paso (see «Thy Name is Sabbath»). Two years later, he identified Mortimer to the Drifter with Many Names (see *For a Few Dollars More*).

JONSON, HANK - eccentric inventor from *EL ROJO.*

In 1868, Hank assisted El Rojo in his quest to avenge his murdered family. During the Civil War , Hank fought for the Confederacy. His plans for elaborate weapons were rejected by his superiors. Hank's invention included a rack of twelve rifles that could be fired at once, and a muffler that acted as a silencer when fitted over a pistol barrel.

Traveling in a covered wagon, Hank sold Jonson's Extract, an elixir which supposedly cured baldness, tooth decay and nagging corns.

Hank was a burly man with gray hair and a beard.

KOWALSKI, COUNT STANISLAUS - alias of Count Salvatore Corbucci from E. W. Hornung's Raffles stories and my «Shadows of the Opera» series.

A high-ranking member of the Camorra in Naples, Corbucci visited America during the Civil War. In 1861, he married Kate Washburn of Texas. The Count took his bride back to Naples. The Camorra was part of the Black Coats controlled by mysterious All-Father of Corsica. During the 1870's, the All-Father was being challenged by Jim Nemo, the leader of the Gentleman of the Night in London. In 1876, Corbucci was sent by the All-Father to the United States to disrupt the Gentlemen of the Night's operations in the United States. While traveling in the United states, Corbucci assumed the identity of Count Stanislaus Kowalski of Poland. His younger assistant, Antonio Nikola, accompanied the Count in the guise of a Swede, Anton Niklas Petersen. Both Corbucci and Nikola had throwing knives hidden under their ties.

In 1876, the Count purchased a machine gun from Gordon Munitions (see «Thy Name is Sabbath»). In the course of this transaction, the Count met Ignacz Djanko. In 1878, Djanko told the Count of his battle with the Red Scarf Gang.

In 1879, the All-Father summoned Corbucci back to Europe to become the supreme chieftain of the Camorra. While in Naples, Corbucci wrote a novel, *The Undertaker's Big Gun*, based on Djanko's exploits. The English translation of this novel was published under the pseudonym of Stanley Corbett. Corbucci was fatally poisoned in London during 1897 (see «The Last Laugh» by E. W. Hornung) .

The idea that Count Corbucci wrote a novel about Djanko is an in-joke based on the director of the film Django being Sergio Corbucci. Sergio used the pseudonym of Stanley Corbett in at least one of the Euro-Westerns he directed.

One of Corbucci's novels, *The Great Massacre*, was never translated into English. The novel was a fictionalized account of the murder of John Gordon. Corbucci's American publisher, Pickman and Sons, rejected the book because of its brutally depressing ending.

LASSITER - Outlaw slain by Degueyo and Jake Sartana in an unrecorded exploit cited in *I am Sartana, Your Angel of Death*.

LEE TSE TUNG - Chinese criminal who ran a casino in Indian Falls, Nevada during 1899 (*Have a Good Funeral, My Friend . . . Sartana will Pay*). He was swindled out of 100,000 dollars by Jake Sartana and Abigail Benson. Lee Tse Tung was still alive at the conclusion of the film.

Lee Tse Tsung pretended to be a crippled rotund man who could only be transported in a rickshaw. In reality, he was extremely muscular and agile. Besides being an expert martial artist, he was an expert fighter with a sword.

LELAND, JONAS - Based on Jonas from *The Hellbenders* (1966).
https://www.youtube.com/watch?v=I70KO0wlSIc

Colonel Jonas Leland was Major Sabbath's commanding officer in the in the Hellbender Regiment during the Civil War. A hellbender is a salamander, and an image of that lizard adorned the Confederate regimental flag, The Hellbender Regiment fought in Tennessee.

In 1862,the Major was wounded at the battle of Stones River in Tennessee. The top joint of the middle finger was shot off. He recovered at a military hospital run by Mrs. Elizabeth Leland, the Colonel's wife. During his 20 days of convalescence, the Major discovered a drunken Colonel Leland beating his wife. The Major warned Leland that he would kill him if he ever beat her again.

When the war ended in 1865, the Hellbender Regiment was disbanded. Colonel Leland took the defeat of the Confederacy very hard. He became exceedingly cruel to his wife, and this resulted in her committing suicide. Holding Colonel Leland responsible for his wife's death, the Major sought to challenge Leland to a duel.

However, Leland had fled Tennessee with his three sons, Nat, Jeff and Ben. Only Ben was Elizabeth's son. Nat and Jeff were the offspring from an earlier marriage. Jonas Leland had embarked on a criminal scheme to steal over a million dollars to fund a revived Confederacy. This scheme resulted in the death of the whole Leland family in New Mexico during 1865. This event is depicted in the film *The Hellbenders* (1967). In that film, the Colonel (played by Joseph Cotton) was only referred to by his first name (the surname Leland comes from a character portrayed by the same actor in *Citizen Kane*).

Before leaving Tennessee, Colonel Leland and his two older sons spread a false rumor that the Major had «chewed» off his own finger in 1862 in order to romance Elizabeth in the hospital. Furthermore, it was claimed that she had committed suicide because the Colonel had refused to resume their affair. Although blatantly false, the story was widely believed by many people including Lieutenant Tervis, who had joined the hellbender regiment in 1864.

At the close of the Civil War, the Major met Pickled Joe (this is Josiah Pickles from *Return of Sabbath*). Pickled Joe was a member of the Hellbender Regiment. A former engraver, he forged documents for the Hellbender Regiment to perform secret missions behind enemy lines. Colonel Leland used Pickled Joe to forge a Union Army military permit to bury Captain Ambrose Allen of the Confederate Army in New Mexico.

Actually the coffin contained a million dollars that the Colonel had stolen from the Union Army. In a series of bizarre circumstances (told in *The Hellbenders*), the stolen millionaire ended up being buried in a military cemetery in New Mexico. The money was in a coffin under a headstone bearing Captain Allen's name in Fort Brent. There are no records of it ever being dug up.

L'OLLONAISE, DELILAH - Original character created for this series. She is conflated with the unnamed woman from Redstone mentioned in *Return of Sabata.*

Delilah L'Ollonaise was a prominent member of the American branch of the Gentlemen of the Night. Her immediate superior was Madame Delphine, and her cousin was Valentin L'Ollonaise.

Delilah ran a casino in Redstone, New Mexico. Holding Major Sabbath responsible for her cousin's death, Delilah attempted to murder him in «Thy Name is Sabbath.» The Major spared her life, but stole a signet ring from her. This ring had been a gift from Madame Delphine.

A later conflict between Sabbath and Delilah is currently unrecorded. Despite the blood feud between them, Delilah and Sabbath had a passionate love affair in early 1878. Sabbath even proposed marriage, but left Delilah at the altar. Nine months later, Delilah gave birth to a son whom she named Valentin after her later cousin. This child became known as Valentin Sabbath, and played a major role in *I am Sartana, Trade Your Pistols for a Coffin.* For some unknown reason, Delilah made her son promise not to kill anyone on a Thursday.

During the events of *Return of Sabata* in 1879. Delilah received a message from Joe McIntock, her lieutenant in the Gentlemen of the Night, that the Major was present in Hobsonville, New Mexico. Delilah had six brothers whom she easily dominated. They were dispatched to kill the Major, but he slew them instead.

L'OLLONAISE, VALENTIN (see BALLANTRAE, JIMMY).

LOST KNOB - fictional Texas town from the works of Robert E. Howard («The Graveyard Rats,» «Garfield's Heart» and «Wild Water.»

In «Thy Name is Sabbath,» Christian Sabbath's widow lived there with her young son.

MARCOS - bank robber in *Sartana Kills Them All.*

In 1869, Marcos was in Lamar, Missouri, where he met the local Constable, who was then Wyatt Earp. As a result of this encounter, Marcos would often compare impulsive people to Earp (such as the storeowner in *Sartana Kills Them All*).

In 1870, Marcos seduced the daughter of Judge Parker of Colorado (a totally different person from the historic Judge Parker of Fort Smith, Arizona).

Beginning in 1870, Marcos was Jake Sartana's partner in a series of bank robberies in Colorado. Jake and Marcos often played cards to settle disputes between them. When in the desert, Marcos and Jake once had a card game to determine who should drink the last drop of water.

In 1871, the events of *Sartana Kills Them All* transpired. Marcos and Jake were betrayed by the Burton brothers, their partners in a Colorado bank robbery. Leaving Marcos and Jake at the mercy of a posse, the Burton brothers ran off with the loot. Eventually Marcos and Jake recovered the money, but it was stolen from them by Maria Anderson, a woman they were both bedding. Maria used the money to buy an expensive saloon. After destroying the saloon, the two outlaws reached an accommodation with Maria. She would once more become their shared mistress as they continued to rob banks.

Recognizing that this three-sided relationship was destined to end disastrously, Jake severed his contacts with Marcos and Maria.

Jake Sartana had an illegitimate son by Carmencita, a former lover of Marcos, in 1872. Carmencita named the boy Marcus in memory of Marcos, Marcos had another Mexican mistress who bore him several sons.

MCDADE, SAMSON - Disguised version of Sam McDade from the «Scar Tissue» episode of the TV series *Hec Ramsey.*

In «Scar Tissue,» McDade arrived in New Prospect, Oklahoma during 1902. He claimed to have served in the Sheriff's Office of Amarillo, Texas, for 33 years. That statement indicates McDade was Amarillo since 1869. However, Amarillo didn't exist until 1887. Hec Ramsey recalled that McDade wouldn't let him carry a gun until he was twenty-one. McDade later claimed that Hec rode across Texas to Amarillo «thirty years ago.» There McDade trained him to be a lawman. Later Hec went to work as a marshal for Judge Parker in Fort Smith, Arizona. The episode entitled «Hard Road to Vengeance» placed Hec in Fort Smith during 1887.

Some massaging of the information needed to be done in order to make it compatible with historical fact. In «Thy Name is Sabbath,» Samson McDade is a deputy working for Sheriff Priam Ramsey in the fictional town of Signo Amarillo, New Mexico, during 1872. One of McDade's duties was to enforce a town ordinance that no one under 21 carry a gun. With Priam's approval, McDade arrested Priam's son (an unnamed Hec Ramsey) for violating the ordinance.

McDade was a Texan. It had been his ambition to become a Texas Ranger, but the Ranger had been disbanded in 1865 with the onset of Reconstruction. In 1873, the Rangers were revived, and McDade left New Mexico to join them. After reaching his twenty-second birthday in 1874, Priam's son left Signo Amarillo to become a Ranger under McDade's tutelage. In 1887, McDade left the Rangers to live in a town originally called Oneda (it would later be renamed Amarillo). There he found employment in the Sheriff's office.

As for Priam's son, he became one of the deputy marshals working for Judge Parker in Fort Smith, Arizona during 1887. In the 1890's, he was a deputy marshal in Texas. From 1901 to at least 1902, he was deputy police chief of New Prospect, Oklahoma.

MCINTOCK FAMILY - one of the major crime families in the American branch of the Gentlemen of the Night. Members included Jason McIntock (killed by Jake Sartana in «Thy Name is Sabbath») and Joe McIntock (killed by the Major in *Return of Sabata*). The McIntocks are subordinate to the L'Ollonaise family.

NINE FINGERS - see TERVIS, LIEUTENANT

PETERSEN, ANTON NIKLAS - alias of Doctor Antonio Nikola from Guy Boothby's novels and my «Shadows of the Opera» series.

Born in Venice during 1856, Niccolo Fosco, emigrated to Cuba with his mother. When his mother starved to death in 1861 as a result of the cruelty of Don de Silvestre, the governor of Cuba, Niccolo, swore vengeance. In 1868, a 12-year old Niccolo attempted to pick the pocket of a visiting Italian tourist. The tourist was Count Salvatore Corbuccci, who easily overpowered the boy. Rather than turn over Niccolo to the Cuban authorities, Corbucci made him his protégé. Niccolo was taken to Naples where he adopted the name of Antonio Nikola. Corbucci entrusted the boy's education to a disgraced Oxford Don, John Charity Spring (from George MacDonald Fraser 's Flashman novels). For copyright reasons, this character can only be called Oxford Spring.

In 1876, Corbucci was ordered by the All-Father of the Black Coats to travel to the United States to interfere with the American operations of the rebellious Gentlemen of the Night. In America, Corbucci posed as Count Kowalski of Poland while Nikola pretended to be his Swedish secretary, Anton Niklas Petersen. In Utah, Kowalski (Corbucci) purchased an early version of a machine gun from munitions dealer Arthur Gordon (see «Thy Name is Sabbath»). In the course of the negotiations, Petersen (Nikola) saved the life of Louis Gordon, Arthur's grandson.

In a story that I intend to write someday, Corbucci and Nikola will discover the Gentlemen of the Night were about to conclude an alliance with Don de Silvestre of Cuba in 1877. The two criminals will then use the machine gun to conduct a spectacular assassination in Cuba.

In 1879, Corbucci was summoned back to Europe by the All-Father, in order to be enthroned as the supreme leader of the Camorra. Nikola went with him. In 1898, Nikola would disappear in the mountains of Tibet (see Guy Boothby's *Farewell, Nikola!*).

PICKLED JOE - Disguised version of Josiah Pickles from *Return of Sabata*.

During the Civil War in Tennessee, Pickled Joe forged documents for Confederate spies belonging to the Hellbender regiment led by Colonel Jonas Leland. When the war ended in 1865, Leland hired Pickled Joe to forge a document permitting him to bury a Confederate officer in New Mexico. This document figured in a scheme to steal a million dollars (see *The Hellbenders*). Once he had the document, the Colonel fled Tennessee.

While serving in the Hellbender Regiment, Major Sabbath had no direct contact with Pickled Joe until after the war ended in 1865. Leland had spread vile rumors about his late wife and the Major. Hoping to challenge Leland to a duel, the Major tried to ascertain his whereabouts. Discovering that Pickled Joe had recently done a task for Leland, the Major questioned the forger. Pickled Joe blatantly lied that he had no knowledge of Leland's whereabouts.

By 1879, Pickled Joe was traveling as a sleight-of-hand artist with a circus. He was dropping off counterfeit money to Joe McIntock when the circus visited Hobsonville, New Mexico. McIntock had Pickled Joe killed when Major Sabbath began to investigate (see *Return of Sabata*).

Pickled Joe was a thin man with gray hair.

RAMSEY, PRIAM - Original character meant to be the father of Hector «Hec» Ramsey, the television character played by Richard Boone. In the episode entitled «Mystery of the Yellow Rose,» we learn certain facts about Hec's family. Hec's mother was a Hunkpapa Sioux. In 1901, Hec had a six-year old niece.

Priam Ramsey's father was a Greek scholar who was an expert on Homer's account of the Trojan War, the *Iliad*. The elder Ramsey named his elder son after the King of Troy. Priam in turn named his son after Hector, the warrior son of the King of Troy.

Born in Texas, Priam was a member of the Rangers prior to their temporary dissolution in 1865. In 1869, he moved to New Mexico to become Sheriff of Signo Amarillo. His deputies were Samson McDade and Giddy Burnett. in 1872, he met Douglas Mortimer. Four years later, Priam would become Sheriff of Snow Hill county of Utah. He rechristened Mortimer Major Sabbath (see «Thy Name is Sabbath»).

Priam had two sons by his Hunkpapa Sioux wife. The elder son became a lawman. The younger had a daughter born in 1895.

RED MARGOT - conflation of Maggie from *Return of Sabata* and an unnamed prostitute in *Hannie Caulder*.

A beautiful redhead, the woman known as Red Margot originally worked as a prostitute for Madame Dora Boyette in St. Louis, Missouri. In 1879, she left Madame Boyette's brothel to work in Hobsonville, New Mexico. there she had an affair with Major Sabbath (see *Return of Sabata*).

In 1880, Margot moved to a Texas town. She tried to run the local brothel on her own, but this proved beyond her capabilities. Therefore, she summoned Dora Boyette who gladly agreed to take charge. In 1882, both Dora and Margot encountered Ana Sartana on a staircase in a saloon (see *Hannie Caulder*). The two ladies went outside to get some fresh air. An outlaw shot by Ana then fell out of the window and landed on Red Margot. Although Margot received only minor bruises, she never forgave Ana for the incident.

REDSTONE - town near Hobsonville in *Return of Sabata*.

The Major allegedly fathered an illegitimate son in Redstone. The town also had a large casino. For some elaboration on those statement, see the entry on *L'Ollonaise, Delilah*.

The existence of a real Redstone in New Mexico has prompted me to put this fictional town there.

REGINA - Brothel keeper in The Great Silence.

In «Thy Name is Sabbath,» she was briefly mentioned as a prostitute in Snow Hill County, Utah, during 1876. By 1898, she was running the brothel. She was gunned down by bounty hunters in *The Great Silence.*

ROJO, EL - protagonist of the film *El Rojo.*

https://www.youtube.com/watch?v=cVW3cqMNXkQ

The film has a confused chronology. It opened with the caption «Territory of New Mexico 1868.» We then see the massacre of El Rojo's family. The action then shifts years later. A character named Hank says two years have passed since the Civil War ended, That statement implies that the post-massacre scenes tale place in 1867. In the conclusion, El Rojo claims to have been fighting the Civil War (1861-65) when his family was murdered. Therefore, some modifications need to be made for the film to be chronologically sound. The massacre happened in 1861, and the rest of the film happened in 1868.

El Rojo's real name was Donald Sorenson. In 1861, his father, brother, sister-in-law, niece and nephew were slain near Gild Hill, New Mexico, by four conspirators. The killers stole a gold mine from the dead family. Donald was away fighting the Civil War in New Mexico. Captured in 1862, he spent the rest of the war in the POW camp of Batterville.

In 1868, the events of *El Rojo* unfolded. Under the aliases of El Rojo («the Red») and Joe, Sorenson arrived in Gold Hill to kill his family's slayers. One of the murderers, Ortega, hired a disfigured gunslinger called Black Bart (see *Gordon, Barton*) to protect him. El Rojo paid Bart to betray Ortega. At the film's conclusion, El Rojo had slain all his family's killers. Black Bart then appeared to coerce El Rojo into taking him as a partner.

SABBATH, CHRISTIAN ADAM (1) -

Basis: *Adios, Sabata* (1970)

https://www.youtube.com/watch?v=udNde1qpczs

Born in 1830, Christian was the son of a Texan and a Tonkawa squaw. His penchant to dress in dark clothes earned him the nickname of the Black Indian. In 1855, Sabbath saw a photograph of King Mongkut of Siam. That monarch had shaved his skull as part of a religious ceremony. Sabbath thought Mongkut looked incredibly handsome without hair, and decided to emulate him by regularly shaving his head.

When Texas seceded, Christian refused to take up arms against the

Union. Instead he smuggled arms to Benito Juarez and the opponents of the Maximilian regime. Profits from this endeavor allowed him to purchase a mansion in Kingsville, Texas. Gaining fame among the Mexicans, he became known as «Sabata» (that name must never be used in our fiction).

Christian used a sawed-off rifle with a horizontal magazine containing seven bullets. The rifle was designed by Leroy Bailey of Gordon Munitions. Besides being lethal with a revolver, Christian also was an expert knife thrower.

In 1865, Christian was hired by the U. S. government to escort Sgt. Boomerang Smith and Sgt. Ignacz Djanko into Mexico in order to sabotage a French chemical factory that was developing a more stable variant of nitroglycerin for Emperor Maximilian. Smith and Djanko blew up the factory, but Christian was able to steal samples of the chemical. He was able to use that explosive effectively against the forces of Heinrich «the Butcher» Von Skimmel two years later.

In 1867, the events of *Adios, Sabata* unfolded. The Juaristas hired Christian to steal a gold shipment being guarded by Austrian mercenary Heinrich Von Skimmel (called Colonel Skimmel in the film). In order to achieve his mission, Christian formed an alliance with the untrustworthy Jimmy Ballantrae (called Ballantine in the film).When Ballantrae tried to steal the gold for himself, he was foiled by Christian. Ballantrae wore vengeance.

When the Juaristas overthrew Maximilian in 1867, they offered Christian Mexican citizenship. When Christian accepted this offer, it caused a rift with his wife (she and their son was visiting relatives during the events of *Adios, Sabata)*. Taking their son with her, Mrs. Sabbath left her husband to live in Lost Knob, Texas. Selling his home in Kingsville, Christian moved to Mexico.

In 1872, Jimmy Ballantrae tricked the man who would later be known as Major Sabbath into killing Christian (see «Thy Name is Sabbath»).

SABBATH, CHRISTIAN ADAM (2) - Disguised version of Chris Adams who appeared in the films *The Magnificent Seven* (1960), *Return of the Magnificent Seven* (1966), *Guns of the Magnificent Seven* (1969) and *The Magnificent Seven Ride* (1972). The character was played by three different actors, Yul Brynner, George Kennedy and Lee Van Cleef. Born in 1859, Christian Adam Sabbath Jr. would later change his name sometime in the 1880's. After altering his name, Christian Jr. became famous for leading bands of seven mercenaries on dangerous missions into Mexico. Of his four known adventures, only the third could be dated with any exactitude. In *Guns of the Magnificent Seven*, there was a young boy who was Mexican revolutionary Emiliano Zapata (1879-1919). Zapata seems at least ten years old in the film. Assuming Zapata was that age would put the movie's events in 1889.

Complicating the chronological placement of *Guns of the Magnificent Seven* is a ex-Confederate soldier named Slater. The character was played by Joe Don Baker, who was 33 years old when this film was made. In order to make the Slater character chronologically fit into 1889, it would have to be argued that a 16-year old Slater joined the Confederate Army in 1865, and that his real age was 40 when *Guns of the Magnificent Seven* transpired.

Like his father, Christian Jr. had a penchant for black clothing. Early in his career, Christian Jr. shaved his head like his father. By 1889, he was allowing his hair to grow. Later in life, he began to lose his hair and also grew a mustache.

SABBATH, VALENTIN - Illegitimate son of Delilah L'Ollonaise born in Redstone, New Mexico, during 1888. She claimed that Major Sabbath was the father. He appeared as a rival of Marcus Sartana in *I am Sartana, Trade your Pistols for a Coffin*. Valentin always wore a white hat and suit. He carried a white umbrella. His weapons were a pistol and a sawed-off rifle similar to that used by Josh Randall (*Wanted Dead or Alive*). Valentin was named after his mother's cousin (who died due to the Major's intervention). Valentin made two promises to his mother: 1) never to kill anyone on a Thursday and 2) never to fight fair when a little cheating would give him the advantage. He carried a book of poetry by Alfred Tennyson. Valentin's favorite poem was «Our Lady of Shallot.» He had brown hair and eyes.

SAN MIGUEL - Recurring Mexican border town which appeared in a least four Euro-Westerns.

In 1868 during the events of *El Rojo*, a corrupt businessman and murderer, Novarro, was slain in San Miguel by the vengeful El Rojo.

In 1873, the town was divided by two criminal factions, the Rojo brothers and the Baxters. As depicted in *A Fistful of Dollars*, the Drifter with Many Names (the Man with No Name) manipulated the two gangs against each other El Rojo was not related to the Rojo brothers.

In 1877, a band of anti-Diaz revolutionaries led by General Santillana in *Run, Man, Run* occupied the town. There Santillana awaited to receive a supply of three million in gold to finance his rebellion. The gold was described as being hidden away by Benito Juarez before his overthrow by Porfirio Diaz. In reality, Juarez died in office of natural causes. It was Juarez's successor, Sebastian Lerdo, whom Diaz overthrew. Probably Juarez accumulate the gold, and his death caused the treasure to fall into Lerdo's hands. Some of the gold must have been used by Lerdo in the secret weapon exchanges with the United States on the Rio Grande that were disrupted by the Rojo brothers in *A Fistful of Dollars*.

At conclusion of *Run, Man, Run*, it was discovered that exiled revolutionaries in Texas and molded the three million in gold into a printed press which was painted black. A woman named Dolores was driving a wagon with the golden printing press towards San Miguel. Did she ever get there? Did Santillana receive delivery of the gold? Since Diaz continued to rule Mexico for decades, Santillana's revolt clearly failed. But what happened to the golden printing press?

In 1918, a group of Mexican revolutionaries seized control of the town in *A Bullet for the General* (1968). After the revolutionaries left, the Mexican army reoccupied the town and massacred all the inhabitants. The film can be viewed here:

http://www.veoh.com/watch/v200924785yFwyYhC

SANCHEZ, «RICHMOND»- Disguised version of Carrincha from *Sabata*. The character had a belt buckle with «CS» on it. Therefore, his first name must be Carrincha, and his last name must begin with an S. Since Carrincha was played by an actor named Pedro Sanchez, I am giving this character the surname of Sanchez. Pedro Sanchez played Escudo in *Adios, Sabata* and Bronco in *Return of Sabata*, but I find it impossible to conflate these two characters with Carrincha.

A burly man with a beard, Sanchez was a bugler in the Union army during the Civil War. He got his nickname from winning a medal in the Battle of Richmond. He told conflicting accounts of the battle. Sometimes it lasted seven days; sometimes nine. Sanchez was a master at throwing knives. He may be related to the other knife-thrower, Manuel Sanchez (see *Corredor, El*).

In 1879, Sanchez assisted Major Sabbath during the events of *Sabata*.

SARTANA, ANA - Disguised version of the heroine of *Hannie Caulder* (1972). Born Ana Racosa in 1857, she married a station master (James Caulder) in New Mexico during 1881. After her marriage, she anglicized her first name to Hannah, In 1882, her husband was murdered by three brothers (the Clemens brothers in the film) who then raped her. Meeting the bounty hunter named Specs (Thomas Luther Price in the film), she persuaded him to train her to handle a gun. When Specs was slain by one of the brothers, Ana became a bounty hunter and slew the three siblings. In killing the final brother, she was assisted by Jake Silver (alias of Jake Sartana). Falling in love with Silver, she went with him to New Orleans to be married.

Invited to the wedding was Major Sabbath. Specs had told Ana about how Sabbath had trained him to be a bounty hunter. When the Major learned that Ana was the protégé of Specs, he adopted a paternalistic attitude towards her. Ana came to view the Major as a surrogate father. At her request, the Major gave her away at the marriage.

Discovering that her husband was really Jake Sartana, Ana learned how he purloined the 100,000 dollars stolen during the Northwestern Bank robbery of 1878. Removing the same sum of money from their joint bank account, Ana gave it to the Northwestern Bank.

When Jake learned of this, he became so enraged that he struck Ana in public. Ana had him arrested for assault. Jake's lawyer, Jeff Plummer, arranged for Ana to withdraw the charges in exchange for a divorce. Using the surname of Sartana, Ana resumed her career as a bounty hunter. She adopted the Sartana name in order to pursue her intention to make amends for Jake's crimes. Unlike her ex-husband, Ana was scrupulously honest.

Ana wore brown pants. Besides a brown hat. The own piece of clothing that she wore on the upper half of her body was a maroon poncho with a gray stripe along the bottom. Her hair and eyes are brown.

Ana used a special revolver devised by Leroy Bailey. It has two triggers: one to cock the gun, and the other to fire. She was one of the few clients of Gordon Munitions allowed to visit Bailey in his home.

The Major's attitude towards Ana was protective, and he would never consider bedding her.

SARTANA, JAKE

Basis: If You Meet Sartana, Pray for Your Death (1968)
http://www.dailymotion.com/video/xq7nsp_if-you-meet-sartana-pray-
for-your-death_shortfilms?start=6#from=embediframe
I Am Sartana, Your Angel of Death (1969),
https://www.youtube.com/watch?v=q4joNhAKUg8
I am Sartana, Trade your Pistols for a Coffin (1970)
https://www.youtube.com/watch?v=AMp4lE629_U
Have a Good Funeral, My Friend... Sartana Will Pay (1970)
https://www.youtube.com/watch?v=DYWpSeJzDqk
Light the Fuse . . . Sartana is Coming (1970)
https://www.youtube.com/watch?v=UKW-OUOYa_M
A Bullet for a Stranger (They Called Him Cemetery) (1971)
https://www.youtube.com/watch?v=0-_NotFNCNg
The Price of Death (1971)
Sartana Kills Them All (1971)
https://www.youtube.com/watch?v=6s4Uilic6Ak

For the purposes of this fictional history, the Sartana played by Gianni Garko in four films is the father of the Sartana played by George Hilton in *I am Sartana, Trade your Pistols for a Coffin*. Also the Ace of Hearts from *A Bullet for a Stranger (They Called Him Cemetery)* and Mr. Silver from *The Price of Death* are treated as synonymous with the original Sartana. The same is also true of the outlaw version of Sartana from *Sartana Killed Them* Although the Preacher from *Hannie Caulder* was played by Stephen Boyd, that character is conflated with Garko's Sartana.

Born in Louisiana during 1842, Jacobo «Jake» Sartana was the son of a Mexican father and a woman of French descent. After the United States gained new territory in the Mexican War (1846-48), the Sartana family moved to New Mexico. Raised as a Catholic, Jake learned how to play an organ while serving as a choir boy in a local church. When Jake was 20. he witnessed the Drifter with Many Names rescue a Mexican bandit from hanging (based on the scenes in *The Good, the Bad and the Ugly*).

Jake was a blond-haired man who usually wore either mustache or a beard. His eyes were blue.

By 1865, Jake was a married man with a wife (Helen) and two young boys (Tim and Mike). When the family moved to Texas after the Civil War ended, their wagon was ambushed by bandits. Helen and the boys were killed. Jake was severely wounded. He was discovered by rancher Clay McIntyre and his wife. They buried Jake's family and nursed him back to health. Once his wounds had healed, Jake left the McIntyre ranch. Twenty years later, he would repaid his debt to the McIntyre family in *A Bullet for a Stranger.*

In order to track down his family's killers, Jake became an outlaw. After killing all the bandits, Sartana became a criminal. For the next few years, he became an associate of several noted crooks including Granville Fuller *(Light the Fuse . . . Sartana is Coming)*, Buddy Ben (*I Am Sartana, Your Angel of Death*) and Duke Boyette (*A Bullet for a Stranger*). By 1871, he and another bandit named Marcos joined forces with the Burton brothers to steal 100,000 from a Colorado bank. Six men were killed in the robbery. The Burton brothers betrayed Sartana and Marcos and left them surrounded by a posse.

At this point, the events of *Sartana Killed Them All* transpired. After a series of misadventures, Marcos recovered the 100,000 money, but deserted Jake. Eventually cornered by Jake, Marcos revealed that the money had been stolen from him by Maria Anderson, a woman whom both outlaws had bedded. Maria used the money to buy an expensive saloon. Jake and Marcos then joined forces to wreck Maria's saloon. Maria made peace with both outlaws, who agreed to share her. The film concluded with the outlaws living with Maria and planning bank robberies.

In the course of *Sartana Killed Them*, Jake had an affair with Carmencita, one of Marcos's girlfriends, In 1872, she gave birth to a boy who would become known as Marcus Sartana. This is the Sartana played by George Hilton in *I am Sartana, Trade your Pistols for a Coffin.*

Uncomfortable with the love triangle involving himself, Marcus and Maria, Jake decided to desert both of them. In 1872, Jake was hired by criminal Valentin L'Ollonaise to be his secret Ace of Hearts. The events described «Thy Name is Sabbath» then occurred. Jake betrayed Valentin to the bounty hunter who would become known as Major Sabbath. In the course of this adventure, Jake gained his signature wardrobe and a powerful weapon disguised as an organ. Two of the outer pipes on each side of the organ could be lowered to fire cannon balls. The four central pipes could be lowered to shoot bullets as rapidly as a machine gun.

After the 1872 sequence in «Thy Name is Sabbath,» Jake became involved in the events of *Light the Fuse . . . Sartana is Coming*. A gravestone for a recently murdered man places this exploit in 1872. Arrested for murder, gambler Grandville Fuller sent a message to Jake begging for help. In exchange for being broken out of a territorial prison, Fuller told Jake about a fortune in stolen gold. After maneuvering through a maze of deception and double crosses, Jake retrieved the gold which he kept for himself. During this adventure, Jake decimated an outlaw army with the arsenal housed in his pipe organ.

This is probably the same organ that Jake used in *I am Sartana, Your Angel of Death*. A graveyard inscription from that film places its events in 1878. This time, the organ was only used to automatically play music in order to distract hired killers. Since automatic players for pianos and pipe organs weren't invented until 1876, Jake's musical device must have been enhanced to have that feature around 1877.

In the course of *Light the Fuse ... Sartana is Coming*, Jake confiscated a silver derringer-like pistol from a corrupt Sheriff, Manassas Jim. This gun would become Jake's most famous weapon. It contained four barrels. The ammunition for this weapon is stored in a detachable cylinder which can be spun like a top when separated from the pistol. The sides of the cylinder are decorated with the four suites of a card deck (a spade, a club, a heart and a diamond). Based on information in *I am Sartana, Your Angel of Death,* the weapon was created by Hiram Crown, a criminal who made weapons for other crooks. Crown was killed by the bounty hunter Philip «Hot Dead» Holden.

Other weapons employed by Jake Sartana include a pack of playing cards that are razor sharp (like those used by the Joker in DC Comics). Jake also owned two pocket watches on chains. One was a real watch with a silver casing. The other was a fake made of lead which Jake used to bludgeon his opponents, Both the card deck and the watches appeared in *Have a Good Funeral, My Friend... Sartana Will Pay*. A box containing at least a dozen throwing knives was featured in *I am Sartana, Your Angel of Death*. Jake was lethal as a knife thrower.

Jake was an expert rifle shot. His legendary maneuver was to shoot a rifle sideways while it rested on his shoulders. This shot was utilized in *Have a Good Funeral, My Friend... Sartana Will Pay.*

From 1873 to 1877, Jake Sartana practiced a career as a bounty hunter. He partnered with other bounty hunters including Phil «Hot Dead» Holden, Degueyo (who lived in a mansion in the American south), Specs (Thomas Luther Price from *Hannie Caulder*) and an Indian called Shadow. In an unrecorded exploit, Jake helped Degueyo killed an outlaw named Lassiter. A grateful Degueyo wanted to give Jake a family heirloom, a watch, as a token of friendship. However, Jake declined to accept the gift.

While functioning as a bounty hunter, Jake dud most of his work for the Northwestern Bank in Wyoming. After the robbery of the El Paso Bank in *For A Few Dollars More*, the Northwestern quickly gained the reputation of being the most impregnable bank in the West.

During the same period, Jake became a valued client of Gordon Munitions. The firm modified his organ to have an automatic player. Jake was allowed to visit the company's gunsmith, Leroy Bailey, in Mexico. As noted in «Thy Name is Sabbath,» Gordon Munitions employed Jake and Ignacz Djanko to smuggle a Bailey machine gun out of Mexico during 1876. Like Major Sabbath, Jake also became a regular client of tailor Gino Di Marco of San Francisco. Jake regularly wore a black hat and a black Inverness cape lined with red. His neckties were always red.

In 1878, the events of *If You Meet Sartana, Pray for Your Death* happened. I placed the movie in that year because there was a scene featuring a phonograph (invented in 1877). In Arizona, Jake became involved with various parties trying to steal a gold shipment. Eventually Jake ran off with the gold.

During this adventure, Jake created the illusion that he was a supernatural entity like the character played by Clint Eastwood later in *High Plains Drifter* (in fact, the opening scenes of both films are very similar with the respective protagonists mysteriously materializing out of the horizon). Jake survived several bullets to the head by wearing a metal object under his hat. This created the false impression that Jake was some sort of Angel of Death. Jake also used the ghostly phrase «I am your pallbearer» before slaying outlaws.

In the same year, the events of *I Am Sartana, Your Angel of Death* also occurred. A gang of outlaws led by a man impersonating Jake Sartana stole 300,000 dollars from the Northwestern Bank. A 10,000 dollar reward was posted for Jake dead or alive. Many of Jake's former bounty hunter friends turned against him in order to collect the reward. Jake was forced to kill both Degueyo and Shadow. A confrontation with Hot Dead was avoided by Jake forgiving a gambling debt of 5,000 dollars that had been owed him for five years. With the assistance of bank robber Buddy Ben, Jake was not only able to clear his name, but secretly pocketed the 300,000 dollars for himself and Buddy Ben.

Despite the bank robbery charges being dropped, Jake Sartana was in an awkward position. His reputation had been severely damaged. It would be necessary for him to adopt a new name. He would assume the identity of Mr. Silver.

The original Mr. Silver was a baby-faced assassin who committed murders for 1,000 dollars. He used silver bullets, wore fingerless gloves, and wore scissor-like nail-cutters on a gold chain, and kept a throwing knife hidden in his hat. His *modus operandi* was to goad his targets into drawing their guns. This way he could claim self-defense. Occasionally he allowed himself to be hired out as an investigator. In his only known exploit, *Killer Calibre 32* (which I'm arbitrarily placing in 1878), he solved a stagecoach robbery. He always insisted that people address him as «Mr. Silver.»

In 1879, an unknown party hired Silver to kill Jake Sartana. In a fair gunfight, Jake slew Silver. In order to track down Silver's shadowy employer, Jake had Silver buried under his own name. With Jake Sartana officially dead, Jake then posed as Silver. After dealing with the person who hired Silver, Jake continued the impersonation.

While using the Silver identity, Jake abandoned his Inverness coat. He also was now clean-shaven. His famous silver four-barreled pistol was replaced with a single shot derringer. Other than the insistence on being called «Mister,» Jake adopted none of the original affectations. Jake's adoption of the silver identity was known to a few close friends including Major Sabbath, Specs, Arthur Gordon and Leroy Bailey. Jake's rival and sometime enemy. Duke Boyette. was also aware of the imposture.

Sartana's famous silver four-barreled pistol was replaced with a single shot derringer. As Mr. Silver, Sartana wore the derringer on his arm under his jacket. A mechanism could slide the gun into his hand. Jake developed the ploy of facing an armed adversary with his hands raised.

After uttering that he didn't have a gun, the derringer would slide into Jake's hand enabling him to fatally shoot his enemy.

In 1882, Jake in his Mr. Silver identity participated in the events of *Hannie Caulder*. This movie is assigned to 1882 because the novelization of the screenplay had a reference to Oscar Wilde's tour of America in that year. Jake was the character whom Ana «Hannie» Caulder, a female bounty hunter, described as being dressed as a «preacher» (the same comparison was made concerning Jake in *Light the Fuse . . . Sartana is Coming*). Jake helped Ana gain revenge on the last of the men who had murdered her husband and raped her. At the conclusion of the movie, Ana and the «preacher» were shown riding off together.

Jake and Ana actually became passionate lovers. They even married and moved to New Orleans, Louisiana, as Mr. and Mrs. Silver. Their marital bliss was short-lived. Ana soon learned of Jake's past as Sartana and his illegal possession of 300,000 dollars from the Northwestern Bank. Withdrawing that amount of money from their joint bank account, she anonymously sent it to the bank. When Jake learned of Ana's actions, he physically struck her in public. She had Jake arrested for assault. Jake's lawyer, Jeff Plummer, arranged for Ana to drop the charges in exchange for a divorce.

In *The Price of Death,* Plummer briefly alluded to defending Mr. Silver on an unspecified charge in New Orleans 1882. He was citing the assault charge described above.

Divorced from Jake, Ana resumed her career as a bounty husband. However, she mocked her ex-husband by calling herself Ana Sartana. As for Jake, he moved to an estate elsewhere in Louisiana. There he resided as Mr. Silver with two mistresses and judo instructor. Jake even re-grew his mustache.

In 1884, the events of *The Price of Death* unfolded. One of Jeff Plummer's clients was convicted of murder. Plummer hired Jake as Mr. Silver to prove the client's innocence.

In 1885, Jake was back in Texas. The events of *A Bullet for A Stranger* happened. Using his Ace of Hearts alias, Jake repaid his debt to the McIntyre family who saved his life in 1865. The McIntyre family was being victimized by a gang of extortionists whom Jake defeated. In an unusual magnanimous gesture, Jake turned over all the extortionists' ill-gotten gains to the McIntyre family.

In the course of this exploit, Jake was opposed by Duke Boyette, a hired gunslinger and friend from his outlaw days. Jake and Duke avoided killing each other, and their contest ended in a stalemate. At the conclusion of this affair, Jake was riding north to hunt rustlers in Abilene, Texas. He offered Duke a temporary partnership, but his rival decided to ride off in the other direction.

Sometime during the 1890's, Jake learned of the existence of Marcus, his illegitimate son by Carmencita from *Sartana Killed Them All.* Jake trained Marcus to be a gunfighter. Under the name of Marcus Sartana, Carmencita's son wore a black hat and Inverness cape like his father (except the cape doesn't have a red lining). Marcus also wore a black tie rather than a red one. Jake even had a duplicate of the four-barreled silver pistol made by one of Leroy Bailey's sons as a gift for Marcus.

In 1899, Jake resumed his Sartana alias to participate in the events depicted in *Have a Good Funeral, My Friend... Sartana Will Pay.* The year appeared on a gravestone in the film. Jake was now 57 years old. The movie has a sign post pointing to Wichita and Sandy Valley. Wichita suggests Kansas, but Sandy Valley implies Nevada. It is more logical to place an 1899 Western in Nevada.Pursuing swindler Joe Benson for a bounty, Jake discovered his quarry murdered. In the town of Indian Creek, Jake and Abigail Benson, Joe's niece and an accomplished con artist, successfully engaged in a swindle that tricked Lee Tse Tung, the criminal owner of a gambling house, out of 100,000 dollars.

Like Major Sabbath, Jake Sartana owned a black signet ring in two films: *If You Meet Sartana Pray for Your Death* (set in 1878) and *Have a Good Funeral, My Friend... Sartana Will Pay* (set in 1899). Possibly Jake had an imitation ring made, or possibly the same ring swapped hands multiple times in poker games between the Major and Jake.

SARTANA, MARCUS - illegitimate son of Jake Sartana and Carmencita from *Sartana Killed Them All*. He was born in 1872. Trained by his father to be a gunfighter, Marcus wore a black hat, tie and Inverness. Unlike his father, Marcus had no trace of the color red in his attire. A duplicate of Jake's four-barreled silver pistol was made by one of Leroy Bailey's sons as a gift for Marcus. Marcus was an expert rifle shot and knife thrower.

The only known adventure of Marcus is *I am Sartana, Trade your Pistols for a Coffin* (1970). This exploit (assigned to 1902) revealed that Marcus and Valentin Sabbath were rivals who joined forces when it suited their interests.

Like his mother, Marcus had black hair and eyes.

SEGUNDO - Disguised version of Septiembre from *Adios, Sabata*.

Segundo was a mute born on the second of September. One of his nicknames was Segundo («Second» in Spanish). In 1867, Segundo assisted Christian Adam Sabbath against the Austrian mercenaries working for Emperor Maximilian.

Segundo had a unique weapon. He would place metal balls on the top of his shoes and then lethally kick the pellets into the foreheads of his adversaries.

Segundo liked to listen to musical watches.

SHADOW - Indian bounty hunter from *I Am Sartana, Your Angel of Death*. Originally a friend of Jake Sartana, Shadow tried to collect the 10,000 dollar bounty on the gunslinger's head that resulted from a bank robbery frame-up in 1878. Jake was forced to kill Shadow.

SHANGHAI JOE (CHIN HAO)
Basis - *My Name is Shanghai Joe* (1973)
https://www.youtube.com/watch?v=iWWikbY8q5g#t=15

Shanghai Joe is a public domain character. There is no problem with using names from the film. There were actually two Shanghai Joe films. The second film was *The Return of Shanghai Joe* (1975, also known as *Shanghai Joe*). The second movie had a different lead actor, a dumb plot, and no continuity with the earlier film. For these reasons, *The Return of Shanghai* is totally ignored in our fictional history.

Shanghai Joe was a character conceived around the same time as Kwai Chang Caine (played by David Carradine) in *Kung Fu*. Like Caine, Shanghai Joe always behaved in a polite and modest manner. However, here's the difference. Caine only fights if he is attacked. He deliberately refrained from taking human life. Caine also ignored racial insults and other slights from bigots. Shanghai Joe was vastly different. If you insult him, he would smash your face. If you tried to kill him, he would either rip off your arm, pluck out your eye, or kill you.

Shanghai Joe's real name was Chin Hao. He was trained as a Champion of Justice by the Fire Lotus Tong. His tutor was Yang. A red tattoo of a fire lotus was on the inside of his left arm (on the joint). He and another student was trained in all the fighting skills of the Fire Lotus Tong. Each was entrusted with two of the four Daggers of Wei and one of the two Dragon Swords.

In 1882, Chin Hao arrived by ship in San Francisco. His exact reasons for leaving China are unclear, but he always claimed that he came to America to become a cowboy. Taking a stagecoach to Texas, he discovered that wealthy cattle rancher Stanley Spencer was enslaving Mexican laborers. Since Spencer had corrupted the Sheriff, Chin couldn't appear to the law. He began to liberate the enslaved workers. Spencer retaliated by sending four vicious killers against Chin, who brutally killed three and maimed one. Spencer then found Chin's fellow student from the Fire Lotus Tong. The martial artist had turned to evil and agreed to slay Chin. In order to defeat the assassin, Chin had to rip out his heart. Presumably Chin confiscated the other Daggers of Wei and Dragon Sword of his defeated enemy. The movie ended without resolving the conflict between Spencer and Chin Hao. The non-canonical sequel didn't feature Spencer.

Chin has a long black pigtail. He was a master of acupuncture and playing poker.

It would be very appropriate to team up Major Sabbath with Shanghai

Joe because Lee Van Cleef made a Kung Fu/Euro-Western called *The Stranger and the Gunfighter* (1974) in which he played an outlaw teamed up with a martial artist.

There is a debate about whether *My Name is Shanghai Joe* was influenced by the *Kung Fu* TV series. The director of the film denied any influence. For the record, the first instance of an Asian martial artist in the Wild West surfaced on the *Wanted Dead or Alive* TV series. There was a second season episode called «Black Belt» in which bounty hunter Josh Randall pursued Sammy Wong, a Korean Karate master falsely accused of murder. The episode was set in 1867.

SIGNO AMARILLO - fictional town in New Mexico created for «Thy Name is Sabbath.»

In 1872, Priam Ramsey was the Sheriff there. Samson McDade and Giddy Burnett were his deputies.

SILVER, MR. (1) - Protagonist of *Killer Calibre 32* (1967).

The original Mr. Silver was a baby-faced assassin who committed murders for 1,000 dollars. He used silver bullets, wore fingerless gloves, and wore scissor-like nail-cutters on a gold chain, and kept a throwing knife hidden in his hat. His *modus operandi* was to goad his targets into drawing their guns. This way he could claim self-defense. Occasionally he allowed himself to be hired out as an investigator. In his only known exploit, *Killer Calibre 32* (which I'm arbitrarily placing in 1878), he solved a stagecoach robbery. He always insisted that people address him as «Mr. Silver.»

In 1879, an unknown party hired Silver to kill Jake Sartana. In a fair gunfight, Jake slew Silver. In order to track down Silver's shadowy employer, Jake had Silver buried under his own name. With Jake Sartana officially dead, Jake then posed as Silver. After dealing with the person who hired Silver, Jake continued the impersonation.

SILVER, MR. (2) - see Sartana, Jake.

SMITH, BOOMERANG - disguised version of Sgt. Jeremiah Smith, the African-American soldier from *Charge!* (a. k. a. *Those Dirty Dogs*, 1973).

Link to the movie:

https://www.youtube.com/watch?v=HPjf3XVa4nQ#t=22

Born a Texas slave in 1840, Smith escaped to California in 1856. There he found work at a mining company where he gained a knowledge of explosives. In 1861, Smith joined the Union Army to fight in the Civil War. In the same year, he invented an explosive which was essentially dynamite (Alfred Nobel would invent the real dynamite in 1867). Smith donated his invention to the U. S. Army, but the government authorities disparage the effectiveness of his invention because of the inventor's racial heritage. However, a Union captain authorized the usage of Smith to blow up the bridge in new Mexico during 1862 (in *The Good, the Bad and the Ugly*).

Smith was fascinated by accounts of Australian natives using the throwing club known as the boomerang. Reading accounts of the weapon, Smith was able to create a replica and master using it.

Smith rose to the rank of sergeant. During 1964, Smith served with Sgt. Ignacz Djanko in Sherman's March to the Sea.

At the conclusion of the Civil War in 1865, Smith and Djanko were sent on a mission to Mexico by the U. S. government. His assignment was to sabotage the activities of Thomas Roch, a European chemist who was developing a more stable form of nitroglycerin for the Maximilian regime. Accompanying Smith and Djanko on this mission as a guide was American adventurer Christian Adam Sabbath Sr. The three Americans blew up the factory where the explosive was being developed. Thomas Roch survived, but the Maximilian government concluded that the explosion was due to defects in the inventor's weapon. Funding of Roch's research was terminated. For the future history of Thomas Roch, see Jules Verne's *For the Flag* (1896). As a result his involvement in this exploit, Christian was able to steal samples of Roch's explosive which would appear in *Adios, Sabata*.

In 1875, Smith together with Captain Chadwell and Lt. Cole Younger, were dispatched to Texas to eliminate General Lopez, a former member of the Maximilian regime who was leading an outlaw army. This exploit is documented in the film *Charge!* (a. k. a *Those Dirty Dogs*). Together with army scout Holy Book (Koran in the film), the trio of soldiers destroyed Lopez's army. Chadwell and Younger were promoted respectively to Major and Captain as a result of this mission, but Smith remained a lowly sergeant.

In 1876, Smith was part of the military force send by the Grant Administration to stabilize Snow Hill County, Utah. There he encountered Major Sabbath (told in «Thy Name is Sabbath»).

In 1877, Smith decided not to re-enlist in the army due to his lack of promotion. At the same time, Holy Book resigned as an Army scout.

Becoming partners, Smith and Holy Book pursued a career as bounty hunters.

SNOW HILL COUNTY - Fictional Utah county from *The Great Silence*.
I have placed Snow Hill between Juab and Millard counties based on the map glimpsed in the movie. The film, set in 1898, erred in having the map be the much larger Utah Territory, which included parts of Nevada and Colorado, rather than the state of Utah (admitted in 1896).

SPECS - Disguised version of Thomas Luther Price from *Hannie Caulder* (1972),
Specs earned his nickname from the fact that he wore glasses. Specs was trained by Sabbath to be a bounty hunter by the Major during the late 1860's. Sometime in the 1870's, Specs encountered Jake Sartana. Specs was one of the few people aware of Jake's assumption of the Mr. Silver identity in 1879. In 1882, Specs trained the future Ana Sartana to be a bounty hunter. Shortly thereafter, Specs was fatally knifed by one of the three killers/rapists whom Ana was pursuing.
Specs had dark hair and a gray beard.

SPENCER, STANLEY - corrupt Texas cattle rancher and archenemy of Shanghai Joe. Spencer purchased laborers from Mexican slave traders. He liked to wear white clothes. He had blond hair and a beard. Spencer was still at liberty at the conclusion of *My Name is Shanghai Joe*.
Stanley Spencer may be the father of Samuel Spencer, the corrupt mine owner from *I am Sartana, Trade your Pistols for a Coffin*. Both were played by the same actor (Piero Lulli) and dressed alike.

TERVIS, LIEUTENANT - Disguised version of Clyde from *Return of Sabata*. Robert E. Howard had a friend and collaborator named Tevis Clyde Smith. Adding an extra «r,» I'm bestowing the name of Clyde Tervis on this Euro-Western character.
In 1864, Lieutenant Clyde Tervis joined the Hellbender Regiment. At the Battle of Nashville in 1864, Tervis saved the Major Sabbath's life. Tervis was awarded a medal for heroism.
Previously the Major was wounded at 1862 during the Battle of Stones River in Tennessee. The top joint of the middle finger was shot off. In 1865, a vile rumor was spread that the Major had «chewed off» his own finger tip to conduct an adulterous love affair during his convalescence. Tervis foolishly believed this rumor.

In 1876, Tervis lost 5,000 to the Major during a game of poker in Fillmore, Utah. Tervis skipped town without paying the debt (see «Thy Name is Sabbath»).

Three years later, Tervis would pay the money back in Hobsonville, New Mexico (see *Return of Sabata*). In the course of this exploit, Tervis and the Major were partners in an endeavor to retrieve a fortune in gold stolen from the citizens of Hobsonville. When Clyde tried to betray him, the Major shot off the tip of his treacherous partner's trigger finger.

In 1900, Tervis surfaced in New Orleans under the alias of Nine Fingers (see my story, «The Last Vendetta»).

VARNO BROTHERS - disguised version of the acrobat characters from *Sabata* and *Return of Sabata*. In the latter film, these acrobats were called Angel and Bionda.

Angelos and Bion Varno were once part of the famed European circus acrobats called the Flying Seraphs. Originally they worked for Ronder's Circus in Britain. A salary dispute with the circus owner caused the brothers to depart for America. In 1878, the two brothers were working as acrobats in Delilah L'Ollonaise's casino in Redstone, New Mexico. There they befriended the Major during his love affair with the treacherous casino owner. When the Major skipped town, he took the acrobats with him.

The brothers then acted as undercover spies for the Major. Hearing that his estranged partner, Lee Galloway, was living in Texas, the Major sent the clean-shaven Angelos there. Posing as a mute Indian, Angelos shadowed Galloway. When the Major learned that a member of the notorious McIntock family was running Hobsonville, New Mexico, the bearded Bion was dispatched there. In 1879, Angelos alone assisted the Major in Daugherty (see *Sabata*), and both brothers helped the bounty hunter in Hobsonville (*Return of Sabata*).

In case you're wondering, the Varno brothers were cousins of Valorie Varno from my «Shadows of the Opera» stories.

Both brothers are adept at using slingshots to knock people unconscious.

VON SKIMMEL, HEINRICH - Alternate name for Colonel Skimmel from *Adios, Sabata*. While no one refers to the Colonel as Von Skimmel in the film, he refers to his own father as Admiral Von Skimmel.

In 1864, Heinrich Von Skimmel was part of a mercenary force of Austrian and Hungarian ex-military officers organized to support Emperor Maximilian's regime in Mexico.

The leader of these mercenaries was Heinrich's cousin, Baron Gustav Von Schulenberg. Due to his sadistic nature, Von Skimmel was dubbed Heinrich the Butcher by the Mexican populace. In 1867, Maximilian entrusted Heinrich with guarding a large shipment of gold. Using a false name, confidence trickster Valentin L'Ollonaise infiltrated Heinrich's household by posing as a portrait painter. Due to Valentin's interference, Heinrich was slain with a knife by Christian Adam Sabbath, an American mercenary employed by Benito Juarez.

Heinrich was survived by his wife Gretchen and his daughter Heidi.

VON SCHULENBERG, GUSTAV - alternate name for Baron Von Schulenberg from *The Big Gundown*.

In 1864, Baron Gustav Von Schulenberg organized a force of Austrian and Hungarian mercenaries to fight for the Maximilian regime in Mexico. Among Gustav's subordinates were Heinrich Von Skimmel and El Diablo. When Maximilian was overthrown, Gustav lead large group of his mercenaries from American into Texas. Among these refugees were Heinrich Von Skimmel's widow (Gretchen) and his daughter (Heidi).

When Gustav offered his services to the American army, but he was rebuffed due to his ties to the corrupt Maximilian regime. However, he and many of his mercenaries were hired as the vanguard of a private security force by the corrupt Brockston-Morton Railways. In the years that followed, Gustav would hire many unscrupulous Americans, including William LeFrank Gordon, to work as Brockston-Morton security personnel.

In 1868, one of Gustav's assistants, Otto Stejar, was murdered by Jimmy Ballantrae (alias Valentin L'Ollonaise). At Gustav's prompting, Brockston-Morton Railways offered a 10,000 dollar reward for Ballantrae. In certain discrete corners, Gustav let it be known that he would offer 20,000 dollars to anyone who turned over Ballantrae to him alive. In 1872, this bounty would be collected by Major Sabbath and Jake Sartana (see «Thy Name is Sabbath»).

In 1869, Gustav married Gretchen von Skimmel. Sigi, their daughter, was born in 1873.

Both Sigi and her older half-sister, Heidi, would die violently in Paris during 1898. See «Kingdom of the Blind» from *Shadows of the Opera: Retribution in Blood* (Black Coat Press, 2013).

In 1876, Gustav entertained Count Kowalski at his ranch.

In 1877, the events of *The Big Gundown* happened. Gustav became part of a Brockston-Morton conspiracy to frame El Corredor (Cuchillo) for rape and murder. At this time, Gustav had slain 24 opponents in gun duels. However, his 25th opponent, bounty hunter Jonathan Corbett, was the Austrian aristocrat's undoing. Although Corbett was portrayed by Lee Van Cleef, the protagonist of *The Big Gundown* is treated as a separate character from Major Sabbath.

YOUNGER, CAPTAIN - disguised version of Lt. Cole Younger from *Charge!* (a. k. a. *Those Dirty Dogs*). The fictional military officer has no connection to the real-life outlaw of the same name.

In 1875, Younger as a lieutenant joined forces with Chadwell, Boomerang Smith and Holy Book to destroy an outlaw army (see *Charge!*). Promoted to Captain, Younger led the 1876 military expedition to pacify Snow Hill County, Utah (see «Thy Name is Sabbath»).

FORBIDDEN NAMES AND ALTERNATE NAMES:

Due to copyright reasons, certain names cannot be used in our stories. However, acceptable alternates are listed

FORBIDDEN	ALTERNATE	SOURCES
Adams, Chris	Christian Adam Sabbath Jr.	"Magnificent Seven" series
Angel	Angelos Varno	*Return of Sabata*
Ballantine	Jimmy Ballantrae	*Adios, Sabata*
	Valentin L'Ollonaise	
Banjo	Lee Galloway	*Sabata*
	Red Galloway	
Bionda	Bion Varno	*Return of Sabata*
Blondie	Rubio	*The Good, the Bad and the Ugly*
Burnett, Gideon	Giddy Burnett	*The Great Silence*
Carrincha	Richmond Sanchez	*Sabata*
Caulder, Hannie	Ana Sartana	*Hannie Caulder*
Clyde	Tervis	*Return of Sabata*
	Nine Fingers (after 1879)	
Cuchillo	El Corredor	*The Big Gundown* and *Run, Man, Run*
Django	Ignacz Djanko	*Django, Viva Django*, and
	The Undertaker	*Django Strikes Again*
Indio	The Crazy Indian	*For a Few Dollars More*
Koran	Holy Book	*Charge!* (a. k. a. *Those Dirty Dogs*)
Man With No Name	Drifter With Many Names	Sergio Leone's Dollar Trilogy
Manco	Lefty	*For a Few Dollars More*
Mortimer , Douglas	The Major (before 1876)	*For a Few Dollars More*
	Major Sabbath (After 1876)	
Pickles, Josiah	Pickled Joe	*Return of Sabata*
Pollicut	Judge Cutthroat	*The Great Silence*
Price, Thomas Luther	Specs	*Hannie Caulder*
Prophet	Isaiah	*For a Few Dollars More*
Red Margot	Maggie	*Return of Sabata*
Sabata	Major Sabbath	*Sabata, Return of Sabata*
Sabata (Indio Black)	Christian Adam Sabbath Sr.	*Adios, Sabata*
Septiembre	Segundo	*Adios, Sabata*
Silence	Louis Gordon	*The Great Silence*
	Mute Shootist	
Smith, Jeremiah	Boomerang Smith	*Charge!* (a. k. a. *Those Dirty Dogs*)
Yant, Delphine	Madame Delphine	Louis L'Amour's *The Proving Trail*

CHRONOLOGICAL ASSIGNMENT OF MOVIES AND FICTION

1862 *The Good, the Bad and the Ugly*
1865 *The Hellbenders*
1867 *Adios, Sabata*
1868 *El Rojo*
1868-76 Rick Lai's «Thy Name is Sabbath»
1871 *Sartana Kills Them All*
1872 *Light the Fuse . . . Sartana is Coming*
1873 *A Fistful of Dollars*
1874 *For a Few Dollars More*
1875 *Charge! (Those Dirty Dogs)*
1877 *The Big Gundown; Run, Man, Run*
Robert E. Howard's «The Dead Remember»
1878 *If You Meet Sartana, Pray for Your Death*
I am Sartana, Your Angel of Death
Django
Killer Calibre 32
1879 *Sabata*
Return of Sabata
1881 *Wanted*
1882 *Hannie Caulder*
My Name is Shanghai Joe
1882-87 *Viva Django*
1883 *Once Upon the Time in the West*
1884 *Sartana in the Valley of Death*
The Price of Death
Louis L'Amour's *The Proving Trail*
1885 *A Bullet for a Stranger (They Called Him Cemetery)*
1888 *Frenchie King*
1889 *Guns of the Magnificent Seven*
1898 *Django Strikes Again*
The Great Silence
1899 *Have a Good Funeral, My Friend . . . Sartana Will Pay*
1900 Rick Lai's «The Last Vendetta»
1902 *I am Sartana . . . Trade your Pistols for a Coffin*
1918 *A Bullet for the General*

LINKS TO FILMS THAT COULD BE VIEWED FREE:

Adios, Sabata (1970)
https://www.youtube.com/watch?v=udNde1qpczs
The Big Gundown (1966)
http://ishare.rediff.com/video/entertainment/the-big-gundown-o-dia-da-desforra-1966-lee-van-cleef-low-/8171974
A Bullet for a Stranger (They Called Him Cemetery) (1971)
https://www.youtube.com/watch?v=0-_NotFNCNg
A Bullet for the General
http://www.veoh.com/watch/v200924785yFwyYhC
Charge! (a. k. a. Those Dirty Dogs, 1973).
https://www.youtube.com/watch?v=HPjf3XVa4nQ#t=22
Django (1966)
https://www.youtube.com/watch?v=6VNSWhhTy8k&list=PLE313F5D7697236E3
Djanko Strikes Again (1987) - For missing prologue, see next link.
https://www.youtube.com/watch?v=UbzQxgE1ROM
Djanko Strikes Again (Italian with English subtitles)
https://www.youtube.com/watch?v=roRaHaThCGk
El Rojo (1966)
https://www.youtube.com/watch?v=cVW3cqMNXkQ
Have a Good Funeral, My Friend... Sartana Will Pay (1970)
https://www.youtube.com/watch?v=DYWpSeJzDqk
The Hellbenders
https://www.youtube.com/watch?v=I70KO0wlSIc
I Am Sartana, Trade your Pistols for a Coffin (1970)
https://www.youtube.com/watch?v=AMp4lE629_U
I Am Sartana, Your Angel of Death (1969),
https://www.youtube.com/watch?v=q4joNhAKUg8
If You Meet Sartana, Pray for Your Death (1968)
http://www.dailymotion.com/video/xq7nsp_if-you-meet-sartana-pray-for-your-death_shortfilms?start=6#from=embediframe
Light the Fuse . . . Sartana is Coming (1970)
https://www.youtube.com/watch?v=UKW-OUOYa_M
My Name is Shanghai Joe (1973)
https://www.youtube.com/watch?v=iWWikbY8q5g#t=15
Once Upon the Time in the West (1968)
https://www.youtube.com/watch?v=MQhZB86WJJU

Return of Sabata (1971)
https://www.youtube.com/watch?v=wdacywm3iiM
Sabata (1969)
https://www.youtube.com/watch?v=Hye7KJOhudY
Sartana in the Valley of Death (1970) - link below has Russian subtitles
https://www.youtube.com/watch?v=cVW3cqMNXkQ
Sartana Kills Them All (1971)
https://www.youtube.com/watch?v=6s4Uilic6Ak
Viva Django (1968)
https://www.youtube.com/watch?v=P8jblBxhQqU
Wanted
https://www.youtube.com/watch?v=dL2bl38yMGs

HIS NAME WAS MANKILLER

Young Jason Mankiller never believed his surname was an omen of his future until the Civil War broke out and he joined the Union Army. Fate took him to the fields of Gettysburg. By the time the battle ended, he was sitting atop a small rise surrounded by the bodies of dozens of Confederate troopers. Days later, while drunk, his fellow soldiers had tears of blood tattooed onto his face. From that day forward, the Man Who Cried Blood's reputation spread far and wide.

Ten years later, Jason Mankiller is in Ft. Rogers, Texas, hoping to find a job and bury his past. But the blood tattoo won't let him escape the gunfighter's trail. Writer R.A. Jones delivers an old fashioned western adventure in the grand tradition of Max Brand and Louis L'Amour. Here are pioneering men and women facing the birth of a new American destiny that will demand their blood, sweat, tears and sacrifice. For Jason Mankiller, that promise of a better life will be claimed at the end of a smoking gun.

HE RODE A
GUNFIGHTER'S
TRAIL

R.A. Jones